"Would you let me kiss you? I believe I can show you the falseness of passion. And make you forget your former betrothed. Just remember, it would be a lesson of the body and not of anything else."

"I really shouldn't."

"Understandable." Adam clasped his fingers and used them, arms outstretched, to pillow his head. "Totally understandable."

He shut his eyes, but when he opened them, his gaze was serious. "After all, I would just give you a soft kiss on the cheek. Just a brush, and it would give me a chance to feel your skin." He spoke the words with the sincerity of a lover. "To experience the moment of touching you. To breathe in the scent of your perfume. To see the flutter of your lashes against your cheeks. To have a closeness with your femininity. For you it would be just a kiss on the cheek. For me, it would be a moment to treasure."

"A kiss on my cheek?"

"Certainly. I would not impose otherwise on your good nature." He said the words as a pact between them.

Marianna lowered her chin and stared at him. "My nature's not that good."

He sat upright, laughing softly. "It is." He stood. "Of course, my cheek is available for you at any time."

Author Note

In Leonardo da Vinci's painting *Lady with an Ermine*, the pet fascinated me even though it didn't appear friendly. So when I began writing *Betrothed in Haste to the Earl*, I remembered the painting and thought my characters should have a similar animal in their household.

I later discovered that da Vinci's patron was the beau of the lady in the painting and that da Vinci possibly added the creature as symbolic. I'll never think of the painting the same way again, but I'm pleased that my hero, Adam, is a pet lover and would welcome many four-legged friends into his household.

LIZ TYNER

—

Betrothed in Haste to the Earl

HARLEQUIN

HISTORICAL

HARLEQUIN®
HISTORICAL™

PLEASE RECYCLE
THIS PRODUCT IS RECYCLABLE

Recycling programs
for this product may
not exist in your area.

ISBN-13: 978-1-335-59565-2

Betrothed in Haste to the Earl

Harlequin Enterprises ULC
22 Adelaide St. West, 41st Floor
Toronto, Ontario M5H 4E3, Canada
www.Harlequin.com

Printed in U.S.A.

Liz Tyner lives with her husband on an Oklahoma acreage she imagines is similar to the ones in the children's book *Where the Wild Things Are*. Her lifestyle is a blend of old and new and is sometimes comparable to the way people lived long ago. Liz is a member of various writing groups and has been writing since childhood. For more about her, visit liztyner.com.

Books by Liz Tyner

Harlequin Historical

The Wallflower Duchess
Redeeming the Roguish Rake
Saying I Do to the Scoundrel
To Win a Wallflower
It's Marriage or Ruin
Compromised into Marriage
The Governess's Guide to Marriage
A Cinderella for the Viscount
Tempting a Reformed Rake
A Marquess Too Rakish to Wed
Marriage Deal with the Earl
Betrothed in Haste to the Earl

English Rogues and Grecian Goddesses

Safe in the Earl's Arms
A Captain and a Rogue
Forbidden to the Duke

Visit the Author Profile page
at Harlequin.com.

Dedicated to animal control officers who rescue rattlesnakes, rabbits and the other animals who need assistance.

Chapter One

Marianna looked up from her book at the sound of her cousin, Cecilia, rushing into the room.

'The Earl of Rockwell is here,' Cecilia said, eyes alight. 'Think of the most stunning formal attire for a male, and then imagine it filled with a man to match, and you have Rockwell. Truly too much perfection to be covered by fabric. I'm surprised his clothing doesn't smoulder off him.' She shuddered. 'That would be utterly delicious to watch.'

'I'm dressed for bed—in my stunning bedtime attire, which is filled with a sleepy, exhausted me, because I arose early this morning to make sure the servants would have everything ready for the guests and Father's event.' Marianna lowered her book and peered at her cousin, giving her an exaggeratedly angry stare. Covering a yawn, she touched the soft, worn fabric of her robe. 'So, go and be the perfect cousin and impress everyone, and let them think you did all the planning.'

'I'm rewarding your hard work by alerting you to him,' Cecilia said.

'I'm reading.' Marianna turned a page and moved so she held the book to block the view of her cousin.

'You must meet him. I wouldn't wait, if I were you. He might fall in love with me before morning.' She stepped closer. 'I've already asked if I might call him Adam.'

She pulled the book from Marianna, put the volume on the sofa and grabbed her cousin's hands. 'Hurry. Now. I'll help you dress.'

'No.' Marianna pulled free and retrieved her book. 'I don't need to attend Father's event. Everything should run smoothly, and if it doesn't and the staff can't correct it, then tell me about it tomorrow. When you wake up—about sunset.'

Cecilia stepped away, frowning. 'I do you the biggest favour I've ever done you, and you throw it back in my face.' She paused and put a forefinger on her lip. 'Well, more decisions for me. It's hard to choose between the Earl of Rockwell and Darius Driscoll. For my next marriage, should I prefer to be rich or titled?' she murmured. 'Decisions, decisions…'

'You live for decisions like that.'

'I do. But you must see the Earl… Adam,' Cecilia said. 'He's not as handsome as Darius Driscoll. But then, no one is. Yet, Adam fills up the space he is in nicely. And the two of you would be stunning in a portrait, which you know is partly why I wed the Baron, whom I still miss—because, even with his advanced age, my dear husband was handsome and charming. May he rest in peace.'

'You are only trying to keep me from spending time

with Darius tomorrow. But, I told you, I am not interested in a romance with him. We are merely friends.'

'Prove it. Meet the Earl. You could just peek in, act as if you're greeting a few people and then vanish again. I'll distract everyone and keep them amused.'

'On purpose?' Marianna batted her lashes.

Cecilia laughed, turning so that her skirt swirled. Then she ran into Marianna's bedroom and returned with a perfume bottle, daubed a bit of the scent on her wrist and left the container on the table.

'Your loss,' Cecilia said. 'I will have both him and Darius to choose from.' She picked at the shoulders of her sleeves, fluffing them up. 'I guess the men will both have to adore me if I can't pick one.'

Marianna frowned, pressing her fingers against her temple. 'I cannot believe we are related. You must not ruin the evening. It's mostly Father's oldest friends, but still… I wanted it to be so perfect for him. You had better behave.'

'Well, I can't stay. I would hate for anyone to die of a broken heart while I'm gone.' She studied her reflection and mused. 'Although it would be talked about.'

'You shouldn't want to be talked about.'

Cecilia swirled round and put her hands on her hips. 'And you—you shouldn't care. But you do.' She puffed out a breath. Her curls fell back into place perfectly and she mussed them a bit. 'I just hope they start early in the day so they will have time to get beyond the best bits and remember all the details.'

'Not me.'

Laughter from the guests filtered through the walls, sounding an ocean away to Marianna, yet she could hear it perfectly. It reminded her of the times when she'd been in love and had believed that it wasn't her father's finances that attracted suitors but herself.

'I'm serious,' she told her cousin. 'Go away.'

'If the Earl is attracted to you, this could be your perfect chance for revenge,' Cecilia said. 'You don't have to do more than throw a few smiles and adoring glances his way, and speak softly so he has to lean in to listen. Everyone will assume you are having a rendezvous later. It's not that difficult.' She laughed. 'I do it all the time.'

'I could not do that.'

'That is your problem.' She blew out a breath, causing the curls to flutter again. 'You'd rather stay up the whole night reading. And you're afraid to risk living outside these walls.'

'I like it here, and so do you, judging by how much time you spend visiting.'

'But I am *visiting.*' Her cousin pointed a finger at Marianna. 'And enjoying myself. You should meet the guests, especially the Earl. Otherwise, I might decide he is perfect for me.'

'That would be wonderful.'

'Blast it, Marianna.' Cecilia glared. 'I know what's best for you. And this would end it with your former beloved.' She tapped her lip again. 'A little more scandal about you won't hurt at this point, and it might be good for you.' She held her arms wide. 'Embrace it. Revel in it. Make people jealous that you can stumble and still rise above all the chatter. The Earl is your next betrothal—you just don't know it yet.' She tapped her finger over her lips. 'You could get caught in a compromising situation with him.'

'Nonsense. I am sick of scandal—last word on the subject.'

'Don't worry. You're always forgiven. Another thing money can buy. Forgiveness.'

Cecilia strolled to the hallway and stood with the door open, resting her cheek against it and studying Marianna. 'Forgiveness. You always forgive, don't you?'

'No.'

'Yes, you do. If someone doesn't do something quickly, you're likely to forgive that dunderhead you almost married.' She bumped her forehead gently on the door in disgust.

'It's my life, not yours. And you can't do anything about it.'

'I'll give it my best try.' Cecilia banged the outer door shut.

Marianna rested her chin on the top of her book. True, she'd received a letter from her former sweetheart, and Cecilia had known how tempted she'd been to read it before Cecilia had taken it from her and burned it. It had taken every fibre of her strength not to write to him. But she hadn't. And she was happy to be free. She repeated the words to herself. She was happy. It had taken her six months to regain her happiness after her broken betrothal. She wasn't going to lose it again.

Adam watched the older man, aware he was somehow being manipulated, but he hadn't been sure what the man's game was until he noticed that Mr Emory kept putting his niece, Cecilia, in his path.

He'd been invited not by a matchmaking mama, but a matchmaking uncle. The man had mentioned his niece's attributes at every opportunity. He'd poured Adam buckets of drink and had kept nodding but not making any comment about the lamp-oil business opportunity Adam had presented.

Now Adam grasped that the woman acting as hostess was the reason he'd been asked to stay a few days—and not because of his suggestion about the investment. Only he and the Driscolls had been invited to stay longer. Everyone else would be leaving at the night's end.

The event had waned enough that he could safely offer a goodnight to his host and ask to be shown to his room. He'd had so many appointments to attend in order to be away for a week that he'd sent his servant along earlier with their things.

The host, ever the matchmaker, summoned his niece.

'Cecilia, show Rockwell to his room and hurry back to the guests,' the uncle said, then smiled. 'Well, you don't have to hurry a tremendous amount.'

'Yes, Uncle,' she said, and she beamed. Adam had seen a menagerie tiger with a more innocent grin than the widow's.

Cecilia led Adam out of the room but detoured past the refreshments first, clasping a drink and lifting it to her lips for a hearty swallow.

He waited. He knew there would be no hurrying her and that she would likely loiter by finishing one drink and then having another. 'I love that man,' she said of her uncle, giving Adam a wide-eyed stare. 'He knows commerce and people. And, if you plan to do business with him, expect to do as he says.'

She giggled, waving the half-empty glass around, but Adam saw nothing humorous.

'The only one who can get away with whatever she wants,' Cecilia continued, 'Is Marianna. My cousin is no saint, because she tries to appear so perfect that she ends up not being perfect at all. And, of course, we all want her happiness.'

He let her talk.

'Am I too old for you?' she asked, steadying herself by draping herself over his arm, drink in hand, batting her eyelashes and almost stumbling from the effort. He felt he'd just been dipped in a vat of perfume and strong spirits.

'You're too young for me,' he whispered.

'That's a good answer,' she admitted.

He leaned closer, voice firm. 'I'm not interested in a dalliance with you any more than you are with me. You are only flirting to make Driscoll jealous—and he is.'

'Thank you for noticing.' She took a lamp from a table top. 'Follow me.'

She led him out of the ballroom into the corridor and led him up the staircase at the end. At the top, she moved further down the hallway and stopped in front of a door. 'Want to invite me in?'

'Nothing is going to happen,' he said.

She paused, laughing softly. 'I'm sure it won't.' Then she held her index finger to her lips, kissed it with a smack, raised her hand in a wobbling circle and dropped the kiss on her own cheek.

'Let me turn up the light for you.' She twisted the knob, lowering it, but hesitating before putting it out. The glow continued.

Adam braced himself. He could tell she'd intended to leave him in the dark, but she'd changed her mind and left on the light.

'My mistake,' she said, and handed him the lamp. 'I was going to turn this out and let you stumble around in the dark, searching for your valet. But I'm just not that mean.' She sighed dramatically. 'Pleasant dreams. Two rooms—don't trip over anything.'

Then she left.

What a mistake he'd made to agree to the invitation. He opened the doorway and walked inside. It seemed to be a pleasant little fusspot of a sitting room, scented just like that Cecilia woman. It must be some floral furniture polish the maids used. From the scant light, he could see scallops on the curtains.

Adam shut his eyes briefly and yawned, stretching it long, savouring the moment of finally being alone. His morning had started near six so he could get duties caught up before leaving for the banker's country estate. A long day and even longer evening… He opened the connecting door, ready to retire.

He noticed the huge bed and the mound of covers and sat the lamp by the door. Blast it, had they put the valet in his room by mistake? He shook his head and took off his coat, placing it on the chair beside him. He'd have to wake Dinsmore and find out what was going on.

He walked to the bedside, unbuttoning his waistcoat and slipping it from his shoulders. He tossed it over the coat and then undid his cravat.

'Dinsmore. Dinsmore,' he said, to wake the sleeping form.

Then the form moved and he caught the scent of

flowers at the same moment the world around him crashed and he realised he was standing in a woman's bed chamber.

Chapter Two

Marianna's eyes flew open.

All her senses seemed to have sharpened. The room was no longer in complete darkness. She could hear movement and smell sandalwood cologne.

Someone was above her, calling out some chant she didn't understand… *Dinsmore…?*

A face came into view and suddenly stilled. His eyes moved closer. She could feel the beast's breath and smell brandy. And then he jumped away.

Without thinking, she grabbed the framed miniature at her bedside and swung at his head. He dodged, moving away from her. The only other thing available was her book. She lifted the tome and threw it towards him, using every breath of force she had. The book struck above his eye as he stumbled and he stopped against the wall. The volume landed on the floor at his feet.

She scrambled to the other side of the bed.

An oath flew from his body as if he'd been clubbed. He swore again and swore once more, and touched the place the volume had hit him, staring at her.

Marianna stood, holding the bed post for support. Surely, if she were dreaming, she wouldn't hear such oaths? She felt a bit dazed, but this didn't feel like a dream. Her dreams had never had such language in them.

The stranger seemed addled. He did not speak, but stood upright and stared at her with anger. One lock of hair covered an eye. If he were an animal, surely he would be snarling and growling?

'Did you and that little witch plan this?' he snapped at her.

'Witch?' Oh, goodness. She was dreaming, losing her mind or the glass of wine she'd had earlier had been aged in a tainted vat and caused some sort of hallucination.

'I hate this place,' he mumbled, pushing himself to his feet but still remaining against the wall.

They stared at each other a heartbeat and she realised everything was real. She wasn't dreaming and a man was staring at her as if she were the one at fault. Marianna blinked. She did not know what a lady did in such a situation. She thought a scream would be proper, but she didn't feel the need. Besides, they had guests, and she didn't want everyone rushing in and *this* being the part of the event that would be shared from house to house.

The man looked at her as if *she* was not supposed to be present. And this was *her* bed chamber. She looked at him. 'Do not touch me,' she commanded. 'Or I will see you shot and hanged and beaten to death.'

This trespasser waited, not moving except for the deep rise and fall of his chest. 'I assure you, I have no wish to touch you—whoever you are.' His voice had the ring of truth in it.

As her eyes followed his movements, she could hardly believe a man of his size could retreat that quickly. She was amazed at the length of those legs—two long flashes of darkness, moving faster than a cat.

She stared for a moment longer.

'I was invited by Mr Emory to stay the week. The woman who directed me here could have been more foxed than I thought, but I suspect this is her foul attempt at humour.'

Marianna felt a surge of anger. 'Would this woman have been wearing an overstuffed yellow gown, have ghastly little, insipid blue eyes, over-styled hair and a mark on her cheek?'

'That was not my first impression of her,' he said smoothly, 'But, now that I examine my memory more clearly, I think you quite described her.'

'It may appear to be a beauty mark, but I fear it's caused by an overabundance of cosmetics,' she whispered. 'I don't expect you to heed my advice, but I wouldn't put a lot of trust in her. We are cousins by birth, and nature played an evil trick. Instead of giving her a conscience, she received stunning form and devastating beauty.'

'Not in my opinion.'

He made a sound which wasn't a true chuckle but more of a groan at himself. 'I apologise for my presence. I assure you, I did not plan this.'

'I know who did.'

'I would leave this house immediately, but Dinsmore is here somewhere. Might you advise me of his location?'

'He is…um… I only told the housekeeper which rooms the Earl and the Driscolls would stay in.' Then she realised she had provided a room for the Earl's servant… 'You're the Earl?'

Before she answered, she heard a door opening in the distance—her sitting room door—and her father calling out.

Then she heard a knock on her bed-chamber door.

The man shut his eyes and jerked his head and she could hear the muttered curse. She remembered the man's reaction and realised he'd been surprised. She knew, somehow, that he had meant her no harm, although that didn't mean he'd had the right to enter her room. But she didn't want an eruption while there were guests still in the house.

'Don't move,' she whispered, jumping out of bed.

'One moment,' she called out loudly. She reached for her dressing gown.

Another knock sounded, and this time she heard her father's voice. 'Marianna.' He opened the door, and she threw her body towards it, catching it as it swung forward, stopping it half-open.

'Marianna?' her father said again, lamp in hand. 'Is everything all right? I heard a thump and I worried you were ill.'

'It was a book,' she answered slowly, clasping one hand in front of herself. 'It fell to the floor.'

She gripped the door harder. 'I think I had a nightmare, and I woke suddenly.'

If she indicated the man, she knew her father would

react without thought for the other guests in his house, and that she would suffer more embarrassment and disgrace. She'd already suffered enough of that for all of her life. Everyone could look elsewhere for their chatter.

She had been paying for one mistake; she didn't need to pay for another one, even someone else's—especially someone else's.

'I just wanted to make sure you are not still ill.'

'I still feel discomforted...' her fingers massaged her temples '...more than I expected,' she said.

'These pains of yours...' His voice was not accusing, merely sad. 'We are fortunate that you only are ill when there are events to attend and that you recover soon after.'

She kept her hand at her head and made her voice woeful. 'I cannot help that I am delicate.'

'Marianna,' her father spoke softly. 'You're hiding away, and you're letting that dunderhead Jules destroy your happiness. I don't care if you don't attend parties, but don't avoid the world because of him. I will not let you continue to do so. I invited Driscoll's son in hopes you would strike up a closer friendship. But what do you do? You hide.'

The stranger could hear.

'That is preposterous, Father.' Her voice rose. 'I have these instances where I am just better staying in my room.' She caught herself and remembered to speak in a frail tone. She put her whole imagination into the words. 'I don't want to have the vapours in front of the guests.'

'Vapours?' her father said and chuckled. 'When you did not go with me to the last assembly because of your illness, I came home to discover you had eaten all the apple tarts,' he said. 'And you had moved my papers and left crumbs on the table.'

'My ailments usually don't last long,' she said, defending herself, and wishing she'd stayed in her room that night instead of this one.

'Daughter, since your betrothal ended, we must be thankful that the eye strain you fear from sunny gatherings, the tiredness that you're concerned you'll feel at meetings past sunset and your fear of rampant poison ivy at outdoor events ends as soon as your attendance at a get-together is no longer required.'

'Poison ivy is extremely vexing.'

He raised a brow. 'Like a daughter?'

'I'm indeed fortunate that, even as I am fragile, I recover quickly.' She shooed him away with her hand, resisting an urge to cough delicately to add some credibility to her frailties and convince him to leave. 'You mustn't linger. Your friends will miss you.'

'My friends are fine. The only ones staying longer are Driscoll and his family, plus that dilletante, know-it-all upstart the Earl of Rockwell, who only wants my funds. Well, I only want his title for Cecilia. He thinks I should fund a ridiculous scheme equivalent to painting slug shells with dots. And they call *me parvenu*!' He turned. 'He's in need of funds, and he wants me to invest in research by some nobody called Michael Faraday, who can make currents go through the air and cause a sudden start to people. There's no money in it. It would be a lifetime before he could have returns on such an investment. If ever.'

He looked across the darkness at her. He stopped for a moment. 'I'm not sure if the Earl is taken with Cecilia. I thought he might make a match with her but he's smarter than I imagined. I let her show him to his room and she was back in a trice.' He clucked his tongue. 'I don't know if it would be worth it to have him in the family just to get a nephew with a title.'

He sighed, but then brightened. 'I did discuss you with Driscoll's son. He said to me that he was so disappointed that you were not in attendance. I'd like you to show him around the estate tomorrow. For me— please. And I just hope that know-it-all Earl becomes taken with your cousin.'

Marianna let out a breath. If she argued, her father might stay longer and that could be disastrous. 'I will certainly see Darius tomorrow.'

He smiled and patted her arm. 'Goodnight, sweet one.'

She shut the door when he left the area.

'I don't believe we've been introduced,' she said softly, after giving her father time to go on his way. She tilted her head up and tried to examine him as best she could. 'I assume you're the Earl?'

'The dilletante, know-it-all Earl of Rockwell himself,' he answered, and she couldn't detect humour in his voice.

'An impressive title,' she said.

'It has been in my family for five generations.'

'How was it obtained?'

'My ancestors stopped an uprising against the crown and kept it quiet.'

'Oh, then perhaps you will have the same chivalry and keep from talking about this as well.'

'Of course. I would have it no other way.' He spoke softly, his voice a deep whisper.

'I beg your pardon for the events.' She put all the apology into her words she could muster. 'And for my cousin Cecilia. She's not as respectable as she seems, and I am much more than I seem. Thank you for understanding.' She kept her voice firm. 'I will deal with my cousin.'

He walked over, picked up the lamp and stopped at the outer doorway, touching it, but then he turned to her. Something in him changed when he looked her direction.

'Don't let your cousin be the only one to laugh.'

The light shone on his face and the shadows didn't dance. It amazed her that he could hold the lamp so still after such a misadventure.

'Let the jest be on her. Don't give her the satisfaction of your anger,' he said. 'But I would suggest you tell your father and let him banish her from this household. Although, I admit, I didn't want you to do that while I was standing here.'

'I don't know if it will be possible for this to be ignored,' she said.

'I didn't say ignore it,' he continued in a tone she found soothing. 'If one of my cousins pulled something like this on me, I assure you, I would consider it a mission to retaliate.'

'I'm not like that.'

'Everyone is like that,' he said, scoffing. 'When the right moment comes along, let her have a taste of her own medicine. For instance, flirt with Darius Driscoll, if she is fond of him.'

'I can't. We're friends, and he would see right through it. He knows me too well.'

'In that case tomorrow, if I seem hopelessly devoted to you when Cecilia is near, please join in the charade. Or rebuff me. Or do as you wish. But don't be surprised at what is said.'

'I won't.'

'I will be on my way,' he said. 'But I don't regret this as much as I should. Otherwise, I would not have got to overhear such an enlightening conversation. And Michael Faraday is a genius,' he added. 'But he probably can't throw a book as well as you.'

'I do have my skills,' she said. 'And I hope yours is leaving.'

He placed his hand at heart level. 'Tonight, one of the best traits I have.'

She opened the door, peered out to make sure her father had gone, looked back at the Earl and led him through her sitting room.

At the door, she pointed in the direction of the stairway. 'Go up, be sure to turn right and you will be directly above my room. You'll have a sitting room, a bedroom attached and your manservant has a room to the other side.'

He lifted the lamp.

'Hurry.'

'I wish that I could say I enjoyed meeting you, but I would rather have postponed it.' He touched the back of her hand then he slipped away, a disappearing shadow in the night.

The whirlwind inside her dissipated the moment he left. She stared out into the darkness, peering at her hand.

The man had given her a gift without knowing it— or a curse. She clasped the hand. She remembered, for the first time in a long, long time, what it felt like to be touched. And now she felt more alone. She should have attended her father's fête, but she'd just not been able to force herself. Since her betrothal had ended, she'd not wanted to attend any festivities. Going amongst a crowd was too overwhelming.

Returning to her bed, she remembered her disastrous courtship. Her former sweetheart had said he adored her tumbling brown hair, which always wanted to wisp around her face, and her eyes, which he'd called 'windows into exquisiteness', and she had practically floated among the clouds. Now she wondered if he said that to all the women he courted.

She had seen his admiration for her sparse, trim shape, and she had thought his expressions and his words had been the truth of undying love. Now, she doubted everything she had ever heard him say. He'd only adored her because he'd wanted to be a part of her family. She'd even suspected he preferred her cousin, but Cecilia had been wise enough to have nothing to do with him.

Had her disposition been stronger, she would have been an excellent spy. She could have walked among the state's enemies and no one ever would have seen her. She could have sat and sketched traitors' faces, and they would have continued on their evil way and wondered later how they'd been uncovered.

Cecilia, on the other hand, would have been an entirely different spy. Men would have given her the coins in their pocket to get a smile from her and, for a kiss, all the secrets in their heart.

She called Cecilia a cousin, and she was, by some

mistake of fate. But now she would be disowned. Cecilia would think something like this quite humorous. She could almost hear her deep-throated laughter, designed to catch the eyes of everyone in a room. She'd heard her cousin practice.

But Marianna was going to take the Earl's advice—let Cecilia wonder.

She flounced down onto the bed.

She'd known the moment her father had invited the Earl that he had plans for a match and had known it was for Cecilia. And she wagered Darius Driscoll had been picked out as a possible son-in-law, someone for her to court.

She thought of Rockwell again and crossed her arms, holding her elbows. Cecilia was right—something about the Earl's voice, his stature, or his assurance, touched her. And she'd not even been able to see him clearly.

Then she turned and saw something in the shadows. She rose and touched it and could immediately see it was a man's coat. Her foot tangled with something else. Retrieving a waistcoat, she gathered the garments. He'd forgotten his clothing.

Her thoughts collided.

The maid could *not* find the clothing in her room in the morning. It would be discussed among all the servants and her father would find out. It would be disastrous.

She peeked out of her doorway, saw the hallway empty and ran up the stairs, hoping Rockwell's valet would not be awake. She could knock, run and leave them outside his door, but he might not even be in his room, or hear the knock. If her father happened by, she wanted no questions about why a man's coat and waist-coat was lying in the hallway.

At his room, she softly opened the door just a sliver, and then a little more, ready to toss the garments inside.

'What the—?' She heard his voice from inside the room.

She froze at first then she pushed the door a little further, and he opened it. The lamplight behind him showed he'd already removed his shirt.

'I—I brought these,' she whispered. 'It would be terrible if the maid found them in my room.'

He reached to take the garments and at that moment a feminine gasp startled her from behind.

'Marianna.' Her name had never sounded so loud.

She turned. Mr and Mrs Driscoll stood in the hall-way, staring at her.

She'd been concentrating on being so quiet in reaching his room, that she'd not looked beyond. Her mouth dried.

Mrs Driscoll clutched at her husband for support.

Without hesitation, the Earl stepped forward and took Marianna's hand. 'We have wanted to keep it a secret because it seems too soon to announce anything so quickly after her disastrous betrothal with Jules.' He squeezed her fingers. 'Can you let them know, sweet-ing?' he asked.

She stared into his eyes. 'Let them…?'

The Driscolls were open-mouthed, and Mrs Driscoll didn't seem to know where to let her eyes rest. Mr Driscoll was taking both of them in with one condemn-ing glare.

'Yes. You may tell them all, or nothing. It is all in

your hands,' the Earl said, soothing but direct. 'Whatever you wish to tell them.'

She took in a deep breath and gathered her strength, but she only needed her mouth, not her brain. That part of her had already quit working. She was compromised and she could only see one way out of it.

'We are betrothed,' she said. 'But it is a secret. I did not want it announced until after a suitable time has passed.'

'Yes. She didn't want to cause undue hurt to Jules.' Rockwell squeezed her hand again.

'Your father hasn't mentioned this.' Mr Driscoll's words frosted the air. His eyes squinted into almost invisible shadows in the darkness.

'It has been so sudden,' Marianna said.

'But every moment memorable,' Rockwell said.

She threw a glance his way, silencing him. 'I did not want to concern Father,' she said. 'I most certainly did not. But he did invite the Earl to spend some time here, so we are in high hopes the two of them will become close.'

'True. I was surprised that he'd invited the Earl,' Driscoll said. 'Though I misunderstood and thought him considering a beau for Cecilia.' He crossed his arms. 'He's not mentioned this to me.'

'And he likely won't,' Marianna said. 'Father is concerned that… You are aware…after Jules…'

'We throw ourselves on your mercy.' The Earl brushed her elbow. 'My dearest Marianna has had such a time with her courtships, and we don't want anyone speaking rashly of her. Nor do we want her father concerned. Can we please keep this among ourselves until a suitable time has passed and we can make a proper announcement?'

'We were young once,' Mrs Driscoll said, conceding and smiling. 'Of course we will keep this between us.' Then she shook her head. 'But do be more careful, Marianna; you do not need any more grief.'

'I agree.'

They walked past Marianna and Mrs Driscoll patted her arm.

But Mr Driscoll glared at Rockwell. 'You'd better not cause Marianna or her father any upset. Between Emory and I, we can have your berries removed and presented back to you with a ribbon on them.'

'Wilmont!' Mrs Driscoll hushed him and pulled her husband away. 'Don't cause any further distress for Marianna.'

The couple continued down the stairs, only Mr Driscoll's steps audible.

For a heartbeat, she and Rockwell stared at each other. 'The Driscolls are very upstanding, and he often keeps business secrets for Father,' she said. 'And she is the same. They can be trusted.'

'You have more faith in them than I do.' He released her hand, leaving a large distance between them. She felt abandoned.

'Do you have a sweetheart?' she asked when the thought occurred to her. It would be horrible if the secret got out and another woman was distressed.

'Oh, don't worry. I have made my pledge on that. None serious.' The quiet words slammed into her. He studied the hallway. 'But you'd best get on your way before we have enough people here to fill a theatre.'

'In time, I can tell them it was all a mistake.'

She couldn't gauge his reaction to her words. She turned, gathered the skirt of her dressing gown and flew down the stairs, not pausing until her bedroom door was shut behind her.

Well, she'd never intended to be betrothed again, but she'd not made herself any promises about a fake one. From the look on the Earl's face, she didn't have to worry about this betrothal going any further than her real one had.

Chapter Three

The next morning, Adam shared the night's misadventure with Dinsmore.

Dinsmore stood, watching him, still holding the steaming water a maid had brought. 'You are the only man I know who can sweet talk his way into a betrothal and out of it again at the same time.'

Adam met the older man's eyes. 'What else was I to do?'

'True.'

'I'm not going to be able to fund Faraday, but I've not given up on the second project.'

'He'll do very well. I'm not concerning myself about his finances. I'm more worried that the carpenters you have working on the estate might not be able to remain within your funds. That lamp-oil idea is truly a good one and it should be funded first.'

Dinsmore dropped a cloth into a bowl and poured enough water to wet it.

'If anyone finds out I'm actually decreasing the size of my home instead of enlarging it, that wouldn't be optimal,' Adam said. 'Even the carpenters and the architect believe I have plans to build a courtyard, add a faux façade and a duplicate of the main house to the side, but I will never spend the money to do anything but improve the gardens. I'd rather invest.'

'Less space to concern yourself with.'

'I don't like Emory, and I'd rather leave and spend the time doing something productive. I've been thinking about my brother.' Adam took the cloth, squeezed out the water then pressed it against his face, letting the heat soften his stubble.

But he didn't really want to leave because the woman he'd seen the night before had awoken something in him.

'Your brother is fine. You keep a close eye on him.'

'I miss the scamp,' he said, speaking around the cloth. 'I believe he would be better off living with me.'

Adam hadn't noticed his half-brother, and had truly not considered the babe a close relative, until after his father's funeral. He'd been discussing the future and the little one had escaped whoever was watching him and run up to Adam with his arms pumping and his head down and had charged right into his brother, then bounced onto the ground.

Adam had crouched, righted him and then Nathan had lifted Adam's hat off his head and tried to put it on his own. It had fallen and, when Adam had tried to retrieve the hat, the boy had clasped at the brim and held on with all his strength. Adam had looked into the boy's eyes and known that his half-brother needed him, just as he'd once needed Dinsmore. And, in that instant, he'd changed his life, working to become someone the little one could look up to.

Dinsmore coughed. 'I really don't want to return home. The meals here are delightful. Food tastes good. It's a strange phenomenon but a nice change. Poor Cook. You should hire someone to assist her and in truth just let Cook sit and watch.'

'I'm fine with her cooking.' Adam laid down the cloth and added some shaving soap to his face. It was true that even the servants in this household would likely turn up their noses at the fare at his house.

'I'm not. She's a wonderful lady, but she missed her calling. I don't know what it was, but it was not anything to do with food.'

'Dinsmore.'

'Remember the time I saved you funds enough to have your sitting room updated?' He put the pitcher of water onto table.

'Yes.'

'And enough to repair the stairway so you wouldn't break your leg? Which I accounted for in the column "saving your life".'

'I put it under "repairs".' He lifted the razor and scraped the whiskers from his face.

Dinsmore lifted his shoulders slightly for a second, then continued. 'Well, this time think about my stomach. Let's stay. Emory invited you for a week, and I am being treated like a guest.' Dinsmore chuckled while he patted his stomach. 'I bet it was novel for you to hear yourself called anything but Rockwell, and then to be told by a woman to get out of her room.'

'If Emory is anything like his female relatives...' Adam gritted his teeth after he spoke. 'They do not need Emory to take care of them.' He tapped the razor against the side of the bowl.

'Which do you prefer? The woman with the over-flouncy room or the over-flounce of a woman? I've never known you not to be aware of a woman's charms.'

'Well, the one who woke up swinging was much more palatable than the beautiful little serpent. I like my snakes with fangs, not beauty marks.'

'The one trying to knock you down could be more dangerous.'

'Yes. She could be. But, even though I admire art, I don't own any. I'm not felled by beauty.'

'What about females with brains?'

'Immune.'

'How would you know?' Dinsmore viewed him through half-closed eyes.

'You're sacked.'

'You can't sack me. Your darling mother was my exasperating sister.' He paused, gathering the shaving items. 'And who would sort out your life so well for you?'

Adam didn't answer, giving the towel a final wipe over his cheeks.

'You know that, if you married one of Mr Emory's relatives, it would be much easier to convince him to invest,' Dinsmore said.

'I will never have it said I wed for funds.' He threw down the towel and rose to his feet.

'Because you have no idea to wed.' Dinsmore sighed. 'You've ideas to hire a good housekeeper, add a few maids and keep the house in repair. For you, women are pleasurable diversions, and you hate that you're like an insect in a spider web when one catches your eye. You think you are weak where females are concerned, but you're not. You don't risk being caught in a web with someone you can't escape from, and you're strong as steel about that.'

'I have had long friendships with women.'

'Yes. But you think all women are like my sister. She was a fluttering, dandelion-fluff of a woman. Or your father's second wife… Who is aware her beauty is a currency, if you'll pardon my saying so.'

'I have no problem with either one.' Then he muttered under his breath, 'As long as they stay out of my path.'

Dinsmore swung up his hand. 'My sister—your mother—saw you, what, once a month? And you only lived in the rooms the visitors didn't see, not the elegant rooms where you might break something or interrupt a guest. What a terrible event if you dared show yourself to their over-exalted friends.'

'I didn't mind.' Adam ran the comb through his hair and winced at the tender spot on his forehead.

'Nor did I.' Dinsmore straightened the cloth on the table top. 'She forgot to visit you on your birthday. I reminded her and she still missed it by a day.'

'I was happy with it, Dinsmore. I had a fine childhood.'

'Only because your parents chose me to take care of you.'

Smiling, Adam extended a hand. 'There you have it. The perfect parents. They hired someone more competent than they were to do the job.'

Dinsmore muttered, 'It didn't take much.'

The valet continued his musings. 'And the young woman who directed me to this room is Emory's daughter?'

'Yes.' Adam said.

'Friendly sort. I never would have believed her to be the heiress.' Dinsmore handed a pair of boots to Adam.

'Me neither. I thought Emory's daughter to be a scatterhead. After all, she was betrothed to that weak tea Walter Jules.' He tugged the boots on. 'To be betrothed to Jules she likely is—'

'Don't put her in the same category as your romances.'

'Why not?'

'You shy away from any woman with an appearance of innocence, but that first woman's innocence was only a pretence. Not everyone is like her.'

'I'm sure. But I still see her enough to remind me of what a fool I was. I will never make that mistake again.'

'Just remember that it is the past and not the future.'

'At this moment, my future is feeling bruised,' Adam said, peering into the mirror and touching the tender spot. 'But it's barely visible.'

'You'd best part your hair on the other side and be thankful it was time for a hair cut.'

Adam stared at his reflection. 'I am going to hoist that insipid little dishcloth cousin by her own petard, and the sleepy heiress will be kind enough to help me. I'm sure of it. It's time she stood up for herself instead of hiding away from everyone.'

The first thing Marianna noticed when she walked into the room was that the Earl wasn't in a pleasant mood. True, he smiled at the right times, and he was genial, but the expression in his eyes was at best one step shy of angry.

Her father and the Earl were standing companionably enough. The Earl's face remained solemn, and for the most part expressionless. He had his hands clasped behind his back and, when he met her eyes, an encouraging smile flitted across his face but faded immediately after.

Now that she saw him in the daylight, she noticed him in a different way. Cecilia hadn't lied about his appearance. In fact, she would say her cousin had understated him.

But then, her father had had many dukes and earls visit, and she didn't remember any of them having the air of assuredness that Rockwell had. In fact, she couldn't remember anyone who'd visited before having such stature.

Her father walked over to her. 'Rockwell, I would like you to meet my daughter, Marianna. My darling niece will join us soon, as…' He said the last three words almost under his breath. 'I sent a maid to wake her—again.'

Marianna's greeting was pleasant and most proper. 'I apologise for not attending the soiree last night,' she said. 'I had to retire early.'

'Our loss,' Rockwell said.

She appraised him, noting the small bruise visible on his forehead. She could see why Cecilia had spoken with him but she hadn't played the game well. However, she found it hard to believe her cousin hadn't intended a flirtation with him. He must have rebuffed her without hesitation. Or Cecilia was truly fond of Darius.

'It's always pleasant to meet friends of my father's. He is known to associate with men of good character.'

'Then I fear he may have made a lapse in my case,'

Rockwell said, smiling. He touched his neck cloth with the grace of an artist. 'I would hope you and your father both call me by my first name—Adam—as I'm a guest in your house.' He touched his temple. 'And it feels like you and I will hit it off.'

He'd lost his remoteness. If that wasn't a gleam of laughter in his eyes, she'd forgo confections for a month. He was confident to the tip of his aristocratic nose— which was not an unpleasant one.

'And are you and my cousin, Cecilia, already calling each other by your given names?'

'I believe that I may have called her by her given name,' he said with all the innocence of a cat with a feather resting on its cheek. 'Hard to recall all that I said about her last night.'

'She's a ravishing beauty,' said Marianna. 'And few men forget her.'

'She gave you direction to your room,' Emory groused.

'I do remember someone unforgettable showing me upstairs. I suspect your daughter has a better sense of direction, though,' the Earl said.

Her father's brows firmed. 'They both have a good sense of direction. Cecilia always goes for what she wants. Marianna might appear to lag behind but is working out different paths to take. She quietly gets what she wants.'

'Would you agree with that assessment?' Adam asked Marianna.

'I would have to disagree. I tend to stay in one place.'

'If that is the place you wish to be, then you should most likely remain in it. But not because you are fearful of moving forward.'

'I will choose whether I remain or not, fearful or not. Reluctance can be an indication that you should stay where you are. Staying in the same location when everyone else wishes you to move can be an indicator of strength.'

'Don't doubt that she will do as she wishes,' Emory said before turning to his friends. Her father moved towards the corridor. 'I was hoping I could take the Driscolls to see the new stables. You are both welcome to come along, if you'd like.'

'I'd rather wait for Cecilia,' Marianna said. 'And perhaps show Darius and Adam the gardens.'

'Fine,' her father said, walking out of the door. 'But it might be a long wait for her.'

Adam watched Marianna, curious about what she would say once they were alone, but she seemed to prefer silence.

Then she appraised his bruise and her mouth opened. 'Is that…?'

'It was dark. A huge object came at me from nowhere. And I survived. We both did. That's all that matters.'

Her eyes grew wide. 'I am pleased it wasn't worse.'

Suddenly, she appeared no more tough than an infant, and that made him feel terrible. It was almost as if he had bruised her, and he was so grateful that the blemish was on him. 'I do apologise for my intrusion last night.'

'You don't have to.'

The thought concerned him. He didn't want her unprotected. 'I insist you tell your father and have him send your cousin packing.'

'I need her, though. She hosts things for him.'

A maid appeared out of nowhere, bringing a fresh pot of tea, the second one since he'd entered the room.

'You can take care of any events he has here.'

'I can't.' She took a deep breath and, without seeming to think, she thanked the maid and waited until she'd left before continuing their conversation.

'Standing and smiling and greeting all the different people is so taxing for me,' she said. 'I just can't.'

'Nonsense. You have a complement of staff to make sure everything goes well. And they did a remarkable job.'

'It has always been difficult for me to attend events, but it has been impossible for me to want to be in public since…recently. I just don't have a lot to say at soirees.'

'That would be much appreciated by some guests, who like to do a lot of the talking.'

'But the silence can be earth-shattering in its loudness around me, and I would wonder if they're thinking about… Did you hear about my betrothals?'

'I know Walter Jules.'

'So, you have heard what happened?'

'Possibly.' He flicked the words away with a light frown and a bump of his shoulder. 'It isn't my concern.' He had heard directly from Jules that Emory's daughter was considered a jilt. That she would appear deeply in love with a man, court him for a long while and then, when he became ready for marriage, she would end it. And then he had complained about the way she had conducted their romance, stating that she had never intended them to wed and changing her mind only days before the wedding.

'Well, it matters a great deal to me.'

He didn't want delve into a conversation about Jules. He was in attendance to discuss business with her father and he'd discovered that, when a woman revealed private thoughts to him, it was because she felt close to him. And he didn't want to foster a false sense of intimacy, although she did fascinate him.

He would never have guessed that a woman who appeared so gentle could possibly wake up throwing things. He would have imagined her screaming for help at the top of her lungs. Oh, that would have been a delightful ending to the soiree. Emory would never have forgiven him.

'Life has a way of reminding us that we're not really in charge.' How well he knew. He always seemed to be wrangling life into a force small enough to be reckoned with, and then whittling away at the problems.

'I agree,' she said quietly. 'I can't always predict what I will do. I sometimes think I surprise myself more than others. I apologise for last night.'

'No need for you to do that,' he said. 'If the Driscolls can be trusted to keep a secret, then time will smooth out the rough edges of this and it will fade away. I am getting to know Driscoll and, eventually, the passage of time will smooth a path for us to explain the situation.'

'I hope so.' She turned, moving to the book case to take a volume she'd left at the top of it.

He couldn't help himself. He laughed. 'You're selecting a book. Does it have sharp corners and does it toss well?'

She hefted it. 'I think it could probably work about as well as a blacksmith's anvil.'

'Then take care with it,' he said.

She left the book alone and returned to the chair, clasping at the back of it, but her fingers not stilling. 'I do beg your pardon for bruising you.'

'No need to. I recover quickly.'

'And thank you for keeping your silence. I could not bear another explosion around me.'

'Fireworks can be an adventure, but that was not the night or the place for them.'

'I can't seem to stay out of their path.' She brushed her hand over the arm of the chair, seeming more intent on the fabric than her conversation. 'People are still talking about my last broken betrothal and I wish them to stop. Father thought to have this event to make me feel better, and yet I could not force myself to attend. If anything, my absence probably made it worse. And then the Driscolls… It doesn't bear thinking about.'

'Don't hide. It makes it easier for others to talk about you and for your cousin to play her games.'

'After all the effort to make everything go well, I was tired and didn't want to attend. I could not paste a smile on my face. It wasn't hiding, but just doing what I preferred over being sociable. I made sure the guests had all they needed.'

He studied her. 'Are you sure you weren't hiding? I would guess that if you planned an evening's entertainments they would be to your liking.'

'Not as much as you'd think. Not at all. I wanted to rest and read. I didn't want to be a social butterfly, flittering about. My wings were tired.'

'You may have been tired, but you could toss a book

with force.' He touched his head and shook it as if it he could still feel the book hitting him.

'I've spent many hours gathering stones to skip across ponds,' she said. 'I suppose that is the secret.'

'I'll let you in on another secret,' he said. 'Don't take anything Darius says this morning seriously. He and I are becoming friends and spoke after breakfast.'

'You didn't tell him?' she asked.

'I told him enough,' he said. 'He was not happy about it. I asked him to help rectify the situation. Don't be surprised if he acts more aware of you than usual.'

'I don't need you to punish my cousin for me.'

'Well, perhaps it is for myself, then.' His lips firmed briefly and he admitted the truth. 'Oh, this is not only for you. And it's not half the retribution I would really choose.'

Chapter Four

Marianna tightened her lips. She'd thought she liked the Earl—Adam—but she wasn't so certain now. Her suitors in the past had all decided they knew what was best for her; Adam had just met her, was telling her not to hide and then saying he would get even with her cousin.

'If you feel you have been treated badly—and you have been,' she said, 'You're welcome to return home. But don't make any other decisions concerning the household.'

'Now you're telling me to leave,' he said. 'I suppose this ends our betrothal.' He put a hand over his heart and looked over her head. 'How will I go on?'

'Out of the door and down the street.'

His dropped his hand from his chest and smiled. 'You don't need anyone stepping up on your behalf.'

'No. I don't.' She tapped her hand harder on the arm of the chair. 'But everyone seems to think they should. I'm getting rather used to it from people I know. From someone I just met, however, I'm not willing to tolerate it.'

'My apologies.'

'And you know what the irony is?' she continued as if he'd not spoken. 'Everyone in the family says I always get my way.'

'Not having to attend a festivity you planned would make it seem that way, especially if you're the host's daughter.'

She waved his words away. 'That's true. But my presence wasn't needed.'

'People might like to meet you. And talk with you.'

'No.' She shook her head. 'The Driscolls know me, and most of the people were friends of my father's, or friends of Cecilia's. She enjoys greeting and speaking with people.'

'Did I hear my name?' Cecilia said as she flounced into the room, parasol at the ready, then paused, stilled and looked around, *joie de vivre* fading. 'Where is everyone?' Then she brushed the back of her fingertips over her chin. 'Not, of course, that I'm not thrilled see my dear cousin, and Adam.'

He gave her an answering nod that he probably used on servants about to be sacked, and she blinked it away.

'Father took them to see the stables,' Marianna answered.

'Well.' She frowned. 'I've already seen the new foal, and the boards surrounding it, but I could always look at them again.'

Then she twirled. 'Are you not in awe that I am awake this early in the day?'

'Yes,' Marianna said. 'It's not even dusk yet.'

'True,' Cecilia said. 'The dinner last night was entertaining. After all, I was looking quite ravishing.'

'You always look ravishing,' Marianna said. 'Except when you look more than ravishing. But it's your decidedly poor nature and sense of direction that results in your having no true friends.'

Cecilia smiled and spoke to Adam. 'And how do you like your room, Adam?' She blinked. 'I just realised this morning that I may have had too much to drink last night and could have misdirected you. If so, I sincerely apologise.'

'I don't think you misdirected me,' he said.

'Did you get that bruise…recently?' Cecilia asked, eyes on his forehead. 'I think the colour suits you, but then I cannot imagine a shade that does not look well on you.'

Adam didn't answer. 'It was a wonderful opportunity to meet the lovely Marianna,' he said.

'Ah,' Cecilia said. 'Please don't hold my *faux pas* against me.'

'I will,' Marianna assured her. 'What you did was hideous.'

The good cousin had had her feathers ruffled, and she'd stilled. The treacherous one needed to watch out for a book coming her way.

'You are the most conniving person that I know.' Marianna stood and put a hand on her hip. 'Father should not allow you in our house, and if I tell him he will be furious. You sent Adam to my room.'

Cecilia made a face. 'I knew you would send him on his way.'

'I was asleep.'

She gasped. 'Not really! That early?'

'Yes.'

'Well, my pardon.'

She turned to Adam. 'Really, was she asleep? Was she snoring?'

'Cecilia!' Marianna gasped. 'I could forgive you for the rest, but that is unforgiveable.'

'I was jesting. Completely.' She spoke to Adam. 'I bet that's really why she is upset. Was she snoring?'

'No.'

'Goodness. Then I have no understanding of why you're angry at me.' She spoke to Marianna, then addressed Adam again. 'She was probably lying there as beautiful as a princess and you walked in, a dashing dark form in the shadows, stood in awe of her beauty and she awoke, gazed at you and said, *"Ah, my lord, are you misplaced?"'*

'In times past, a woman like you might have been banished. For good reason,' Adam said. 'And it's more than due.'

Cecilia put a hand at her throat. 'I can't believe you don't thank me. How incredibly rude to Marianna.'

'Cecilia,' Marianna said. 'You *are* being banished—from my home. I will tell father and he will send you back to your parents.'

'I will make it up to you.' She pursed her lips and looked at the ceiling. 'Besides, I forgot to tell you that Jules wrote to your father and told him how he misses you and that he's reconsidering everything, including the marriage settlement. As if Jules couldn't have wed you and had you with him for ever. That worm.' She pretended to squash something under her foot. 'That's what I think of him for treating you so badly.'

'My good fortune that he did,' Marianna said. 'I am very thankful for that. I am destined to be a spinster.'

'I lie to other people. You tell other people the truth and lie to yourself. I do beg your forgiveness. But please let me spend more time with Darius before you send me away. I do adore him, and I only woke up this early so I could be with him. He said he wanted to go for a walk this morning.' She moved to the door. 'I'll go and collect him.'

Cecilia left in a swirl of peach and trail of lilac scent…or perhaps it was brimstone. Marianna didn't know what brimstone smelled like but she wouldn't put it past her cousin to make it smell good.

'You really should send her away.'

'She saved my life once, which makes it harder. Sometimes I wonder if I should be more like her. She does seem to weather the storms of life easier. Nothing seems to touch her. She bounces back from everything bad as if it is occurring to someone else, no matter what happens.'

'In that respect, and that alone, you could be more like her.'

Marianna wondered if that was why she preferred to stay in her room—the serenity of not worrying about what others thought. And wondered if she really did lack the courage to strike out on her own.

'Not bouncing back could mean things matter to you. That you don't brush them away easily because you feel they're important.'

Cecilia strolled back in again, Darius behind her. 'Look who I found in the hallway,' she said. 'Only one of the most endearing men in the world.'

Darius didn't seem to hear her.

'Oh, Marianna, you look lovely today,' he said, after greeting Adam when he walked in.

'Doesn't she?' Adam said. 'I'm so looking forward to taking a walk in the gardens with her.'

'So am I,' Darius added.

'I've enjoyed her insights on life,' Adam said.

'She is one of the most thoughtful people I know, and I heartily recommend her advice. On many occasions after she's spoken with me, I've been grateful to have heeded what she says.'

'I'm hoping Marianna and I might spend the day together,' Adam said. 'I want to talk with her.'

'Not without me,' Darius said, walking past Adam, taking Marianna's hand and gazing into her eyes. 'I've been giving her time to put Jules in her past, and I refuse to stand aside while someone else discovers her rarity. I made that mistake once. Never again.'

'But, Darius, we have known each other for ever,' Marianna said, and then she remembered that Adam had suggested that Darius would appear attracted to her...

'That only shows what a fool I've been,' he said. 'I should have been the first to propose to you. The only one to propose to you. We could have had children by now. Imagine.' He lifted his hand slightly and tightened his fingers. 'Children—ours.'

'You did wait too long again, Darius. I discovered her now, and I am fascinated by her,' Adam said. 'If you couldn't see what a jewel Marianna is years before now, I don't think you're the right person for her. You don't deserve her.'

'I agree,' Cecilia said, tugging at his arm. 'She is not right for you, Darius. She isn't.'

'I have to disagree.' Darius walked closer to Marianna. 'You are more lovely than a summer's day after a lifetime of winter.'

'Get away,' Adam muttered, and stepped in front of her. 'Stop thinking about her in such a way. You are a family friend, not a suitor.'

'And you think you are her suitor?'

'I might be,' Adam said. 'I know her father invited you here as a chance for you to get closer to her, but it's too late. You had your opportunity.'

'It's never too late. I have always cared deeply for her.'

'It seems everyone falls in love with her,' Adam said.

Darius sighed. 'Let's let Marianna decide between us. Our fate is in her hands.' He put his knuckles to his forehead.

'I wouldn't want either of you to get blood on your clothing fighting over me,' Marianna said. 'So, let us postpone this for another day.'

'Alas. I am alone.' Darius' lips quivered in laughter. 'I will go to the gardens and suffer.' He paused as he left, throwing his head back and giving a gasp of desperation. 'Come with me, Cecilia, while I tell you how my heart is broken.'

Cecilia glared at them and then ran after Darius.

'Darius really isn't that good an actor,' Marianna said. 'But it was a nice performance. Thank you.'

She stepped forward so she could see out of the window. Darius burst into the gardens and then doubled over in laughter. Cecilia stormed out behind him and started tapping him about the head and shoulders with her parasol.

Adam stepped behind Marianna. 'Her actions have repercussions. She needs to grasp that. Darius truly is a friend to you. He didn't like that she'd done it.'

'You told him all of it?'

'No. But, he's a good sort. Our paths haven't crossed much in the past, but I suspect they will more in the future. I wouldn't have thought it, but he does enjoy a jest.'

'Not normally.'

'You don't know him as well as you think. I'd wager he's been like a piece of furniture to you—always around, never in the way. He would have been a good person for you to court.'

'You're starting to sound like my father.' She turned. They were standing so close that she noticed how thick his lashes were, and the way they gave authority to his face. But it might just have been the strength in his gaze.

'Emory wishes the best for you. I'm sure of it. His voice embraces your name when he speaks it.'

'Oh, my. That is a sweet thing. No one has told me that before.' She touched his arm in gratitude.

'It seems obvious to me, a near stranger.'

'Father has tried to ease my path. Especially now.'

He wanted her to hold up her head up, to stand firm. 'That's what some parents do.'

'I admit, I was feeling very low when the courtship ended, and didn't want to go about if I might see any former suitor or anyone who knew of my losses in love. If I was seen out having a good time, I thought it would reflect badly on me. But now I'm used to it.'

'You have to give your side of the story. It's no crime for a woman to be selective.'

'My last suitor's side of the story is that I cancelled the wedding after the banns were read.' She firmed her lips. 'I did. I could not force myself to wed him, even though I loved him.'

'So much better than discovering after you were married. That would have been regrettable.'

'I just wish I had changed my mind earlier. That I could have seen him for what he was.' She left the window and stopped by the side table.

'You saw him for the person he presented himself as. He wanted you, so he acted the part you would like. You wanted him, so you believed the charade.'

'Thank you for your empathy.' She tapped her fingers on the table.

'Marianna…' he said softly, stopping her before she left the room.

She looked at him and waited.

'Does it matter? Truly?'

'It matters a lot to me. A lot.' With his back to the window and the light shining around him, he seemed more imposing than ever, but his eyes had softened more than she'd imagined possible.

'You made your views known. You chose to be alone rather than with him. If anyone criticises you for that and you let it bother you, then yes, you might have a problem.'

'That's not what you're supposed to say.' It hurt her that, even though he appeared to care about her, his words were so frank.

'The truth?'

'Well, you could make it a little sweeter.'

'Sweeter? Then what if I say that you look very lovely today and that, if you kept yourself from being trapped in a marriage you didn't want but you let that bother you then, yes, you might be the problem.'

'I'm so pleased you sweetened it up.' She grimaced broadly at him.

He smiled and reached out to her, giving her shoulder a gentle caress. 'I'm beginning to think the weakness in you is that you need to hear it. You should believe it from your marrow. It's not a good idea to base your opinion of yourself on what you *think* other people's judgement is, whether you think it is harsh or favourable. Besides, you can't change a blasted bit of the past.'

'I suppose,' she said. 'But I don't have to stare it in the eye.'

'You don't.'

She indicated the teapot. "May I?" she asked.

He nodded.

Then she poured a cup of tea while he spoke.

'But as long as you live," he said, "as long as people are people, your past will follow you. And people are going to look at your past with a tremendously powerful spyglass, with all the facts gained by passage of time. All of them, real or imagined. The only time people forget your past is when you are irrelevant to them. And it sounds like that's what you're trying to do—become irrelevant to everyone outside your home. And it's wrong.'

She offered him the cup of tea and he took it.

'Did your tutor teach you that?' She asked.

He sipped, then put the cup back on the saucer and set it aside. 'In a sense. My uncle.'

'My governess taught me that nodding and agreeing with everything might benefit me.'

'She wasn't good at teaching, I see.'

Marianna paused. 'Perhaps not.'

He moved so he could reach her shoulders, and look directly into her eyes. 'Give up on it. You already have, but you've not realised it. Calling off a wedding was a big statement. Telling the truth as you believe it is kind, when you are in private conversation, even if it has jagged edges. In public, it can be different. It's best to be noncommittal if possible. In public, people see any disagreement as a personal affront. A challenge, a request for a verbal duel.'

Jagged edges. Verbal duels. He made conversation sound like warfare.

'Well that all sounds good but practising it is entirely different. That is my viewpoint with a spyglass.'

'Maybe you need to check for dirt on the lens.' He stepped closer. 'I forgot to tell you that. These lenses collect dirt, dust and all things unpleasant. Cleaning them is a constant battle.'

She cocked her head. 'What else did you forget to tell me about spyglasses?'

'They come in various sizes, shapes and some of them aren't solid.'

'Well, I hope mine is sturdy.'

'Perhaps you do need some of that nonsensical praise. But you need to hear it from yourself.'

He studied her. Then he took her by the shoulders and peered at her as strongly as a lost sailor studying the horizon in search of land. 'Forget about the man and the past. And when you get up in the morning, every morning, look in the mirror and tell yourself the compliments or praise that you need to hear. And don't take any nonsense from that cousin of yours.'

He stepped away and she had to strengthen herself to keep from wobbling once his hands left her shoulders.

'You don't lack assuredness.' She stared at him. It was like watching a rock in heavy waves which didn't move while the other pebbles were tumbled about.

'We're all just animals in clothing,' he said. 'Hungry wolves don't pick the strongest creature when they attack, now, do they?'

She blinked at him and took a small step back. 'I'm not the most robust. And I can't forget that everyone knows how foolish I was.'

'Just pull out a measure of the strength you must have had when you called off the marriage.'

Marianna studied the door—much easier than meeting his eyes. 'It wasn't strength. My father spelled out the truth for me probably a thousand times before I listened. I couldn't face anyone. I knew what a foolish person I was, and I know I could continue to be.'

She grasped that. It had been cowardice as much as anything that had caused her to call off the marriage—and Cecilia telling her to stand firm. She had made the mistake of not listening to the inner voice and the outer truths, and it had almost landed her in a lonely marriage with a husband who wasn't overly concerned about fidelity or discretion but was a firm believer in her forgiveness and funds.

'I was weak.' And she had been, to wait so long to

end it. To have given even half a speck of thought about returning to him. She remembered the whispers she'd overheard, and ignored—that Jules had been another of her suitors who'd seen bank notes within his grasp.

'But now you have him behind you. And get up every morning, look in the mirror, give yourself a speech about your strength and howl like a wolf, if that's what it takes to get power to continue to do the right thing.'

'Is that how you gained your confidence? By looking in the mirror and acting tough?'

'No. I fought. I fought boys who were bigger than me, and tougher. Sometimes I was batted about a considerable amount. Sometimes I challenged the biggest one just to see how he would react.'

She could imagine him doing that, being unafraid of fighting. 'Were these boys, perhaps, your brothers?'

'No. At that point, I had no brother.'

'Wasn't your father angry?'

'He didn't know.' He studied her as if the possibility hadn't occurred to him. 'I chose to do it. I liked proving myself. I would run with the tenants' sons, and the young men hired to work in the stables and such. They wanted me to know that they were strong, and I had to show them my strength time and time again, and I did. Not just for them, but for me.'

'Did no one reprimand you?'

'Dinsmore—my valet—would be upset sometimes about me destroying my clothing and having bruises, and he'd worry that I or one of the other boys would break a bone. But he was often irritated with me.' He paused. 'In some ways, getting him angry was part of the enjoyment.'

'My life hasn't been like that.' She'd had a governess, Cecilia and a maid keeping watch over her. Rarely had she been without supervision in her childhood. In fact, she couldn't remember being alone except when she went to bed.

'Perhaps it was your loss, then.'

'Let's see… So, is this your advice…?' She couldn't howl in front of him, but she put up her fists, adopted a pugilistic pose and grumbled. Then she cocked her head. 'See how unfrightening I am when I do that?'

'I have to agree.' He lowered his chin and stared at her. 'It's not about the other people. It's against yourself that you need to win the battle.'

'I think I'm happy not to win. Perhaps, in my own way, I'm strong. Your way was best for you and reading a book is best for me.'

He shook his head. 'I give up. You are defeating yourself.'

'That's why I like to be alone. I tried another romance the first time I had a betrothal end. But that led to a much worse situation. Besides, I could not use someone that way.'

'You shouldn't use people.'

She supposed those poundings he'd taken from the other boys, and had given, had made him far stronger than she would ever be.

'It would have been a lot more difficult,' he continued, 'If you didn't have a safe haven, and you do, in your father's home…as long as your cousin isn't around.'

She walked to the window and peered out. 'Well, she and Darius have left now.'

He took her arm. 'Now that they've wandered off,

would you be kind enough to show me around the grounds?'

'You must be brave. You've not recovered from the first time we were alone.'

She tapped her forehead in the area where the bruise on his head still showed. 'I'm stronger than you realise.'

'I will keep my eyes on you.' He studied her, eyes intent. 'That will be a pleasure.'

'Should I get the book?'

He chuckled and raised an arm to protect his head. 'I will keep a safe distance. Why don't you take a chance that a walk with me will be a pleasant diversion?'

'I will, if you don't offer any more advice.'

'Not offer advice?' he mocked. 'I consider my words not to be advice but great wisdom.'

She rolled her eyes and pretended to have a rebuttal caught in her throat. Then she strolled out of the door, head high.

'Come along,' she said. 'I can show you Father's version of a folly, but Cecilia and I always imagined it ours. It was a good place to play when I was a child. I acted out dramas there and pretended the trees were my audience. Sometimes Cecilia would join in, but she was older and didn't enjoy it as much.'

'I would like to see it.'

She led him outdoors, happy to feel the sunshine on her face and pleased to have him at her side.

She hoped he would feel the same imagination she had in the area. It had been her favourite place to play, and she'd pretended it was a castle, or a cottage or a dungeon, even though it was completely open on one side.

'I had wooden swords, and sometimes Father let us stay out until late at night with torches all around.'

He saw a small house in the distance that really didn't seem large enough for a servant. 'What's that?' he asked.

She dipped her head and waved away the answer. 'Oh, it was one of Father's ideas. When I was a child, he said I had so many dolls that they needed a house of their own.'

She strolled along without taking any real notice of what she had said, and he took a second look at the little house. It even had a small chimney. And then he took another glance at her, wondering if she was oblivious to the fact that she might be the only woman in the world whose dolls had a heated home.

They walked down the stone path and found the folly and the small pillars designed to hold lights.

On three sides it was shaped like a fortress, with two huge windows facing east and a stone floor that extended around it, making a small pavilion.

'This is the best place to watch the sun rise,' she said. 'In winter, a fire built at the open side can keep a person warm, and Father would have servants cover the windows with oilcloth, and sometimes put a covering over the top. The governess told Father she did not want me to get ill in the cold, but she admitted later she hated the temperature. The younger maids told me they enjoyed playing soldiers with me, except the housekeeper didn't like them to shirk their duties.'

She hadn't just had a dolls' house at her fingertips, she'd had a whole village of people. He glanced back to the main house, rising above the treetops—a fortress around her, protecting her innocence.

'I can imagine a child loving this,' he said, not meaning the structures, but the world she'd been nestled into.

He'd actually slept under the stars at one of the fairs when he'd been young, not too far from a rowdy group who'd spent the night singing lusty ballads. Dinsmore had searched him out and had given him an earful. No one else had even noticed him missing.

He smiled, relishing the memories.

'I did like this pavilion, but sometimes I wished it brighter,' she said. 'While I like the coolness in the summer, it does attract bugs, but my governess swept them out for us.'

He didn't remember ever noticing a bug in his childhood, although he was sure they must have been there. She had grown up in the same world as he had, but the distance between them was as great as the earth to the stars.

She reached out and patted the unpolished stone. 'I was happy I wouldn't have to leave my father when I wed Jules because there is plenty of room for families to live privately on father's estate.'

He frowned. 'Oh, please say his name once more. I never get tired of hearing it.'

'That is definitely honesty. Of a fractured sort.'

'But I made my point.' He lifted a broken twig and tossed it out of the folly. 'He gave you passion. A feeling mistaken for love. It's not that difficult. It's natural; as easy as a kiss. And, if you need one, I'm available.'

'Really?' she asked. 'I'm not going to ask you for a

kiss.' Then she paused, studying the strong jawline, the shoulders, the dare in his eyes. 'Probably.'

He sat on the bench and stretched his legs in front of him, leaning back, his elbows on the stone arm. 'I'm not so proud. If you want to kiss me at any time during this visit, I'm available. You can consider that a request in stone.' His eyes danced along the rocks and his smile was a dare.

She chuckled. 'You swore at me last night.'

'Not you. The situation. I was surprised.'

'Not as much as I.'

His face turned serious and his voice soft. 'Would you let me kiss you? I believe I can show you the falseness of passion. And make you forget your former betrothed. Just remember, it would be a lesson of the body and not of anything else.'

'I really shouldn't.'

'Understandable.' He clasped his fingers and used them, arms stretched back, to pillow his head. 'Totally understandable.'

He shut his eyes but, when he opened them, his gaze was serious. 'After all, I would just give you a soft kiss on the cheek. Just a brush, and it would give me a chance to feel your skin.' He spoke the words with the sincerity of a lover. 'To experience the moment of touching you. To breathe in the scent of your perfume. To see the flutter of your lashes against your cheeks. To be close to your femininity. For you, it would be just a kiss on the cheek. For me, it would be a moment to treasure.'

'A kiss on my cheek?'

'Certainly. I would not impose otherwise on your good nature.' He said the words as a promise between them.

She lowered her chin and stared at him. 'My nature's not that good.'

He sat upright, laughing softly. 'It is.' He stood. 'Of course, my cheek is available for you at any time.'

'It looks a bit scratchy.' She touched her bottom lip. 'Probably feels bristly. And you might smell like boot leather. And I bet your coat retains the scent of smoking, and nights out at the club, and just plain decadence.'

'If that were true, Dinsmore would never forgive himself.' He briefly held his arm to his face, sniffed strongly and said, 'I smell good.'

She laughed.

She walked closer, took a pinch of his coat sleeve and pulled his arm to her nose. She sniffed and waited a moment. 'Yes. Smells like…flowers.'

His eyes narrowed. 'No, it doesn't.'

'Yes. It does.'

She didn't release his sleeve at first, and he moved his arm to his face.

'It does.' He frowned. 'Dinsmore is going to answer for this. I smell like a lady.'

'You do not.' She smiled. 'I like the way you smell. Manly, but with a hint of floral.'

He looked skyward. 'A man never smells like a flower.'

'I would disagree.'

She moved in closer, tiptoed, wobbled and put her nose near his cheek. 'Definitely floral.'

'No.' He clasped her waist, steadying her. With his free hand, he lifted her wrist to his nose. 'This is floral.'

She stumbled against his chest and put her palm flat to steady herself, then brushed her finger down his cheek. 'Manly.'

She put a soft kiss on his cheek, surprised that she didn't notice stubble but just the warmth of him, the moment of closeness. 'Reminds me of kissing a rose petal.'

'A manly rose petal?' he asked, daring her with his perusal.

'Of course.' Her eyes sparkled.

He took her hand. 'I feel concern for any of your future suitors. You can be a trial.'

She moved outside, pulling him along with her hand in his, but released him as soon as they stepped out of the folly. 'I will show you the rest of the gardens.'

'Thank you for the kiss,' he said. 'And if you were thinking of anyone else, anyone else in the entire world in those moments, then it was not a success.'

She pursed her lips for a second. 'I would say it was a success.' She studied him. 'Were you only doing that to prove to me that I am over him?

Lifting her hand, he studied it, rubbing a thumb against her knuckles. 'Innocent Marianna. I did want to put him in your past, both for you…and for myself. At another time, I hope you might go with me on a carriage ride in the park?'

He took her arm and draped it over his. They fitted perfectly side by side, and he made her feel cherished, and tiny and larger at the same time.

Then she saw her father and everyone else returning from the stables. The way they were standing so close was almost a declaration of courtship.

Her father's glare could have flayed leaves from the trees: Mr Driscoll's was even worse. But Mrs Driscoll gave a knowledgeable smile and waved to them.

He spoke softly. 'Head high. You control this moment.'

Chapter Five

She was summoned to her father's private sitting room, her feet feeling heavy on the rug.

She opened the door and he entered from his bedroom, holding a comb.

'Marianna, I saw you returning from the folly with that earl. He wants me to finance his oar-building business, or whirligig endeavour or some such. Be aware that he could be sweet-talking you to get to me.'

'You invited him here as a conquest for Cecilia.'

'She reminds me of her mother, and I can't stand that woman. I'd be getting an earl by marriage and losing a niece. A perfect situation.' He finished combing his hair.

'Father. We do need to talk about this.' She sat in an over-stuffed chair.

'I fear we are about to have a discussion,' he said, voice weary, pointing the comb at her. 'I would like to know in advance if I am to be angered, lose money or lose sleep—and I would guess all three.'

'That is unfair,' she said. 'I have not given you one moment of anything but peace for several months.'

'True,' he said. 'And I have not thanked you for it. I know that it has been hard for you,' he said.

She raised an eyebrow. 'And now you are matchmaking for Cecilia and me. Only, it's not working out like you planned.'

'I invited the Earl to introduce him to Cecilia, to get her settled. She's… Well, it would be nice to have an earl for a nephew. The Driscolls' son was half in love with you, but you're letting your cousin steal him away. He's thoughtful, smart and he will inherit their fortune.' He stared into the distance. 'My grandchildren could have an empire.'

'We are friends, but nothing more.'

'Well, that's a better start than your other romances.'

'I am not good at them. I have accepted that I may never marry.'

He used the comb to tap his cheek. 'In that case, I should take more care over who I introduce to Cecilia.'

She nodded.

'Marianna, you should not judge all men by one,' he said. 'But it is fine to compare the Earl to Jules. The Earl has swaggered around town here and there for years— that's why I've never wanted you introduced to him. His father died while he was just becoming a man, and he and his stepmother go their separate ways, though she is barely older than he is.'

He threw the comb onto the table. 'In some respects, he is like you. He shuns parties, though I am sure he gets invited. He goes as he wants, where he wants.'

'Is that a bad thing?'

'Not in your case, as you had rather be home taking care of things here or visiting your aunts or some such.'

He put his hand on her shoulder. 'Marianna, for you, industry is what you prefer. The housekeeper didn't tell me the plans for the guests and ask approval—you told me over dinner. The butler informed me you wanted the new walkway completed well in advance, and you narrowed the choices down before the stone mason even discussed it with me.'

'I am your daughter. And I like rock pathways.'

'True,' he said. 'And you should give Driscoll's son a chance. He's studious, adept at business, devoted to working with his father. He would make a match for you.'

'I know,' she said. She searched her heart. If she was being sensible, Darius would be perfect for her. He worked side by side with his father, and he was ever so polite, and she truly did like him in a distant but caring way. It would be so unfair to compare him to the Earl, but she did.

Darius's eyes glazed over if she discussed anything of feelings, commerce or plans. Now, he could discuss events and horses *ad infinitum*, and how the sun shone on Cecilia's hair. Marianna could only talk of society for so long, horses even less and, whenever he started on Cecilia, she put her fingers in her ears and started humming. He laughed and the conversation changed.

She wondered what her problem was that she always seemed most interested in men who could cause her grief. Perhaps her spyglass was more of a kaleidoscope.

'I have always liked Darius, but it will never be more than that. I have known him since we were children— he is more like a brother than a sweetheart.'

Her father puffed out his cheeks momentarily, then

admitted, 'I invited Adam because he was so persistent about an idea he had. He was so earnest. But he's also aware of women.'

She prompted him to elaborate with a small wave of her hand.

'If an attractive woman enters the room, he is aware of her. He always remembers their names. I had noticed that before our event. Then, last night, he talked solidly with me concerning tariffs, licences and fees for transporting soda but, when Jacobson walked up and asked if we had seen his wife, Adam mentioned that she had moved to the garden with Susanna. I was facing the garden door and had noticed them going through the doorway. Adam's back was to it. He must have seen from the corner of his eye. But he hadn't wavered in his discussion.'

'He's observant.'

'He is much like that scoundrel who courted you, except he has a title. Don't make the same mistake twice, or three times,' he said. 'I love you dearly, and respect your decisions, but if you keep repeating a mistake it's not the mistake's fault.'

He slapped his palm against his head. 'I never even noticed it, or I wouldn't have invited him. Same height as Jules, similar appearance… Yes. It's Jules all over again.'

'No, it's not.' Marianna paused, wondering if her father was right. 'He asked me if I might accompany him on a ride in the park.'

Her father held up both hands as if he were imploring the heavens to impart wisdom on her.

'That is the same as courting…courting disaster.'

'No.'

'Accept his invitation, then,' he said, biting out his words. 'But you are not to allow yourself to be the subject of pain caused by him. I do not want you hurt.'

'I have no intention of it.'

Her father swung his hand low and snapped his fingers. 'No intention. But if you travel a road to Bath don't expect to end up on the west coast. And do not become betrothed if you don't intend to go through with it. I will not step in this time. He's got a title.'

'I do like him,' she said, waving his words away with a flick of her wrist. She looked at her father and spoke quietly. 'And he has completely erased Jules from my thoughts.'

'Marianna, you—you are quickly losing all semblance of propriety,' he sputtered in his haste. 'At this point you need to settle with a nice man like Driscoll. Society will accept you having a few romances to find out you prefer a solid man. But, if you are seen as pursuing the Earl, people may jump to the conclusion you rid yourself of one man because you saw another with a title.'

'I wouldn't marry to have a better social standing. Mine is good enough for me. Almost too good.' If she wed an earl, she'd have to be in public more, and she wouldn't like that. He would likely expect his wife to attend many events with him and would have more soirees than her father did.

'Well, you cannot go about with him without a chaperone. Cecilia will go with you.'

'Cecilia?' Her voice rose. 'She is apt to lead me into more trouble.'

'You are well old enough that no one should be able to lead you into any trouble you don't want to find on your own. Don't forget that.'

'That is unfair.'

'To watch you suffer through another heartache is unfair to me, and to give me a son-in-law interested in my funds is unfair.' Then he studied her. 'Oh well, if you err this time, get that ring on your finger. Get me a peer for a grandson.'

'Father. That's cold.'

'Not in my opinion,' her father said. 'He's an earl—four letters. Wipes away so many errors. Like "*coin*". I don't see why you worry about the past. With your appearance and my funds, you can court any unmarried man.'

'That is the problem.'

'Yes. You find the ones who would make a good husband uninteresting. I brought Darius here and you have mostly ignored him. Cecilia is keeping him company. But do you think she truly sees him or his purse?'

'And do you think he sees her or her appearance?'

'You are far more attractive than her, have better manners and would make a much better wife. Any dolt could see that.'

'You are my father, so of course you believe that.'

'I am a businessman first, father second. You have always known that.'

'And I have always known that you groomed me to know as much about your business, if not more, than a son would have.'

She stepped over to pick up the comb he'd put on the table. 'You hired the best to teach me. And, yes, you have always said "*business first*". When we had breakfast together; when I sat in your library and you made the man of affairs wait when I wanted to talk with you. When I was ill and you spent the entire week at my bedside. When I cried over my ended romance. Yes, business first, family second. You said it over and over, but your actions were opposite.'

'Well, no one is perfect.' He slammed the door shut as he left. Then he opened it and looked back. 'Business first. And, if anyone cares for you, they will put business first because it will make the best life for you. I have enquired about the Earl's finances. They are better than they used to be. I don't know if it is worth looking into further, but I would do business with him if you were his wife.' His brows furrowed. 'Because you are my daughter and can make good decisions in finance, even if you cannot where the heart is involved.'

He shut the door more quietly this time.

Marianna returned the comb to her father's dressing room, and then checked the mirror. Her comfortable, wrinkled dress would not do for an outing.

She quickly summoned a maid and changed her clothing, choosing a blue gown with a bodice trimmed in a darker blue ribbon which continued around the hem in several rows. The lace fichu was not as soft as she would have liked, but was matched at the hem of the sleeves. Then she hurried down the stairs, anxious to see Adam again.

She walked into the room, and his eyes rested on hers. Her heart jumped two steps ahead of her, then three, then four.

Adam stood, thumbing through a book on Greek architecture. He was as appealing as any display of syllabub, comfits, marzipan or macaroons, even with the bruise on his forehead.

She moved to the sofa and lifted a poetry book from the side table, pressing her hand over the embossed lettering, before re-shelving it. 'My cousin is to be our chaperone, and I want to apologise for her in advance. Plus, I can explain why I have so much forgiveness for her.'

'I can hardly believe the two of you are related.'

'I have thought the same thing. But she would fight someone three times her size for me. She once proved her compassion by throwing herself in front of me when I was standing near a carriage that started rolling towards me without my realising it. She jumped forward and pushed me out of the way, taking the brunt of the hit. Later, neither one of us could believe she'd been so brave. She risked her life for me, and it was weeks before she could walk comfortably. She admitted she didn't know if she'd do it again.'

'Your cousin sacrificed herself for you?'

'Yes. And there were witnesses, or I might not have believed it myself. She's been an older sister to me, and sometimes almost a mother, albeit one without much conscience.'

'You'd think she could borrow yours on occasion.'

She laughed away his words. 'Again, proof of my inability to make the best decisions. I do care for her.' She tucked a tress behind her ear.

'I would suggest you enlarge your circle of friends.'

'I have done that with betrothals and it hasn't worked

out too well.' She studied his face. 'No opinion. No kind words.'

'I'm sure you had a good reason to call the wedding off and, even if you didn't, better Jules find it out early than after the wedding.' He shut the book and slipped it back into the bookcase.

She let out a puff of breath and raised her brows. 'That's not what you're supposed to say to me.'

'Well, it's what I said to him when we were at the club and he told me. Plus, I told him he was about as suited to marriage as he was to be a vicar.' He peered at another volume and took it out, one her father had purchased on modern farming practices. 'I don't think I've ever heard of a marriage being called off and it being a mistake.'

'The two of you discussed me?'

'Somewhere between the taste of the ale and him telling me about his new carriage. He mentioned he had not seen me about much and wished to thank me for that, and wondered if I had a new sweetheart or was visiting an old one. I told him that he should keep wondering, and that he should be so fortunate as I.'

'And what was the conversation about me?'

He slipped the tome back without looking at it.

'He told me the betrothal was off, that you were too fickle for him. And I told him he had confused the meaning of the word "fickle" with "intelligent".'

She hadn't really considered him discussing her, although she knew she'd been a topic of conversation among the ladies.

'He called me fickle?'

'It was only an attempt at salving his pride. It really

didn't matter to me. And it still doesn't.' He walked away from the bookcase and stood closer to the doorway. He raised his chin. 'He called my horse an old nag, and Mercury is a rare and wonderful beast, so I knew he was feeling low.'

She'd not thought of Jules being dismayed by the broken betrothal, so aware had she been only of her own feelings, but perhaps he had been. But that was the past, and Adam was standing in front of her. Her mind returned to her father's comment about Adam's romances. She knew nothing further about them.

'Have you had many sweethearts?' she asked.

He stilled and raised a brow, pointing out the personal nature of her question. 'Not now. And it's always singular, not plural. But I don't think a man could be my age and not have a few indiscretions. I'd feel I was in error if I didn't. That's how we mature. Though we don't have to make every mistake to discover the truth of them. Or even most of them.'

'But it's a convenient way.'

'And inconvenient too,' he informed her. 'But not as much to me as it is you. I don't hide away after a romance ends—the opposite. If I wasn't happy about it, I try to use revelry to put it in the past.'

'That is what Father is trying to get me to do with the soirees, but I'd rather be by myself. He worries about it. That's why Darius is here.'

'I would have thought the title would have put me first in the competition for your hand,' he said, and chuckled.

'You would have thought it,' Marianna said, and

paused. 'But, you have to admit, Darius has the qualities a father would prefer for his daughter. He's reserved and agreeable.'

'And you're the nice cousin?'

She paused. 'I could have been wrong on that.'

He continued, 'Remember what I said—we are just animals in human form. Think of the animals fighting for dominance, for food, for territory. We see their claws and fangs, and think ourselves superior because we speak our opinions. But sometimes we joust for position just as much as the lower life forms. And we are civilised—somewhat.'

Marianna was so civilised. A woman raised in a house of privilege, unaware of anything else. He'd seen more footmen in her house than he had servants in his.

'Did you know before you visited that Jules was not my first betrothal?'

'I had heard,' he said. 'But again, idle conversation. That was not nearly as interesting a topic among my friends as how our drinks tasted, the weather and whether Miss Susie used her spare stockings to accentuate her ample bosom.'

'It's ghastly that you would talk about such things.' She didn't hesitate. 'And I have it on good authority that she does.'

'See? We are all animals.'

'I'm imperfect, as we all are, and I'm reminded of that imperfection when I think of my last romance.'

It bothered him to think of her betrothed to Jules. It had ever since he had kissed her. The moment had sparked something in him. He had been trying to show her that Jules was nothing more than a memory, and yet it had ignited an awareness in him of her femininity.

Her eyes had shown an awareness too, and seeing the change in her had taken his breath. He'd not believed it possible.

She touched a finger to her lip. 'Tell me you have no regrets.'

'I'm human. I do, but I try not to dwell on them. Sometimes, I might try to be aware of them, so I'll make better decisions going forward, but that's about it.'

Until that moment it had been true, but now regret flooded into him. Regret that he had not met her long ago and spent lazy summers with her, and long winter nights.

Inwardly, he gave himself a shake and pushed those feelings away, telling himself they were an aberration caused by the rarity of being close to someone with her innocence. He would not let that inexperience affect him. He had believed in that kind of innocence once, and that had led to his biggest regret. He had once fallen in love with his whole heart, and she'd had no heart at all.

He'd learned that either innocence was fraud, or it was a lack of guile caused by an unawareness of the world and an inability to form a lasting bond with another person.

'I wish I could be so untroubled about things,' she said.

Her intense perusal of him almost made him smile. 'I didn't say that is always a good course. But yours causes too much concern. Choose either to be wed or live unwed happily.'

'Good advice. But much too simple.'

'Perhaps then you should have friends and not a husband. Find a good parrot.'

'A parrot?' she asked.

'If you only want to hear your own opinions.'

'You would obviously not make a good parrot.'

'I would not,' he said. Their eyes met, and in that moment he forgot his promise to himself about keeping his distance from her. 'But I could make a good lover.'

Blast, he'd jested with her.

Her eyes widened. 'You are impertinent.'

'Yes,' he said, and moved his head closer to her so he could speak even softer. 'Don't forget that.' He studied her, smiled and said again, 'Please don't forget that.'

'Well, I have a whole carriage ride to look for flaws in you.'

'I could probably point you to some people who would fill you in on plenty of them.'

'People…or women?'

'Both. But again, that is hindsight, and if every experience changes us slightly then it might not be accurate as an assessment. And it might not be correct if we are different with every person we meet, and most of us are somewhat.'

Footsteps sounded in the corridor. Her father and the Driscolls passed by the door, discussing the horses, but then her father returned.

Her father took in the room for a moment 'Are the two of you still going on a carriage ride?'

'Yes. We're waiting for our chaperone.'

'Well, try to come home with all the horses you leave with.' He looked at his daughter.

She waved away his words explaining to Adam. 'That is a family jest…that I try to exchange horses for something I like better.'

'As a child, she tried to convince me to trade her horse to the proprietor of the confectionery shop. She would have happily emptied the stalls for a shop of treats.'

'I thought it was a grand bargain.' She laughed at the memory. 'I am still not uncertain. Father thinks he should purchase an entire shop for me on my birthday, but he can't find the right location.'

A shop? He didn't think they were jesting.

'Location is an important factor,' her father agreed. 'But what was the other?'

'You make your profits when you buy the supplies, not when you sell the goods,' Marianna repeated. 'The original purchases are most important. You can almost never correct a misstep you've made at the original acquisition, either with land or with merchandise.'

'Yes. The purchase is the most important part of the agreement,' her father repeated, before giving Adam a silent appraisal and returning his gaze to her. 'That can be true of many things. I raised you to think for yourself, not for anyone else.' He spoke again as he strolled out of the door. 'Particularly anyone else.'

'Oh, she can think for me,' Cecilia said, strolling down the stairs and flouncing into the room. 'But, even if she does, I can ignore her good plans as well as I ignore everyone else's.'

'Oh, hush Cee.'

Cecilia rolled her eyes. 'I might if you will not call me that ever again.'

Adam held out his arm to Marianna. 'My carriage is outside.' Adam indicated for Cecilia to proceed him.

'I brought a book so I could read. And,' Cecilia said to Adam on the way to the carriage, 'I wondered, why haven't you married before now?'

Adam looked at Cecilia. 'I've not met the right woman.'

Cecilia waved her hand as if relegating his answer to the coals. 'What about the truth?'

'I haven't met the right woman,' Adam repeated, shrugging and looking at Cecilia as if he would bat back whatever she asked.

'And where've you been looking?'

He helped them into the carriage and spoke as if it were of no consequence. 'Apparently not in the right places.'

They settled into their seats and the vehicle rolled away.

Adam's eyes had a shuttered look, but then he turned to Marianna. 'I hope you did not tutor her on those questions. They were similar to yours.'

'True. But I would feel free to ask you any questions I wanted answers to.'

'Good,' he said. 'And I would hope you would understand if I declined to answer.'

'Probably not.'

Marianna was glad she was not completely immune to his charms. If the apothecary could have bottled Adam's smile and sold it, the chemist wouldn't have needed the other medicines he dispensed. A look at Adam could cure a lot of minor ailments, and a few major ones, she imagined.

Of course, the apothecary would need to keep some kind of new medicine for curing broken hearts, though...

He used his thumb to dust at a speck of something on his coat sleeve she couldn't see.

She compared his hands to her own. His had a beauty borne of strength. A strength not so well hidden, and an assuredness that she would never be able to match. If his ancestors had received the title in the same way she suspected most peers had, his forebears had probably assured the continuation of their title through bravery and intelligence—and fate, nature or luck had passed these on to him.

No wonder he did well in the world. When he stared, he could make men back away, and when he smiled, he drew all eyes to his face.

'Talk amongst yourselves,' Cecilia said. 'I'll read.' She opened her book. 'Aloud.'

Adam glanced at Marianna and his lips turned up. 'I suppose we'll listen, then.'

Momentarily, Marianna's gaze locked on him. He flicked a glance her way and his lip quirked up, almost in the same way two people would share a private jest.

Cecilia's droning voice read on, but finally Marianna could stand no more about the tale of people who shared castles with their ghostly ancestors.

'Adam, would you mind stopping the carriage so that I might walk a bit? I would so like that,' Marianna asked. 'If we can leave Cecilia behind with her book?'

In moments he had stopped the carriage and jumped from the vehicle, landing so gracefully it looked as if he'd swung to the ground. Marianna took a moment to let her mind linger on the image of his legs leaving the carriage.

Cecilia's cough was not at all discreet. 'Don't do anything I wouldn't do.' She cleared her throat. 'And don't do anything I would do.'

'Don't worry about it,' Marianna said as Adam helped her disembark. Then he shut the door behind her.

They began to walk the path that she had taken many times with different suitors, but with Adam at her side even the sky felt brighter, bigger and clearer.

Adam seemed far more astute than her former suitors—quieter, more introspective, holding his cards closer to his chest. More of a potential mistake.

'Do you wager?' she asked.

'Occasionally.'

'Do you lose?'

'Sometimes.'

'I try not to wager. If I win nine out of ten times, I am still angry at myself.'

'You shouldn't be so afraid to lose.'

'You don't know me. I have a low tolerance for mistakes, but I do keep a tally sheet with some of Father's business endeavours. He asks my opinion, and I tell him, but he has promised that the final decision will always be his.'

'Do you come out ahead?'

'Usually. He helps with the decisions so much, though.'

'In his finances?'

'Yes. I really do assist him. But he explains it all so perfectly, the decision is easy. I wish I could have made the right conclusions with my beaus.'

'With them, you only have to be fortunate once, and keep that one close.'

A bark disrupted her thoughts.

Weaving around the carriages and dodging a thrown hat, a dog ran out. It appeared fonder of mud than food and bounded up. Adam stepped in front of Marianna. The dog jumped on Adam, panting happily, paws connecting with his chest, adding streaks of mud to his clothes as Adam lowered the creature's paws to the ground. She heard the oath under his breath.

A little boy appeared out of nowhere, a ragamuffin, looking no cleaner than the dog.

'Pardon, mister. Pardon,' he called out. 'We was walkin'. He got away.'

Then Marianna saw the sad rope, little more than a frayed thread, that had been used to lead the dog.

Her father would have been furious at the muddy dog, the unkempt boy and the distraction in his day that would force him to return home to clean up.

'He's new and he ain't used to me yet,' the boy said.

'What's his name?' Adam asked.

'Maximillian-Maximillian,' the boy said. 'I thought he was good enough for two names.'

'Well, I suppose he is,' Adam said, patting the mongrel on the head and grabbing the frayed end of the rope. Then he reached into his waistcoat pocket and pulled out a coin. He flipped it to the boy, who caught it while Adam still held the frazzle of hemp. 'Why don't you treat him to a new collar?'

The boy's eyes widened as he examined the coin. 'Mister, I ain't ever seen this much money.'

'Maximillian-Maximillian probably hasn't either. If

there's any left over, a treat for both of you.' He returned the frayed rope to the boy.

'Thank you, mister.' The boy took the dog, fingers clutched tightly around the coin. 'We be gettin' a right fine collar right now.' And he scurried off, with the dog panting happily behind him.

Adam dusted off the front of his coat. 'It will take more than a coin to get Dinsmore's forgiveness.' He chuckled.

'But he's your servant,' she said.

'He's not really a servant,' Adam said. 'He's been more of a father to me. And if letting him grumble makes it easier for him to handle the task of cleaning this—' he indicated his coat front and trousers '—then I will let him have a bit of a protest.'

'My servants would never dare.'

'As they shouldn't,' he said, looking at the splatters on his coat.

She reached into her reticule and took out a white, silk embroidered handkerchief to dust off his coat. He clasped her wrist gently, stopping her, the responsiveness to him replacing all other awareness in her body. His clasp could almost have encircled her wrist twice.

'No,' he said. 'The handkerchief you have is too elaborate.' Releasing her and reaching into his pocket, he took out an unembroidered one that appeared twice as big and many times as thick as hers. 'This one is better.'

He dusted the front of the garment, making the cloth brown and not doing a lot for his coat.

'Well, I tried,' he said, and laughed. 'That dog reminded me of one the stable master had when I was a youngster. Dinsmore allowed me to play with the dog, but I didn't have one of my own.'

She folded the silk handkerchief and put it away, watching Adam. 'Has he been with you all your life?'

'Yes. Dinsmore is my uncle. He was charged with looking after me, and then tutoring me. And then he started taking care of my clothing when I needed a valet. And some days he promotes himself to butler. He does whatever he thinks is needed in my household.'

Surprise flitted across her face. 'Doesn't your butler mind?'

'You could say I have a bachelor's residence,' he said.

'That sounds delightful.'

He saw the imagination behind her sparkling eyes. Thoughts of him lounging around in an elaborate dressing gown, with the biggest problem being which drink to select. He didn't correct her.

'I suppose,' he said. 'I am happy with it.'

'Where were your parents when you were a child?'

'My mother died when I was fairly young, but she had her own interests, and I was generally not one of them. Father was too busy searching out life's enjoyments. Yet, I can't complain of my childhood. It was as idyllic as a boy's can be. Poor Dinsmore had to follow me around occasionally to keep me safe and keep me out of my father's path. And I was able to play with other boys, as I mentioned. When I had lessons, Dinsmore tried to keep them interesting for me. He tried to stay one step ahead of me and I tried to keep one step ahead of him. It's amazing he didn't leave, but truly, he had nowhere else to go.'

Marianna tried to imagine Adam as a young boy,

having to keep out of his father's path. 'Was your childhood happy?'

'Yes. Most of Dinsmore's days were spent watching over me and making sure I had plenty to keep me amused. Dinsmore would get my father's ledgers when he was away—without his knowledge—and we would go over them. Later he somehow convinced my father to let the man-of-affairs also tutor me, and as I matured I began taking over father's decisions. Paying father's bills was our biggest challenge. He could spend more in an afternoon than the rents for a month. Now, that is a difficult problem to navigate.'

'Were you able to?'

'We were able to get the man-of-affairs to negotiate before Father made purchases. To suggest places to him and talk grandly about items that the merchants had agreed to let us return for a small fee later, if they were unused. It became a game. Instead of trying to keep him from spending funds, we tried to find things to tempt him to buy. Or items that would keep him occupied.'

'It sounds like you were the parent.'

He studied the direction in which the young boy had disappeared. 'I knew what was going on. I doubt my father did. By the time he passed away, I was already managing our household, although I had to let my father think he was still in charge.'

Without his father to side-step, Adam had made swift and far-reaching decisions. In hindsight, he should have taken more care, but enough ventures and plans had worked out that he'd managed to make the estate sturdy and do right by his brother. And he knew part of it was because he'd remained in public, attending as many events as possible and listening to everyone's talk of ventures.

Attending clubs, events and having a grand time had been his last duty of the day. He'd never been able to sequester himself and have the life he wanted.

Chapter Six

Adam had been the eyes and ears for the man-of-affairs and Dinsmore. He had gathered information so the decisions could be made, and they had carried out his instructions. Without their help, he would not have been able to make enough for the extensive the repairs on his home but, even so, the structure did not live up to the standards that Marianna took for granted.

Adam watched her fingers as she slipped the delicate handkerchief into her bag. He'd never seen one so fragile, delicate. A sneeze would have shattered it.

She stood so close, her arm brushed his.

The grace in her movements captured him, holding his attention. She'd tried to help him with the dog, but it would have been little more than trying to put out a fire with a thimbleful of water. But it had ignited a pailful of his awareness of her. The woman who'd awoken and thrown a book at him had awoken something in him he'd not known existed. He wasn't sure he liked it. It felt like a weakness. The sort that caused a man to lose himself in a woman.

As a youth, he'd discovered how that folly could be crushing, and he'd been ever so careful to avoid it since. And he would again. He would soon leave Marianna's house and relegate her to another pleasant memory.

Besides, this was a woman who had servants to oversee her other servants. A woman who'd spent her life with her father standing in the background, letting her suitors know he could destroy them if they did not tread carefully. He'd heard the drunken talk at clubs about how Emory prized his daughter more than anything else, and could be less than heartless if he thought her slighted. Some had thought Jules too daft to know what dangerous ground he'd been treading on.

He used his handkerchief to wipe his hands, and whistled for the driver.

'Why do you think your courtships ended? Truly?' He wondered if she searched among the wrong men to give herself a reason to reject marriage.

'I don't think I've been sensible. I may be like your father in finding things to amuse me. In fact, I think I am—not sensible. It seems easy to have a man court me, but not always wise. I only have to start a conversation and it seems to continue along on its own. I agreed to my first betrothal because the question took me by surprise. One man claimed to love me desperately, and he was nice enough, but he was furious when father started talking about settlements. And yet one suitor, a widowed man, was someone I didn't consider and he seriously tried to catch my attentions.'

'Why did you not consider the widowed one?'

'He was too mundane, too safe, I think now, looking back. I was too young and he was serious. It was all rather tedious to me, sitting beside him in a carriage. We could not always find things to speak about. He found someone else easily enough, and wed her and they have a family.' She paused. 'I watched from afar and wished him well. I knew it could have been me but was so happy it wasn't.'

She hesitated. 'I truly don't have any deep fond memories of the first man I had privately said I would marry, but the question was unexpected, and I agreed without thinking. I instantly felt sick after I left the room, and told my father what a mistake I'd made. Father spoke with him while I hid.

'Jules and I laughed a lot. I suspect that was not enough to build a marriage on. Now I don't understand what I saw in him. I should have found the parrot.' She shook her head. 'In fact, it surprises me that you are acquainted with Jules.'

'We were at university together. We are friends much in the same way your dear cousin Cecilia and I are friends.'

'Oh,' she said. 'At least you are not sworn enemies.'

'Not yet,' he said, giving her an almost imperceptible wink.

A man walked in their direction, and he changed paths to give them a wide berth.

Adam saw the puzzlement in her face, and then she studied him.

'You can appear rather foreboding. The seas seem to part for you,' she said.

'As they do for you?' His words were almost a challenge, and he wondered if she knew how much sway she had in her world.

'Yes.' She pursed her lips. 'They do. And I rather

like it. I pretend not to notice, but I do, and try not to take advantage of it. Plus, Cecilia points it out to me. She thinks it's amusing, the things my money can buy for both of us.'

'Why don't you pursue Darius Driscoll, then, as I suggested before? His father is as wealthy as yours.'

'I thought of it,' she said. 'But it never felt right. He is a brotherly friend. It feels too late now, anyway.'

'How is that?'

'Cecilia admires him. In truth, that's really why she sent you to my room. It had little to do with me or with you. She knew Father had invited you to partner her, and Driscoll for me.'

Adam questioned whether that had been Mr Emory's strategy. What if he had invited both Driscoll and him to give Marianna a choice?

The carriage rumbled up behind them.

Cecilia stuck out her head. 'You look as if you fell in a puddle of mud. But it was kind of you not to get angry at the boy. And Marianna…' She stared at her cousin. 'Was that a handkerchief I gave you?' Then she disappeared back into the carriage.

Adam shook his head in wonder. 'She's a better chaperone than I expected.'

He helped Marianna into the vehicle.

Cecilia kept the conversation flowing all the way back to the Emory residence, only this time it didn't seem to be done to irritate them, but was more companionable chatter.

When Adam stepped out to help the ladies alight, the butler came out of the house and approached him. 'The master would like to talk with the three of you.

He said he wanted Miss Marianna to join him in the drawing room.'

'I wonder what he is thinking,' Cecilia added, patting her cousin's shoulder. 'I hope you don't mind that, when I saw him alone the last time, I told him I would be happy to wed and provide lots of little grand-nieces and –nephews, should you not feel inclined.' Laughter glittered behind her wide eyes. 'You would have thought Uncle had just eaten a wasp, thinking of his fortune ultimately being inherited by my children.'

Marianna and Cecilia preceded Adam into the room. She wondered how her father would react to Adam returning with mud on his clothing.

Her father's eyes took in Adam's coat, but he didn't mention it. Instead, he spoke to her as she entered, his voice frosty. 'A package arrived for Marianna.' His words hung in the air like a bell tolling.

She paused.

'What is it, and from whom?' she asked.

'From the confectioner's, I would imagine,' her father said, eyes stern.

She stilled, examining her father's face. 'From…?'

He pointed to the parcel.

'I couldn't say, but it is of the exact same look as Jules used to send. It is on the table.' He scowled. 'A few weeks ago, Jules asked how you were when I saw him at the club. I reassured him you were well. He has also told me he would be willing to consider again the conversation he and I had earlier. I told him it is not my decision at this point, but yours, and I would stand behind any decision you make.'

'He said he would reconsider?' She didn't expect that.

Her father nodded.

She remembered her father had decided to have an event the day after he'd returned from his club…to which he'd invited Adam and Driscoll.

He studied her.

Marianna stared at the parcel and looked inside. 'You can have it, Cecilia. I don't like marzipan.'

Cecilia strode over and peered inside the package. 'He made a good choice. The heart shapes are so—convincing.'

'Marianna can select her own treats.' Her father growled.

'Oh, a note. I see a note,' Cecilia said. 'Tucked here among the sweets. How touching. Would you like me to burn it for you?'

Marianna took the note. 'Take the marzipan and go.'

Cecilia offered the confection to Adam, who refused.

'I will see if Darius wants to try this, and explain to him how it is a very, very poor choice for a reconciliation…in case he ever needs to be aware of how to ask for forgiveness.' She tasted a piece of the treat and scowled, as if she'd just taken a bite of salt.

Then Cecilia stared at her cousin. 'Remember, Marianna, he is the one who has spent long hours suffering over that letter. Not you.'

'I am done with him.' It was true. Seeing Jules' spiked handwriting actually made her feel sorry for him and blame herself for not noticing his failings earlier. She had no ill will towards him, but…

She ran a hand over the paper. Adam had stood in front of the dog to shield her without thinking. Jules would have protected her as well, but his limited abilities would have made him unaware of the dog until it had been too late. She would have been hugged or bitten, depending on the dog's inclination.

She felt sorry for Jules, but it was over between them. And, if it meant being embarrassed in public because she'd jilted him at the last moment, or dealing with her father's irritation, then it was worth it—a thousand times.

She looked up.

Both her father and Adam were staring at her.

No matter. She would go to the kitchen, say a few words of thanks and then she would throw the letter into the stove. She would let that symbolise a burning of her time with Jules. It would be liberating.

She smiled, raised her head, told them she had something she must complete and left the room.

'She's still fascinated by him,' her father said. 'I cannot believe after all the training I gave her, and all the discussion we had about why he is wrong for her, she still…'

Adam stood, again seeing the mud left on his coat, suddenly irritated by it beyond measure.

'Yes,' her father answered, interlacing his hands and stretching while leaning back in the over-stuffed chair. 'She's aware… She took the letter with her. She didn't make a big show of crumpling it. And that little whimsical smile right before she left… She was thinking of him—of returning to him.'

Adam stared at the man, not certain Emory wasn't being manipulative.

Her father rolled a bit in his chair, more like a sleepy hedgehog than a man whose daughter risked making a life-changing mistake. 'Of course, none of us really know her, as she goes her own direction and sometimes doesn't listen to advice.'

Adam took a step forward. 'I should leave and return home. While the visit has been—'

'Of course,' her father interrupted. 'Or you can stay longer.'

Her father wasn't listening, still musing about Marianna. 'She was happy. She had his letter in her hand. She couldn't wait to be alone and think about it. Or read it a dozen times more and convince herself he could mean something again in her life.' Emory tapped his two longest fingers over his lips, but didn't speak at first.

Adam could see machinations behind Emory's eyes. 'She's smarter than that.'

'I suppose you could be right,' Emory mused, but then he sat alert and stared at Adam, eyes speculative. 'You can't count on people to know what's best for them. Emotions get involved.' Then he stood. 'I'm going to find out for certain if she has any affection left for that scoundrel. It may take me a few days, but I will put it all out in the open.'

'How?' Adam asked.

'Stay and you'll see.'

Adam stood fixed to the spot. Emory knew what he was doing. Adam would be staying longer. Even though he knew he was being manipulated, he was unable to step away.

Chapter Seven

'Well, now that we're all here…' her father said. A maid walked in with a soup tureen and waited for them to get settled.

Adam expected the meal to have business talk scattered around it, but it didn't. Mrs Driscoll and Cecilia quietly discussed the merits of embellishments for gowns and where to find the best laces. The older woman smiled encouragingly at Marianna, and gave a similar glance at Adam.

The soup was unusually thick, with spices sprinkled on top of a froth, and he didn't ask what kind it was. He supposed, as an earl, he should know such a thing, but the finer points of eating didn't interest him much, only the taste. It was good, if a bit salty. Emory was enjoying it, but Marianna hardly did the food justice.

Later, a plate with a berry sauce and meat was given him. Two servants for each person stood at the ready. He wondered how they decided who should respond if help was requested, and then he realised the one nearest the door was to answer a summons for something not in the room. The one at the sideboard was to serve anything needed from there. A servant for each diner, and the one looking half-asleep in the corner was probably more a display of wealth than anything else. He could never provide such excess.

When the meal was over, Mr Driscoll asked if he and his wife might be excused as they planned to leave early in the morning, but Emory asked them to please stay at least one day longer, as he'd invited a few friends for dinner and music the following night.

Darius stood and Cecilia walked up to him, slipped her hand around his elbow and asked if he and his parents would be so kind as to look at the night sky with her, as she so loved gazing overhead, particularly in good company.

She was smart, even courting his parents.

Adam had to fight to keep from rolling his eyes. Then he caught Marianna's gaze on him. He didn't apologise, but slightly shook his head, as if to question if he'd heard correctly.

Just a flicker of her eyes in response, and they'd shared a moment.

Then Emory asked Adam to accompany them to the library, and he suggested Marianna join them also. In the library, Emory said he must fetch a ledger and thought he had left it in his sitting room, so he needed to collect it.

The man had had six servants in the dining room. He was as determined as his niece.

Marianna moved, stopping him as she reached for the bell-pull. 'I will send someone for it, Father.' She tugged on the rope and again their eyes met. He could have sworn she was thinking she didn't need a matchmaker.

He gave a slight uptick of his chin.

Her father stopped, unaware of the silent conversation going on around him, then grimaced. 'Well, now that I think of it, perhaps it is in my desk.'

Marianna's smile at her father was returned with a scowl.

He moved to his desk and pulled out a book. 'The maid always puts my things away. Hard to keep up with them. I've reconsidered…once I had my man-of-affairs study your endeavour a bit more,' Mr Emory said. 'It may be a consideration.'

Adam studied the placid eyes that were now giving nothing away.

Mr Emory made a fist and with his other hand cracked his knuckles. 'Yes. I do want to look into it more. I've thought about his idea, and it sounded much more beneficial after I deliberated on it.'

He opened the book and glanced at it, appearing to peruse figures. 'I'm thinking, Adam, that it might be wise to invest with you. I am definitely going to delve further into it.'

The book closed with a soft snap. 'But not tonight. I've had a long day and the old bones are bothering me.' He tapped his hip and looked at the servant who appeared in the doorway.

'Would you bring some of the filigreed biscuits and refreshment for the Earl and Marianna?'

Then he turned to Marianna and Adam. 'I must retire my achy bones. I wouldn't want my infirmary to ruin your evening.

'Adam, tomorrow my friend, Lemuel Jules and his son Walter, plus some others, are coming round in the evening. There will be lots of good food, and some music has been procured, but there will be very little dancing, though the wives will be along as well. The ladies don't have much to do with planning it so the intention is to talk business. The music is a distraction for them.'

He smiled and glanced at Marianna.

Now Adam knew how her father intended to find out if Marianna still had any feelings for her former betrothed.

'Father?' Shock vibrated in her voice. 'You didn't tell me you were inviting people. An event? At such short notice?'

'I know. I wanted it to be simple so I told the housekeeper and sent a footman round to let a few friends know. I invited Lemuel Jules and said he might bring his son.'

'You didn't!'

Her father moved to sit at his desk. 'I saw the younger Jules the other day when I was out. I don't think the meeting was entirely by accident. He very much regrets that you did not become his wife. And, when I saw your reaction to the treat, I sent a footman to invite him so he could see what he missed and will understand you have moved on with your life. He is no longer a part of it. And you must be entirely sure you have put him behind you.'

She put her hand down on the arm of the chair. 'I really would prefer not to be with him.'

'You don't have to be there, Marianna. You don't.

But you should. He needs to know that you are finished with him. You can buy your own confections, in whatever form they are presented.'

'Hearts,' Adam said. 'Hearts. As if that means anything. He thought of you, penned a note, sealed it and possibly sent a servant to shop for him and then, of course, to deliver it.'

'That's a cold way of putting it,' she said to Adam. 'At least he thought of me.'

'Adam,' Emory said, glaring. 'Don't push her back into his arms.'

She gasped, turning to her father. 'I am not going back into anyone's arms. And I don't know what you were thinking to invite him.'

'I was angry and wanted it to be settled,' her father said. 'We live in too small a society to avoid him for ever. Everything needs to be out in the open. You need it permanently decided between you. One way or the other.'

'It is.'

'Then he had better accept it. You would have made such a good wife for him if he hadn't been such a dimwit, forgoing a wife such as you to quibble over… I know it is not done to discuss such things.'

'I don't want to talk about it,' she said. 'The past is over.'

He gave Adam a sideways glance. 'She may be unsettled at events, but if you give her a ledger book she will sort it out without any effort. She would have made a good wife for him.' He strolled out of the room, his shoulders swaggering.

Marianna shrugged the words away as her father left.

'He said he was going to make certain you were finished with him,' Adam said after waiting long enough to be assured they were alone. Adam wasn't convinced that this wasn't a push to get him to pursue Marianna.

'Perhaps he is right. Jules still has hopes that we will be together again, but we won't. Over. Done. Finished.' She studied him, and he gazed at her, an expression of neither agreement nor condemnation in his eyes.

She shook her head and her words came slowly. 'I wish Father wasn't planning a gathering so soon after the last one. I don't want him meddling. It's not like him.'

'Sounds very much like him to me. He's meddling constantly.'

Adam didn't think he'd ever seen a parent who interfered as much as Emory. No wonder Marianna seemed so innocent about life. She had a wealthy man as a barrier between her and the rest of the world. She would likely have crumpled under the stresses of his life.

'He wasn't happy I'd let things go on so long with Jules when the marriage plans fell through. I think I was being manipulated by Jules. And I would never go back to him—ever. Even if he were to crawl in and agree to everything he'd disagreed with in the past. Never.'

'I think it was wise of you to stop the wedding.'

'And how did your romances end?'

'Much better, as I practised how to do it.'

She gasped. 'That's direct.'

'It's true. After the first one, I learned not to let it continue too far or too deep. I always ensure I let the other person know there is no future in it. It puts everything out in the open, and I believe it acts as a barrier for tender feelings.'

'You want a barrier?'

'Sometimes it is good to have.'

'And why are you not in a romance?'

'It takes effort and time. My duties have always been first in my life, even before I officially inherited them, because so many people depend on me: my stepmother; my half-brother; my estate; the people who work for me. And not in that order.'

'Work before play.'

'Work in addition to play, and sometimes they are almost the same.' He blinked. 'I see myself like a honeycomb in life.' He interlaced his fingers and held them in front of him like a basket. 'To hold things together while others are combing for flecks of pollen and storing honey.'

Then he waved a hand at his shoulder. 'No wings. No sweetness of my own. I'm merely the hollow container.'

She took a step towards him and peered, eyes squinting. 'Surprising. I was sure you had little fluttering wings hidden.'

'Your trustworthiness is now in question.'

A little upward sweep of her lips and he'd been captured by her. She'd released something inside him that he'd not known existed. Erasing everything but his awareness of her presence.

He could have watched her all night and fallen asleep with her in his arms, waking to kiss the day alive.

'I must leave,' he said, knowing that to stay longer, to be in her presence, was lighting something inside him that he wished to keep extinguished. He didn't want to be ensnared by her, to become so entranced by her he could not think clearly.

'You can't,' she said, stilling him with her smile. 'Wait until you've had the biscuits. They are the best on the earth.'

She moved closer, whispering. His body breathed in and reacted to her closeness. 'Cook was hired based on them.'

'Well, then, in that case, I could not leave.' But that wasn't what kept him in place. The sparks in her eyes lit the air around him and trapped him.

'You will not regret these biscuits.' She held his hand. Her side brushed against him. 'We don't serve them to just anyone, or even at events. We do not want the secret discovered and the risk of someone luring her away.'

'Am I being offered them because of my title?'

'Oh, that alone would not get Father to offer you those biscuits.'

But he was fairly certain he knew what her father's motives were. He saw the title and unmarried status.

'If you were to begin a romance now…' she said. 'Would you tell the person there is no future in it?'

'I might not have to. The person might tell me so herself.'

'What if she didn't?' her eyes danced, jesting at him, daring him.

'I suppose it would depend on the person.'

'Are you at a stage in your life where you think of marriage?'

'I don't rule it out completely. There could be one chance in ten thousand that might make me consider it. Are you asking me to wed?'

'No,' she said. She shook her head and a smile wafted past her lips 'I would surely be branded a jilt when I called it off.'

'Do you think you wouldn't go through with it?' He stepped closer, pretending to study her. 'I'm crushed.'

'You shouldn't be,' she said. 'I think there is a chance of two in ten thousand that I would consider you, and that is far more than anyone else at this point.'

'I think I could raise that to a three,' he said. 'Or a five.'

'Truly?' she said.

A servant rapped on the door and entered, putting the biscuit platter on the table.

With her eyes, Marianna motioned for Adam to take one.

He did. It was a fluffy cloud of buttery, sugary sweetness.

She took one and shut her eyes as she tasted it. He watched her. She was a vision of sweetness. She had already raised the numbers on the odds of considering marriage to him.

'What do you think?' she asked, taking another.

'It's the best thing I've ever tasted.' He took another bite, finishing the treat.

Then he dipped his head, dropping a whispery kiss on her lips, not a true touch at all, but more a hint of one. 'Well, I must correct myself. The biscuit is the second-best thing I have ever tasted.'

'That may have raised the number to two and a half. Or two and three-fourths.'

'It was only about half a kiss.'

'Should I be insulted that I only received half a kiss, not a whole one?'

The next kiss was moist, bringing alive the taste of the confections, the woman and a warmth that could only be stirred from deep inside the body.

Her arms went round his neck and she pulled him closer, and in the last second, before he was lost for ever, he stepped away, taking her arm and sliding his hand along her skin until he held her fingertips, then released them, letting them part.

Neither spoke. The game had ended.

His world had erupted, crashed, soared and flown.

Then he kissed her cheek and left.

Because he had to.

Adam spent the day reading paperwork he'd been neglecting, which Dinsmore had collected from the estate, but when the time for dinner arrived he selected a fresh cravat and coat and found her father.

'Marianna says she won't attend. She sends her regrets,' Emory said, glaring. The man scowled more than anyone Adam had ever seen.

'Does she?'

'Yes.'

'Why?'

'She said she is not feeling up to speaking with my friends. She sent a message before I left my room.'

The sound of a carriage arriving interrupted them, and Emory excused himself, sending Adam a challenging glance.

In seconds, Adam was knocking on Marianna's door. There was only silence from the other side.

'Marianna,' he called out. 'If this door isn't locked and you don't answer, I'm going to open it.'

The latch turned and the wood swung back.

'Yes?' she said, eyes sparking ire. Her hair was piled high on her head and her dress was a particularly frothy creation he'd not seen before. Even her face appeared to glow more. He stopped moving, taking her in.

He let the moment pass, and then he spoke softly. 'This is one time you need to show your face and your smile.'

'I don't have to prove anything to anyone. This is a gathering of my father's friends. I'm not needed.' Her chin came up, her voice starting as ferocious but quietening at the end.

'Yes, you are. By me.' He waited. 'I want you to be there.' He made certain she could see the truth in his face.

She half-turned away and held onto the door. 'I don't enjoy the long evenings, talking about fripperies. It just seems pointless.'

'And I was going to tell you about the riding boots I'm planning to order. With buckles in the back.' He moved his head closer, almost close enough so that his breath touched her.

'Were you really?' she asked.

He propped himself against the frame. 'I was thinking of three small buckles. Above the ankle in back— plain. Because I wouldn't want too stylish a buckle that goes out of fashion.'

'How tall are you planning the boots to be?'

'To the knee. My boot maker always says that ladies like boots and no expense should be spared on good footwear. He says he knows for a fact that the difference between a woman being attracted to a man or completely ignoring him is often solely based on footwear and the quality of the leather. He believes several families have been started because of his skills in crafting elegant boots.'

'Well, now I grasp why my betrothals truly ended,' she said, leaning closer, her voice a whisper. 'Their boots.'

'It's understandable,' he said.

'A good pair of boots is a work of art.'

'That's what my boot maker charges for—art.'

He held out his arm for her to take. 'You look perfect. So, will you come with me to have dinner? I'm hoping the cook will allow us a few more of her biscuits. I remember how wonderful they tasted before... Or it was something afterwards.'

'You are charming me.'

'I hope so.'

She dithered a moment, looked heavenward, then her lips turned up, she clasped his arm and stepped out, moving down the stairs with him and into the ballroom, where the guests were assembled before dinner, the air scented with shaving soap, perfume and wool coats.

'Will there be an announcement?' Mrs Driscoll walked over to them and whispered.

'It would be in poor form,' Adam said. 'Jules is going to be here.'

'Ah,' she said, agreeing, and walked over to her husband.

'Perhaps we should tell her the truth,' Marianna said softly. 'I feel guilty for misleading her. She's a dear.'

He shook his head. 'Most certainly not. She's enjoying being part of the secret.'

'I fear she might let it slip.'

'I don't think she will,' Adam said. 'Particularly not tonight. She seems too kind.'

Adam and Marianna stopped, standing by Darius and Cecilia, and together the four of them spoke with the guests who entered.

Her father watched with the precision of Wellington reviewing his troops, but Adam ignored him. When Jules and his father arrived, Jules greeted Marianna and told her he'd missed seeing her about, and she thanked him. His eyed widened when he saw Adam, but they spoke a few pleasantries and he walked away to speak with her father.

Then she glanced at Adam and he didn't move, letting their eyes lock briefly. Adam saw nervous irritation in Marianna's face. She was over her former beau. There was no question in Adam's mind.

More conversation erupted around them as Darius spoke to Cecilia, but Marianna didn't contribute.

He linked her hand over his arm. 'You appear as exquisite as the best boots the best boot maker has ever made.' He said the words softly and she burst out laughing, then blushed when the eyes turned to her.

'I would have told her she's lovely,' Darius said. 'And she would have told me I don't know what I'm talking about.'

'Well, don't you agree that she is exquisite?' Adam asked.

'Yes,' Darius said. 'The Emory ladies are always the most entrancing at any event.'

'Thank you for saying that,' Cecilia said, dragging him away. 'I don't want you telling me I look like an old pair of boots.'

Marianna waited until their conversation was more private. 'Please tell your boot maker his insight into footwear is appreciated. I may visit him myself and order some half-boots.'

'You don't need them. Jules is looking as if he made the biggest mistake of his life and is fully aware.'

'Wasn't that the plan?'

'Your father's, I suppose.'

He could quite happily have put his face against hers, shut his eyes and stayed that way for hours, her smile softly creating a world around them.

Easing her worries had brought a change in him. When he had complimented her and she had reacted, he'd felt a warmth in his body. Instead of making him feel like a giant, the desire he felt for her weakened him. It made him hungry for a smile from her. For hints of approval. A glance.

They moved into the dining room, and the conversation flowed easily. When the dinner finished, Emory took them all into the ballroom.

He had to look away from Marianna or his attraction would reflect in his eyes for all to see. He didn't want everyone to think he was another suitor and that she was going to throw him over. But then he decided it didn't matter. He would land on his feet—in this case boots.

He went to get them drinks, not because he was thirsty but because he needed something to hold onto, to have in his grasp, but he made sure to be quick while he was away from Marianna's side. He didn't want Jules sidling up to her, although he was certain she could send him on his way.

When he returned to her side, Emory stepped over to them.

'A lot of business will be conducted tonight,' she said.

'If the feathers dear Ethel Richards is wearing on that bonnet do not distract them,' her father added. 'Obviously, it is a windless day outside, or she would have fluttered away.'

'I know she is one of your dearest and closest friends,' Marianna said. 'And that is why you invited the widow and her brother, even though you can barely tolerate him.'

'True. She brightens any event.'

'Because she is your sweetheart.'

'I love you almost like a daughter...' he said, and tapped her elbow so that her lemon drink jiggled. 'An annoying daughter, though.'

Adam watched the interaction.

'Father if you cause me to spill this on myself, I swear I will tip the rest of it onto your feet.'

Her father laughed richly. 'I am in public and must remain parental.'

'You are always parental,' she said. 'And I am always your daughter. And, if you wed again, be sure to find a widow with a lot of daughters to enrich your life as I do.'

'Oh.' He tapped her drink again, but she didn't spill it. 'I will think long and hard before I wed a woman with even one daughter. Sadly, Ethel has three children, and not one is a boy.'

Adam did not speak. He had never seen a father and

daughter who actually spared time for more than pleasantries with each other. His father had so little time
for him, and vice versa, but truthfully Adam hadn't
minded. The former earl had been nothing like Emory.

Her father moved away, strolling directly to Mrs
Richards, greeting her brother and her.

Adam put a hand on Marianna's back and whispered
close to her ear, 'We can talk about boots, the weather—
which is good—the taste of the drinks—again good—
or whether Ethel Richards' hat is going to be taken by a
golden eagle flying to Scotland for an elopement with
the hat.'

'I don't think those are eagle feathers.'

'Nor do I. But ostriches would have more trouble
getting her hat to Scotland.'

'You are trying to relax me.'

'And is it working?'

Studying her, he waited for a denial, but it didn't
happen, and the pleasure he felt in making her feel better surprised him. But she was Emory's daughter and
Emory was an overly caring father. Jules had said that
Emory had hinted that he would destroy Jules' father
financially if the betrothal continued.

If it was true, it didn't seem to matter that night.
Emory had invited Jules.

His eyes flicked to Jules and he saw the challenge
in them. It was so hard to turn away from a challenge,
particularly when Marianna was aware of the stare.

Chapter Eight

Marianna enjoyed Adam's nonsensical chatter, until she saw how closely Jules was watching him. But when she peered up at Adam, and he turned to her so no one else could see his face and gave her the briefest wink, all the trepidation faded.

Adam stood tall, lean and his frame was full of confidence. He wore his evening clothes as comfortably as he wore the simple clothing he had had on in earlier in the day. She thought several of the women looked their way, and from the look in their eyes they were not seeing her.

'Darius is well and truly under your cousin's spell. Do you think we should gather your father and sit down after this and have a long talk with Darius?'

'No,' she said. 'They will be happy together.'

Darius stepped towards Cecilia, smiling, and almost collided with a footman. Marianna suspected he didn't realise how close he'd been to an upset. 'I would think her romance chances are about nine thousand nine hundred and ninety-nine in ten thousand.'

'Still less than yours if you put your mind to it,' Adam whispered. 'You could add another three-fourths.'

She stole a glance at him. He wasn't looking at anyone else but her. 'If you are saying this to bolster my confidence, you don't need to any more.'

His brows rose in question. 'I may be saying it to bolster mine and in hopes you'll consider it.'

Her body reacted as if embraced, her senses heightened.

She gazed around and the feelings evaporated as quickly as a drop of water hitting a hot grate. Jules was still watching them.

'He's staring at you,' Adam said, ire in his words. 'And those boots he's wearing… I wonder if he lost a wager.'

She jolted herself back into the moment.

'Well, if we are to speak frankly…' She turned so that she almost brushed against him as she regarded his face. 'I have heard he is already interested in someone else and that he just wants to make certain that there will be no reconciliation. My cousin is the source of the information, but I believe her.'

Adam was silent.

'Do you think I was told the truth?'

'I don't believe I should comment on it,' he said.

'I'm happy if he has someone new,' she said.

'He does,' Adam said.

She shuddered against Adam. 'I missed such a disaster. It was like standing below a cliff watching the beautiful waves and all is wonderful. Then you step aside, and suddenly the cliff crumbles away and a huge boulder lands just where you were standing.'

'Do you feel that way?' he whispered, the words flowing over her like a caress.

'Yes. A few pebbles struck me and it took some time to recover, but now...' She stared up at him. 'I am ready to celebrate and make up for lost time and emerge like a butterfly from a cocoon.' She spread her hands at her side. 'No more worrying if I am wearing a dress that a suitor might not like. No more fretting about saying the wrong thing.'

'You should never worry about that. You have a good aim, and that is what is important.' He touched his forehead.

'A good aim and possibly new boots. I will be so admired.'

'You already are,' he said. 'Ask Darius or your father and, if Cecilia were to admit the truth, she is probably jealous of you—very jealous.'

Marianna glanced at her cousin. 'Look at her,' she said to Adam. 'She is so enthralled with Darius. Oh, my, she is all fluttery. Cecilia is *never* fluttering, but his smile causes such a stir.'

'What?'

'Watch,' she whispered. 'Watch closely.' And she and Adam peered at the couple.

'A weak smile like that and it causes a stir?' Adam's brows furrowed. 'Are you certain?'

'Well, not with me, but I hear the ladies talk about it. It's endearing, I suppose.'

'I will take your word for it. Looked like he was fighting indigestion to me.'

She smiled.

'Now, that is a stir-worthy smile.'

He gazed at her face and traced his fingertips slowly

over the top of her hand until he grasped her fingers in his own.

'Will you dance the waltz with me?'

'I can't. Father prefers to let the musicians play softly and have little dancing at all, unless someone requests it.'

Adam walked away. She watched and saw him give something to a musician, speaking with the man.

Then, he returned.

'Marianna, let us dance, and for those moments you are to forget everyone but me. I will try to make certain of that, and it will shine from your face and my own that we are enjoying ourselves.'

He pulled her fingertips to his lips, stopping just before kissing her. 'Don't forget it. Now, dance with me. I took the liberty of giving your father's musicians a vail in order to have a waltz. I want this night to be memorable for you for all the right reasons.'

Her mind was empty of all things, except the look of Adam standing in front of her, his eyes on hers.

'We can't. It will be scandalous if we're the only people dancing.'

The music began.

'It is apparently going to be a night of scandal, then.'

He swept her onto the dance floor.

In moments, Cecilia and Darius began to dance too, and then her father danced with Mrs Richards.

'I must thank you.' His head bent so close that his breath fanned her cheek. She looked into his eyes and could think of nothing but him. She did not even think of her feet; she only let herself feel the music with Adam, and she could have danced the night with him.

His body was not touching hers other than one hand on her waist and the other on her fingers, but she could imagine the length of his body and, when he turned with her, her dress twirled against his legs and his hand pressed against her back. She felt a tingle and an explosion of awareness but kept her face impassive. This was just a dance, not a courtship or a rendezvous.

And then he smiled at her. Not a half-smile, or a mere pleasantry, but a smile of adoration. Of shared moments and hopes for more shared interludes. Time stopped. Her gaze locked on his lips, his eyes and she felt the consciousness of herself in his arms. She forgot to follow the steps. and he nearly had to pull her off her feet to keep another couple from dancing into them.

Momentarily, they fought the tangle of their feet, and then finally they regained the dance. Never before had that happened. She looked at Adam's face, they both laughed and he gave her a gentle squeeze of camaraderie.

'Who knew?' he said softly. 'A smile.'

'I could have guessed,' she answered, thinking of how his grin affected her.

'I am sure I have smiled at others and not one has reacted as you did,' he said. 'Are you sure you don't have some kind of upset?'

'It's gone,' she said. 'Your smile took it away.'

'That bump on the head changed something inside me,' he said.

'I could tell by the way you swore when you stood up.'

'It wasn't an optimal place for me to be. My host's house, in a woman's bedroom. But looking back…'

She felt carefree. Free of memories of heartbreak and loneliness.

He held her hand close to his heart as the dance stopped, lingering just a bit, looking into her eyes, and then walked her to the corner.

She saw him look at Jules and their eyes met. Jules took a step back and Adam gave him a nod and a smile. Jules turned and left.

'Hmm,' he said. 'I don't think the smile works for everyone.'

'Oh, I believe it works as intended,' she said.

Adam did not touch her, but he held her with his gaze.

Her senses were engulfed by him. She could feel the warmth of his body, hear him as he breathed and smell his spicy cologne.

'You are an enchantress.'

'You know what I think of when you are like this?' she asked.

He barely shook his head.

'I think of you reassuring me by saying that you are meant to be a honeycomb, holding the honey together while the bees work. But I don't think you're a hollow container. I think you are the backbone of your world.'

'I do not want to disappoint,' he said, his lips giving a scant smile. 'As I know how much work everyone else has to do to hold me upright. But I am honoured if tonight I can help you. And if simple words will help, I will be happy to rain them upon you.'

'I am sure,' she said. 'You seem to be quite good at it.'

'My boot maker has taught me a lot.'

He looked at her. She could feel every inch of her

skin above her bodice, and for a moment she felt they were alone in the room and the world.

'You're quite lovely,' he said. 'A jewel.'

'You make me near-breathless with your words.'

'Now you are flattering me.' He leaned towards her and spoke near her ear.

'Marianna,' she heard, and reality surrounded her. The voice belonged to Jules. He'd returned.

She reached to touch Adam's arm and he guided her with his eyes, infusing her with confidence. He stepped aside so that he faced Jules, and somehow seemed to create a barrier between the two of them.

'Hello, Jules. I hope you are doing well,' she said, and was surprised to find that she could speak with him.

'I could not leave without talking to you.'

As she looked at his face, she realised she felt nothing for him but dread at the memories of the times they'd shared together, once seeming precious, but now nothing more than a heap of ash.

'I am fine. And you?'

'I made such a mistake with you. Please forgive me.' His voice cracked at the end.

'Nothing to forgive,' she said, her lips in a smile, a true smile.

Adam gave a monosyllabic greeting to the other man.

They stood with her between them and she could feel the antagonism of each man towards the other. In another era, she thought each might have hefted a club and given a throaty bellow.

Jules gave a polite nod and said, 'Rockwell. Or perhaps I should say, *Your Lordship?*'

Adam smiled and he acknowledged the greeting,

but the nod was the only bit of civility about it. 'I suppose you could. But don't let it make you a lesser man.'

Jules' lip curled at the side.

'I'd like to talk with you, Marianna,' Jules said, putting a hand on her arm.

Without a thought for propriety, Adam touched her shoulder and moved her aside, running his hand down her arm until his hand had replaced Jules'.

'While I am sure you might wish to catch up on old times with Marianna, I am more concerned about her current thoughts,' Adam said. 'If you were to invite her to a future event and she were to accept, then I would not intrude on your time with her,' Adam said, eyes like a winter storm, icicles at the ready.

'Marianna and I have a lot of fond memories,' Jules said, his eyes challenging.

'Memories fade,' Adam said, smiling. 'Especially when they are replaced with more pleasant ones.'

'Are you replacing those memories?' Jules rasped out. Tension overtook his body and his chest heaved.

'Whether he is or not, it is none of your concern. Those days are past.' Marianna stepped back so that her shoulder brushed Adam's chest. His hand went to her elbow. She let the silence linger and she looked into Jules' eyes. 'Adam is such a gentleman, it would be difficult not to enjoy my time with him,' she said.

'I know him. He is not always a gentleman.'

'He is with me. And that is all that matters,' she said.

'I must talk with you,' Jules said again, eyes catching hers.

'This is not the place,' Marianna said.

'I agree. Then may I call on you?'

Marianna's eyes widened. 'I don't think it would be a good idea.'

'She said no, if it wasn't clear enough,' Adam said, voice low.

'I must do as you request, Marianna,' Jules said. 'But you are still in my heart. I will always love you.'

Adam cleared his throat. 'That's nice.'

'Adam…' Marianna silenced him.

'If you reconsider, Marianna, I promise you will not regret it,' Jules said, clasping his hands and giving her a lingering glance. 'I just wanted you to know.'

Adam turned, as if he couldn't stand the sight of Jules near her.

'This is not the time or place to speak of it. But I have already put our friendship behind me.'

Jules stared at Adam. 'Well, I suppose this means you won't be reuniting with your lost love. The first one who married the Earl of Rockwell for his title.' He took a step away and studied Marianna. 'How fortunate for you.' He strode away.

'Have you been married before?' she asked.

'No. He's talking about my father.'

Adam caressed her back. 'Say the word, Marianna, and I will drag him to you with one arm behind his back and he will beg your pardon.'

'No,' she said. 'I just feel relieved. I didn't expect a confrontation.'

'He is all talk,' Adam said. 'He blusters and grumbles because he's skilled at it. Just be thankful you avoided a lifetime of it.'

'I am.'

'Your father is watching,' Adam said. 'Why don't we go and speak with him?'

She nodded.

Adam put a hand on her back and led her to her father. He moved towards them. Adam stood close enough that she could hear his breathing, low and measured.

'He didn't act as I expected,' her father near-whispered. 'I shouldn't have invited him. I didn't think he'd act so bereft. He damn near ruined my daughter's life and now he's acting like a love-sick puppy.'

The two men communicated without speaking.

'Let us step outside for some air,' her father suggested.

'That's a good idea,' Marianna said. 'Please. You are both standing so close to me that you are nearly taking all my breath, and I fear to walk because I might trip over you.'

They both stepped away.

'Can we take some refreshments with us? I daresay it would do us all good,' she said.

They stepped outside with their drinks. Others milled about.

Her father spoke softly, staring at Marianna. 'I can't see why I ever thought Jules would be a good match.'

'It was my error,' she said.

'He's a toad,' Adam said.

Her father inclined his head towards the door. 'I let her down by not remarrying,' he said, shaking his head. 'I tried to keep her close at my side as she grew, and filled her head with financial matters.'

Her father turned his attention to her. 'If you'd only had a mother, and not been so close to Cecilia…' he said. 'I should have found someone and got married again.'

'No, Father. It's not your fault. I make my own mistakes.'

He ran his hand through his thinning silver hair. 'When I fell in love with my wife, she was my world, and nothing else meant anything. I would think anyone would do the same with Marianna. Even a fool would be able to see what a gem you are.'

'Father...'

'You don't have to say a word,' her father said calmly to Adam, 'But you can jump in at any point.'

'We all know what a treasure she is.'

'I believe I will go to my room now,' Marianna said.

'I wish you wouldn't,' Adam said.

'Too early,' Her father agreed.

'Do I not have a say in this?'

Adam took her arm and spoke more softly. 'You should stay until the night is near over. Don't let it appear as if you left because of him. Give yourself a chance to enjoy it.'

'In other words,' she said, quietly, 'I should not leave until I have shown everyone what a wonderful time I am having.'

'Precisely,' Adam said.

'Well, if I am to be trapped at a gathering,' she said, 'I suppose this one is as good as any.'

'I'm surprised Jules didn't cry when he saw that dance,' her father said, taking Adam's measure. 'A waltz in my house, with my daughter, was as good as an announcement of a courtship.'

Marianna glanced around to see if the Driscolls were watching. They would easily believe that she and Adam were betrothed now, and finding a way to tell Mrs Driscoll that the betrothal was off could be difficult.

'It was merely a dance and a statement for Jules.' But every guest had seen it.

'A loud statement.' He turned to his daughter. 'Let's go back to the guests, *ma petite mal de tête,*' her father said.

Marianna laughed, a wafting sound.

'At least I am but a small pain for your head,' she retorted.

'And my purse and my sleep and my digestion.'

'Just like your favourite desserts.'

'But a belly ache afterwards is a belly ache.'

'I could see her causing discomfort,' Adam said.

'She is the perfect daughter.'

She turned her head away from the men. 'Both of you are thinking about my life too much. It is mine,' she said as they moved back inside. It was hers, but she seemed to be the only one who thought that way. Even society kept its attention on her actions, yet she didn't want to be an outcast.

Several guests were saying their goodbyes to Cecilia, and her father went over to bid them farewell.

Adam waited and turned to Marianna. 'What did Jules say when you told him that you were calling off the wedding?'

'Not much. I sent a request for him to visit me and told him it was vital. We had a discussion, and I told him I had had a change of heart. He seemed unable to speak then, but I gave him back every gift he'd given me. It was horrendous—for both of us. I told him I was choosing my poison, and it wasn't him.'

He took her hand. 'I'm sorry that happened.'

'Don't you have any women in your past that you regret?'

'Every one of them, when I am standing next to you.'

'That's the kind of thing a sweetheart says. Tell me the truth.' She searched his expression, needing to know what he felt.

'Or it's the kind of thing a friend says. And I did tell you the truth.'

'Are we—friends?' The thought curled its way into her heart, giving her peace and strength she'd not expected to feel. Now she understood his concern more.

'That would be your choice.'

Silence surrounded them. 'I would like to think we are close friends.' At first, she couldn't read the expression on his face. Then she saw warmth, and it created and compounded the same feeling inside her.

'We are,' he said. 'If you want to be.'

'I do.'

'Or more, if you want to be.'

'I might.'

He caressed the outside of her elbow.

'If you will excuse me,' he said. 'I would like to speak with the Driscolls.'

'Not about our…pretend betrothal?' She whispered the words.

'Oh, I'd already forgotten about it,' he said.

She placed a hand over her heart and took in a breath.

'Not truly,' he said. 'But I thought you'd prefer it if I did.'

She wasn't sure she wanted him to forget about it.

'Are you coming back?' The words tumbled from her.

'If you mean tonight, I'll be going to my room.' He

didn't take his eyes away. 'But I can always change direction. If you ask.'

He strode towards the Driscolls.

And then she wondered about what he said. Was he warning her that he had always changed direction with his other sweethearts? But she knew the truth, and that hadn't been what he'd meant.

'Is Adam speaking with the Driscolls and Cecilia?' her father asked, after saying goodbye to the other guests and summoning a footman to bring him a glass of wine.

'Driscoll's wife keeps singing Adam's praises to me,' he said, grimacing. 'Like she's trying to be a matchmaker. Or make me like him. It's not like her at all.'

She swallowed. 'That's nice.'

'I have looked into Adam's business,' her father said, leading her into the hallway so the servants wouldn't hear. 'He's not as sure on his financial feet as I would like.'

'It doesn't matter to me. And you should not be asking questions about him.' Again, he was meddling. He had done so before but she knew that she would have made a mistake had he not done so. But she only blamed herself for trusting Jules.

He used his glass to point at her. 'Cecilia likes Driscoll and is doing all she can to further that.'

'Good for her.'

He took her arm and led her to his sitting room, opening the door to let her precede him.

'I like the way Adam stood up to Jules. The Earl might work out well as a suitor for you. First I brought

Driscoll here knowing he could help you put Jules behind you. Now I'm seeing the value of Adam. As you see an error, you should always change course.'

'Father…how would you feel if I tried to select a wife for you?'

He tapped his glass after entering the room. 'You tried. You have introduced me to the widow Barstow and Lady Crumb, and I enjoyed spending time with them, but not any more than that.'

'I suppose that is best for me also. Not to wed, but to experience life with friends.'

She moved her head so her father couldn't see her expression. Friends…like Adam.

'Before you discard the idea of marriage, I hope you think more about it. I don't want you to make the same mistake as I have since your mother died. She and I married young, which was good for us, and we grew together. After she died, I waited for a woman as perfect as she was to come along again. She doesn't exist. She couldn't.'

'I know how much you loved my mother, so that is understandable.'

A hint of a smile touched his lips.

'Yes. But I don't know that we were in love when we decided to wed. She was the most beautiful woman I'd ever seen. And, in truth, it was not always sunshine. It was an adventure in romance, you could say. I wouldn't trade those memories for anything and wish you had had a chance to know her. We were maturing together and it was a precious time in my life.' He sighed. 'Though, we often had disagreements.

'Marianna, if you are waiting for the perfect man, remember—he does not exist. We are all flawed.'

'But some flaws are insurmountable to me.'

'Of course. And that is the correct way to be. But don't give up on marriage because you have made errors in the past. The heart is not reliable. It is flawed when it comes to choosing a mate.'

'If you're pointing out to me that Darius is a good man, I know it, but I have never been interested in a courtship with him.'

'Sadly, I know.' He glanced around the room. 'If you were to wed Adam, you would have to attend events, large ones, and you definitely shy away from them. I should have insisted you greet people more. It is not that difficult.'

'It is for me.' She took a pin out of her hair and tucked the lock back in place before settling the pin back again. Then she moved to the door. 'I must go and make sure the servants get some rest.'

'Marianna,' her father called out, voice sincere. She hesitated and waited.

'A woman as arresting as your mother would not have wed a toadstool of a man like me if I were poor.' He spoke matter-of-factly, and yet there was sadness in his words. 'Without that marriage, I might never have had the wife I ended up loving so devotedly. I would never have had a daughter.'

'Father, I know you've had many more women express an interest in you in the past years and you've not got any taller.'

'Yes. I'd even say I've become shorter and broader, but I have become richer. And Adam will always be an earl.'

He stared at the spot on her finger where a wedding ring would have rested. 'Your mother would be so proud if you were to become a countess.' He pursed his lips. 'You would have everything. Everything.'

'I would have a husband in addition. And I don't know Adam well at all. I'm blinded by his charm and I know it.'

'Your son would be a peer. Think of that—a peer.'

'And that would mean, if I were to want to live apart from Adam because his actions upset me, that he could easily insist my child be left behind. That is a big risk to take for a title.'

Chapter Nine

Adam stood in Emory's private sitting room. He'd been summoned, no doubt about that. And Emory was used to having his own way. He'd asked Adam about his plans earlier, during the meal, but he hadn't felt like talking about them then, because too many people had been there and it had been best to keep the chatter mindless.

Emory's true concern was getting his daughter married, but that felt like a dull razor against Adam's skin—too blunt to do a proper job, yet plenty sharp enough to cause irritation. He and Marianna got on well and he could imagine her father mucking up their friendship.

Emory had sent for her as well, even though Adam had suggested she was tired after the gathering.

When Marianna entered, his thoughts changed from their normal direction regarding business and wrapped themselves around her. She did look ready to go to sleep. Her eyes had a dewy softness, and her hair had had enough time to begin escaping from its knot.

He schooled his features to be unmoved. Her matchmaker father already had too many designs for her future.

'We were about to give up on you, Marianna,' her father said.

'I was finishing a few things with the servants.'

'Thank you for that, dearest. Adam has been talking about the merits of paraffin and how it will revolutionise lighting,' he said to Marianna.

Now the man had all the enthusiasm of a scientist thinking he could excavate Pompeii with only a few shovelfuls of digging.

She found a chair and almost cuddled into it, like a kitten relaxing in its owner's arms.

'Marianna may not be interested in this,' Adam said.

Emory snorted. 'She usually brings her embroidery and sits sewing while I discuss business with my man-of-affairs, and then he leaves and she has beautiful stitches to show me—and insight on what was said.'

'Whale oil may not be sufficient to continue to meet the city's needs, and an alternative will be needed,' Adam said, his focus on Marianna. 'An associate of mine mentioned a soda plant, and I thought it might be a good investment,' he continued, 'As soda is needed to make paraffin. We know many people have been using it to burn in their lamps.'

'Sensible,' her father said. 'You said you planned to own a soda plant... How soon will you begin seeing profits?'

He doubted he'd ever forget the image of Marianna relaxing, appearing intent on nothing, studying the curve of her fingernails.

'Profits?' Emory nudged.

'Not for some time.' He had to stop being so aware

of Marianna. Emory would surely notice and strengthen his matchmaking efforts.

'Then why do you wish to buy a soda plant?'

He looked at her father. 'I am looking to the future. I know it will take time to unfold as I wish, but I will build it up, even if there are no returns at first.'

Marianna unfurled a bit.

Her father scratched his chin. 'Why won't there be?'

'Rain could delay transport too easily,' Adam said. 'The roads are not always the best.'

Her father nodded. 'And the winter would be a problem. But, not insurmountable.'

'All has to be considered. It's not whether something goes wrong, it's how much goes wrong.' He let out a breath. 'It's why I always prepare for the possibility of doubling the planned expenses,' Adam said.

'I would invest in something like this.'

'You don't need to. Darius Driscoll is interested and has agreed to add the funds I need.'

Emory sputtered. A ghost of a smile wafted across Marianna's face.

Her father glared. 'And you did not ask me first?'

'Well, you were to be my second choice.'

Emory frowned.

'Father doesn't like to be the second choice,' Marianna said.

'No one does.'

'True.'

She stood and dusted non-existent wrinkles from her skirt, a habit he suspected she was unaware of. He couldn't take his eyes from her. His body changed. His senses changed. And it irked him that he was falling into her father's plan as easily as raindrops splashed onto the ground during a rainstorm. He needed get his thoughts back on oil, paraffin, soda and anything but how close she was to him.

He had spent months with the soda plant on the periphery of his mind, and then for another month it had consumed him so much he'd been studying it every moment he could spare. It had taken over all his thoughts. Yet while he stood next to Marianna it hardly seemed important.

She had some inner presence, like an invisible breeze within her that swept her nearer, and took so much of his thoughts that he didn't want to back away. He only wanted to remain. To have again the feeling of being pulled towards her.

Emory smiled at his victory and Adam moved a step away from Marianna.

'I have been making enquiries,' Adam continued, 'And heard of a structure that is now empty. I thought it suitable for my purpose.'

'An investment like this is almost like a sweetheart,' her father said. 'A man shouldn't let that perfect one get away.'

'A man will make his own decisions. Only he knows what is right for himself.'

'So he must find the best investment,' her father continued. 'One that is special and will make him richer. That adds just the substance he needs in his life to make his world stronger. Better.' He paused, and his next words were pointed. 'If he is any kind of man at all.'

Adam didn't speak, but Marianna seemed to understand his expression. *Yes, your father is matchmaking, but we are going to do as we wish.*

'And, while her former suitors will live to regret not marrying her, Marianna will be an asset to any sweetheart.'

'No one has argued with that,' Adam said. 'But you need to let Marianna make her own decisions, and stand or fall by them. She's not an infant. You are interfering. You keep pushing her to wed, and she cares enough about you that she doesn't want to hurt your feelings. But you're only making it harder for her. If she hasn't worked out the hazards of marriage and betrothals by now, then she never will. You need to let her do as she wishes.'

'He kept me from making a horrible mistake before.' Marianna defended her father.

'Well, let him keep you from making mistakes. Don't let him push you into one.'

'I am not,' she said. 'My father cares for my future as much as he does his own.'

'Your father is definitely in the market for you to wed. If he wants to see a marriage so badly, he should find his own wife.'

Emory said. 'You need to open your eyes. You should be on your knees begging my daughter for a courtship. That you don't says you are not of great intellect.'

That was a slap in the face, but Adam ignored it. He knew Emory was goading him.

'I think you would be better off letting someone else pick her suitors in future. Do you really have her interests at heart or do you just want an heir?'

Her father sputtered. 'I'm a wealthy man who commands a lot of money, and you'd best take care what you say to me, or your finances will dry up like a cup of water in the desert.'

'You try to command everyone in your world. You use your money to control everyone who steps into it. If you can't control them, you punish them financially.'

'You're an impoverished earl who thinks he can tell me what to do.'

'I am not as wealthy as you, but I turned my financial world around, and I know the difference between a spotted slug shell and a good business investment, even though you said I didn't.'

His eyes flitted to Marianna. 'You told him I said that? The night of the party when you claimed to be ill and I spoke to you in your room?'

She didn't answer.

'You did,' her father stated, and he appeared punched in the stomach.

'She did not,' Adam said, not wanting to cause any distrust in their relationship. 'I heard you.'

'But how would you—?' Silence flashed, bouncing from the walls, and even the sound of their breathing faded. 'You were in her room.'

Adam saw the balled fist and the changing pupils. The man lunged forward, flailing his arms, and Adam stepped aside, deflecting him. But Emory didn't stop, like an overactive windmill of erratic punches.

Her father swung an arm again, charging forward. Adam dodged and made a fist, ready to fight back. But the man was a head shorter than he was and apparently had never thrown a punch in his life. Emory reached out for Adam and they both crashed into the bookcase. Glass shattered. The man stumbled to his knees and a clock toppled from the bookcase and hit him on the cheek.

Emory pushed himself up, cheek cut, and swore at Adam.

Adam took a step towards Emory, and put up his free hand to deflect Emory's fist.

Marianna threw herself between the two men, screamed and latched on to Adam's right arm. 'Do not hurt my father. Do not. Do not hurt him. He is half your size.'

Adam tried to get a hand on her father's chest to move him back, but Marianna had him half-trapped. 'You're going to injure her,' he snapped, but Emory was beyond hearing.

He cradled Marianna, turning himself into Emory's blows so he could keep his body between her and the fists. He dodged two hits from the other man, and finally grasped Emory's cravat and held him firm. Again the man swung an upper cut that barely missed Adam's chin.

With his free hand Adam rotated him into the wall beside them, where he stopped and stumbled, and Adam helped him slide to the ground. Then Adam moved himself and Marianna away from her father, half-lifting her off her feet before disentangling himself from her.

Emory stood.

'No more. She might get injured!' he shouted.

'My father is frail!' she cried. 'You cannot hit him. He is all I have.'

Adam spoke softly and his arm went around her. 'I would never hurt him.'

Marianna saw the blood on her father's face. She put a hand on her mouth. 'He's cut,' she accused Adam, whirling to stare at him.

Her father put his hand on his cheek and felt the blood, then felt his temple. He looked at his red fingers. 'I think it was from the clock, Marianna.'

'Oh,' she gasped.

Adam put his hands on her waist, holding her. 'It is over, Marianna. Settled. Though I don't know who won or what the outcome is.'

'If he does not get his hands off you,' her father said, 'I will get the broadswords from the wall and run him through.'

Adam released her. 'I am sorry, Marianna.'

The room smelled of spilt oil, and Marianna didn't appear to know what to do. She gathered handkerchiefs from the desk and handed one to her father and one to Adam. 'Your head,' she said.

Adam put the handkerchief on his forehead, and blotted the blood. But then he saw her watching him, and his heart catapulted.

'I am so sorry,' he whispered to her. He wanted to make the scene go away. Wanted her not to look so stricken.

Her father sat in his chair. He wiped his temple, forehead and cheeks and crossed his arms. His voice smooth as a windless lake, he said, 'So tell me, Adam, how did you hear what I said to my daughter in the privacy of her bedroom?'

Adam shut his eyes. He righted a chair, turned it to the desk and sat. 'The revelry was doing me no favours,' he said, biting out the words. 'I was tired. I was to go to my room…' He looked at Marianna. 'And her cousin sent me to the wrong one.'

'Cecilia could have made an error accidentally, Father.'

'Just as she could be flying about in the night sky scaring little children, although that's more probable,' Adam said.

'Remember the noise you heard the night when you checked on me in my room?' she asked her father.

'You fought him?' Her father glared.

'No,' she said, shutting her eyes and shaking her head. 'I am not sure he realised his error fully until he— Until I woke up.'

'I was sincere when I apologised,' Adam said, straightening his cuff before gazing at her father. 'I assure you I was surprised to see her, and then jumped back, and was surprised to feel the floor.'

'I would think so.' Her father raised his brows. 'It comes at you quicker than you'd expect.'

'I did not tell you because it was a mistake. Honest on his part—not Cecilia's.'

'Did you keep the incident a secret to protect him?'

'No. It didn't want a fracas at your event. Think of such a debacle playing out in front of guests. But the Driscolls saw Adam with me that night, and…'

Her father narrowed his eyes.

'And now they think Adam and I are betrothed,' she continued.

He rubbed the cut on his forehead and then held his fingers out, extended in question. 'Are you trying for an increase in the number of broken betrothals you have, Marianna?' He clamped his teeth.

'Cecilia is to blame for the error the night of the event,' Adam said. 'And I apologise if it seems I even hint that Marianna was at fault.

'Well, all the servants still awake surely heard this fracas, and most certainly they will tell the others, who will spread the news.' He waved a hand at the broken bookcase, the clock, his own face and then pointed to his knuckles and Adam's chin. 'This will also be noted and duly recounted.'

'I am sure there will be some speculation,' she said.

'A tremendous amount of it,' her father agreed. 'I am sure it is extremely quiet in the rest of the house now, with many ears listening. This will be talked about.' Shutting his eyes, he tilted down his chin and pushed back his hair.

Adam knew that, with as many servants as Emory had, there was no way of assuring silence.

'Then you need to be certain it is talked about with the emphasis you want,' Adam said. 'Trying to conceal it will not do Marianna any good.'

'The problem is she does not make the best choices in suitors,' her father said to Adam.

'At least she corrected the betrothal with Jules by ending it.'

Marianna didn't speak.

'Marriage is not meant to be all joy. It is an endeavour like any other. A business of a home.'

'It's supposed to be more than that,' Adam said.

'That is a tremendous undertaking,' her father said, 'And I do not ever expect you to know the true joy of being wedded to a woman such as my daughter, even though you are not worthy of a flicker of a single eyelash of hers.'

'She can cause trouble with no more effort than a flicker of that eyelash.' Adam picked up a paper that had fallen to the floor.

'My father and I have lived peaceably for years together. And he is a good man. That is what it takes for harmony in a household.'

'I don't think it's that. I think he does all you ask and, since you are given your way at every turn, you don't complain much.'

'He does not give me my way at all times. We just agree on most things,' she said, tapping her chest before crossing her arms.

His eyes locked with hers. 'Because you are the centre of his world and he has trouble saying no to anything you might ask.'

'I rarely ask for anything.'

'Because it is at hand. You have servants seeing to your every whim and, if you choose not to go to an event that your father is hosting, you are given the choice to stay away. You shouldn't be encouraged to hide.'

'I am definitely not encouraged to hide.'

'And what of your accepting betrothals and then changing your mind?'

'When new things come to light, I do make corrections.'

Her father frowned. 'You should know the complete truth. I wanted her to have someone to watch over her,' he said, voice stone-cold, hand on the door. He stared at it before turning to Adam again and giving him a nod. 'I hoped for a wedding, but I drove such a hard bargain financially, and the men thought it meant she didn't love them and that I would be a factor in their married lives, and were reluctant. Jules agreed to live here, but quibbled over the amounts I wanted to settle on her. I admit, it was a mere pittance, because I thought her worth the world. And the men took umbrage. She is not the jilt. They were.'

So that was why the betrothals hadn't gone forward. Her father had driven a hard bargain over the marriage settlement, wanting his daughter loved for herself and not her money. And the men had walked away. They'd been driven away by her father, but she saw it as a lack in herself.

Marianna had no confidence in her worth as a woman…but she should.

Chapter Ten

Marianna studied her hands. 'It doesn't matter. I will not leave my father. I don't want him to live alone.'

Adam acted as if her father were not a consideration.

'He has about a hundred servants under his roof. I'm surprised he doesn't move out for some peace and quiet. Besides, he can wed.' He snapped his fingers.

Her father interrupted, with a puzzled shake of his head. 'Oh, and now you are telling me to wed again. You see how easy it is to direct others?'

'The both of you should. Marianna is afraid to leave this house. She is afraid to act as a woman. She is afraid to act as a wife. She should marry,' Adam said. Just not the dunderheads she courted in the past.'

'My daughter's marriage is none of your concern. It is mine.'

'No. It's mine,' she said. 'I do not need a matchmaker. I can make my own decisions and I can change my mind.' She crossed her arms. 'Imagine—two unwed men who both have reputations for squiring around many ladies and remaining single are giving me advice about marriage. No, thank you.'

'I married your mother. That very much qualifies me for giving marriage advice to my daughter.' Her father dotted his brow again. 'It's my role.'

Then he picked up a pen and tapped it against the top of the desk. 'I am not seeing the conflagrations again that I saw the last two times. I am tired of tears. First that bumbler you were fascinated who with ran out crying when I spoke with him. And you cried for days after the negotiations ended with Jules. I hate tears. Let's settle this quickly.'

'I agree,' Adam said, biting out the words, righting a chair. 'But Marianna doesn't truly want to marry. It is a lie she tells herself.'

Marianna picked up several books, dusting them off, and picked up several shards of glass. 'I can tell myself any lie I please.'

'No. You can't,' her father said. 'You created this. You will not be meandering through life, picking one flavour of sweet and then changing your mind for another. You will step into the confectionery shop, pick the sweet and take it home with you. Is that so difficult an idea?'

'Father, marriage is more than picking a sweet. And you are the one who ran off Jules.'

'Of course. He was a....' He stared at Adam. 'A lout. And a son of my friend, although I doubt we will ever be true friends again.'

Her father brushed his handkerchief over his head. 'Let us just forget this has happened. In part, I blame myself. I overreacted, and I see now that Adam was an innocent in this family's machinations.'

'Emory, I understand you are upset, and I appreciate

that you know I respect your decisions and your care for your family's honour. I realise that Cecilia causes problems. None of this would have happened otherwise, and you were merely defending your daughter's honour. A great thing to do, and something I deeply respect.'

He sighed. 'Now, may I please borrow your daughter's hand for a moment?'

'Of course.'

Reaching inside his waistcoat, he took out the small telescope he carried with him. It was hardly larger than a child's toy, but it worked.

He placed it in her hand, and he watched her eyes as she felt the metal that his body had warmed. His fingers clasped around hers as he bent slightly and held her hand firm.

He felt her grab hold of the small telescope. She pulled out the brass fixture and, as she held it in her hand, he pulled the hand up and held her fingers captive, only moving his aside enough so that he might kiss it. 'You may have this.'

She held her head back. 'I can't keep it.'

'Why?' he said. 'I want you to open your eyes to the world around you. Particularly in the same room with you. It has been in my family for a very long time, and no one seemed to care about it but me.' It was one of the few things he'd kept besides the actual estate.

'When I was a child, it was my favourite plaything, because I imagined I could see myself sailing around the world, fighting dragons and living a life of challenge. And I did. Here, in the town of my youth. I didn't have to go far to find what I wanted.'

She handed it back to him. 'I can't.'

'You need it as a memento. To remember to see what is there. What is really in front of you. Not what you imagine is there.'

She gave it back to him, their fingers touching, and aware of the moment. He slipped it inside his pocket.

'Whenever I see a beautiful woman," he said, "I touch my coat and I remind myself that the beauty is what is nearest me now, but I must not stop thinking of my future. I don't want to be distracted by beauty.'

Then he turned and left for his room, unwilling to leave the house. This time, he didn't touch his coat to remind himself to look to the future. Perhaps a romance with Marianna would be worth it.

'That sweet-talking scoundrel.' Her father took out a handkerchief from his pocket and wiped his forehead. 'I should not have let him get the better of me.'

'Father… He is a guest in our house. He shouldn't fight you for any reason.'

'In case you didn't notice, Marianna, he only defended himself. You're the only one who got a good blow in, and he just held me back, and didn't have to work too hard at it either.'

'He wanted to give me the telescope that he had had as a child.'

'Yes. I carry a handkerchief. For mopping my brow.' He swaggered. 'That was an easy tussle for him. The man I went after was more concerned about my daughter hurting me than anything else. And then Adam told me how much he respected me.' He shook his head. 'What a fool,' he grumbled. 'Me, that is.'

A sigh erupted from deep inside him. 'If you had

married that widower, one of the first you courted— a decent sort, albeit a bit of a mouse—then he would be my son-in-law and we would all be living peaceably.'

Marianna stared at her open palm where the telescope had rested. 'No. He was impoverished and he wanted the funds. I grasp that he wanted them for his children, but still, it wasn't how I wanted to begin a marriage. I wanted a man who would not care for my fortune.'

'Of course, but even you do not want to be poor. So you can understand others being willing to wed you for the funds.'

'I do. I truly do. And I understand people wanting to provide for their children. I just don't want to be viewed as an investment.'

'I know. I sometimes wonder if the women I squire around would see me if I were poor, and that's an easy answer—they would not. Your mother was just so beautiful, I didn't care. And then, after we married, I fell in love.'

'Surely she loved you for yourself?'

'I suppose I will truly never know.' He sighed. 'That is my burden. I know she wouldn't have noticed me without my wealth, and I hope her love became sincere.' He paused. 'Tread carefully, child. It's true I drove a hard bargain with your suitors, because I wished they would walk away from the money and provide for you. Society believes you are fickle, and at the time I didn't realise they would think that. I didn't want them to know the shallowness of the suitors, and didn't want to speak about their wish to have your fortune.'

He took her hand. 'Speculation is going to make its way around society.'

'So, Adam is right.'

'He is, but let's just consider it a fortunate guess on his part. I am not sure I am fond of him at all, and yet I'm willing to let him be a part of our family. Perhaps I will learn to like him, and if not he is still a good man to have on our side.' He chuckled. 'He fought us both off, Marianna, and did not even crumple his coat.'

'We are wealthy. Everyone understands and forgives us.'

'But I do not bank on that, Marianna. I bank on being an honourable man. And, to carry on our legacy, you must be an honourable daughter. And, while you are reserved, you almost appear to be competing with Cecilia in the rumours. In fact, I feel you are out-pacing her.' He patted her shoulder. 'Please take care.'

Marianna was ready to turn out the lamp when a light rap sounded at her door, and Cecilia rushed into the room, her hair down, in her dressing gown.

'You are being talked about,' Cecilia said, giving her cousin a knowing smile. 'My maid told me. She knew I would not want to sleep through this.'

'She woke you?'

'Yes. She said the house is all aflutter. The maid said that your father was begging Adam not to kill him and things were crashing around. I checked in the sitting room, and the clock is broken.

Marianna tensed. 'That is not what transpired.'

'Good. I could not imagine Adam so vile,' she said. 'What happened?'

'I'm sure it sounded worse than it was.'

'And I'm sure you'll make it sound better than it was.'

'It was partly your fault, truth be told, because you sent Adam to my room that night.' Marianna glared at her cousin. 'You should not have done that.'

Cecilia laughed. 'True. But I wanted you to meet him. It's the thought that counts, and I don't have second thoughts about what I do.'

'You have none to begin with.'

'Well, I admit my error. I'll leave first thing in the morning. I'm sure my parents miss me. I would like to have them invite Darius so they can get to know him, and I have already extended an invitation on their behalf.'

'Do not lead him astray.'

She paused. 'I like him. You should take a lesson.'

'From you?'

'Yes. You let Uncle push suitors away. If a man starts getting close to you, you get scared. You dangle him in front of Uncle and he drives a hard bargain. The men realise Uncle will be controlling their lives if they wed you.'

'Not true. My standards are just high.'

'If you say so,' Cecilia said. 'But really, you are like a person told not to touch a pot because it's hot, and you do and then you run away. At least stay long enough to enjoy the meal.'

'I don't think I should take any advice from you.'

'If it is good, you should,' Cecilia said, moving to the door. 'Don't discount a good thing just because you don't like the way it is delivered.'

'I just know better than to listen to you.'

'I'm leaving tomorrow. But do not forget about our outing. Darius will be visiting my parents next week and I hope to have some new frocks ordered for the honeymoon.' She winked. 'Take a lesson.' She lifted a brow. 'And even people in not so wonderful marriages can have wonderful times. Don't keep running away. I run into romances and I trudge right through them. You run from things. I don't know what you're afraid of, but you're definitely not afraid of being hesitant.'

'Father believes I should marry and can't let the idea go. Will you give me a haven, should he get insistent?'

Cecilia considered this. 'For you to be living at my house will not put you in a good light, even though my parents live with me. Everyone knows I'm trouble.' She shut her eyes. 'And Darius said he likes that about me.'

Marianna knew that Cecilia's parents actually lived in a cottage next to their daughter and both kept their privacy.

'But, yes, I will put you up. But do not be surprised if the situation doesn't change. I'll also expect you to wed. The choices I put in front of you might be more delightful, but seriously, you are turning up your nose at most available men. Darius is the first man of my own age I have been attracted to, and I never thought a nice man would spare me a second glance, or the other way round.' She paused. 'Perhaps I see the finances before the man.' She put a palm on her forehead. 'I am so shallow, and I suppose I am the last to work that out. I am so fortunate that I've discovered it after it is too late to be corrected.'

Cecilia shut the door, and the quiet of the house didn't seem peaceful any more. It felt like a simmering kettle that could overflow at any moment.

Marianna doused the light and settled with her pillow

under her head, then she adjusted it, the soft scent of the covers nestling around her comfort she couldn't enjoy.

The events of the last few weeks kept reappearing in her thoughts. Perhaps her cousin was right. Perhaps she had a fear of closeness. Of leaving the safe world of her home, where she could control the house as she wanted. After Jules, she'd sworn not to marry, because she'd learned that she could not trust her choices.

Then Cecilia stuck her head back inside the room. 'Oh, and Darius and I had a disagreement concerning you. He says you are a dear person, but that you purposely choose bad suitors so you will have an excuse not to wed.' She rubbed her palms together. 'But I know how much Uncle has meddled in your romances. My uncle doesn't give up easily when he settles on a plan. I would never have been able to wed someone as influential as my former husband had not Uncle been involved.'

'Father is going to let me decide on my own future.'

Cecilia nodded. 'Of course.' She winked and snickered as she shut the door.

Chapter Eleven

The next morning, Cecilia's father sent a maid to wake her and ask her to join Adam and him at breakfast. She firmed her shoulders, unsure of what would happen next.

The scent of bacon and fresh bread greeted her before she stepped into the room. She knew her father would be having his usual boiled egg and tea, as he believed it was the only breakfast food a man needed. There would be a glass of chocolate near her plate. Two servants waited near the sideboard, as was usual when they had guests.

Both men stood to let her get seated, and she couldn't help herself—she met Adam's eyes. He had a new bruise in the same spot where the first one had faded. She wanted to reach out to him. He seemed to be pushing her away with his eyes.

Her father watched, studying them both. That was unlike him. He rarely did more than look up from his newspaper and give her a 'good morning' grunt.

Marianna stared at the men. She'd thought they would be over their upset, but it was obvious they weren't.

'The Driscolls left earlier,' her father said. 'They wanted to get an early start. And I told them that, if they heard anything of my temper the night before, to disregard it.'

Marianna knew she would never have to give the Driscolls a reason for a broken betrothal with Adam. They'd most likely heard the tussle in the household the night before and decided to depart.

Cecilia stuck her head in the doorway. 'Is Darius gone? I woke up early for no reason? Well, I'm returning to bed.' Then she hesitated. 'Marianna, don't forget we have shopping to do today. I will catch up with you later. That is, if you don't desperately need me now.'

She raised her brows at Marianna as the two men bid Cecilia farewell. Marianna gave her a quick shake of the head.

The only sounds breaking the silence after Cecilia left was the whisper of a spoon or fork against a dish. Then Adam asked her if she'd slept well. She told him she had, and her father said, his voice a grumble, 'I didn't sleep well. If anyone is concerned.'

He stared round the table.

'Adam and I had a long talk this morning,' her father continued. 'He sent someone to see if I was awake long before my normal time of rising and we have apologised for our misunderstandings about concerns over my business dealings.'

'I am pleased we discovered early that two explosive personalities such as our cannot always see the same on purchasing matters,' Adam inserted.

'True,' her father said. 'We do not always see things the same.' He glared at Adam. 'And I do not normally have an explosive personality.'

Marianna saw the servants' bored faces, but she knew the ears were noting every utterance.

'I am so pleased you are both seeing eye to eye again,' she said, taking a delicate sip of her chocolate, keeping her expression bland.

'Yes. I'm leaving today.' Adam smiled. 'Since our business plans fell through, there is no reason for me to impinge upon your hospitality any longer, Emory.'

'I understand. Adam.'

Oh, they were cordial, and smiling—or at least gritting their teeth at each other.

Marianna felt a moment of sadness that she had let another unsuitable suitor into her life and he was leaving. This time, even before a betrothal or a true romance. She took another sip, making sure her voice was lacklustre when she responded. Adam was leaving her life. 'We have enjoyed having you here.'

Adam's expression showed warmth and she wondered if he was still acting. 'I'm pleased I visited,' he said.

'Oh, do stay for another day,' Emory said, sipping his tea, and with absolutely no enthusiasm in his words.

'Thank you for your invitation,' Adam said. 'I believe I will.'

Her father choked on his tea.

She could feel the tension between them, and was certain the servants would also. This would be reported throughout the house. But the altercation would hurt none of their reputations. A financial difference of opinions was just business, nothing else.

'I will also have the glass in your case repaired,' Adam said.

'Oh, no.' Her father finally caught his breath. 'I would not hear of it. Perhaps I did cause it. I hope my punch did not cause a great deal of distress to you, Adam.'

'I hardly felt it.'

'And you have no reason to feel any concern about this small bump on my head.' He glared at Adam, a truly spiteful look. 'I stumbled into the bookcase, and the clock fell. At my clumsy feet.'

Marianna sipped her chocolate. The two servants shared a darted glance.

'I'm finished,' her father said, and a servant stepped forward to help with the chair. 'I hope you have a good journey home tomorrow. If you don't change your mind and leave sooner.'

He left the two of them alone. She knew both their actions were being watched closely and so did Adam.

She tried to act the same as she did every morning, but she lingered over her chocolate instead of taking it to her room. Torn between leaving and staying, she rose from the table.

Adam stood, giving her a nod. 'I appreciate the help you have offered with your father. Please don't let the disagreement cause bad feelings between us.'

'And I hope you will do the same.' She walked to the door but could not help looking back. Adam tossed his napkin aside.

'Care to meet me in the sitting room?' she asked.

Inside the room, he looked around and studied the many framed pieces of embroidery on her wall. It was a room a grandmother would feel comfortable in. 'You like stitching.'

'It's how I often spend my time, and some are gifts from friends.'

He took her hand and walked around the room, studying the different frames. She told him which ones she'd completed, and her relationship with the people who'd sewn the other ones.

He took her hand and lifted it to his lips. 'I suppose I should tell you goodbye. I only told your father I'd stay longer to irritate him.' He moved to the door.

'Perhaps you should stay another day.'

'Are you sure?'

She closed the sitting room door, holding it shut with her hand. 'Yes. It will help things settle after the argument you had with Father, but that's not the real reason. I enjoy being with you.'

'Isn't that risky for you?

'More for you. You are the one who keeps getting bruised.'

'True.'

'But every time two people meet and go deeper into their relationship, they are always taking a risk.' She couldn't stop herself from wanting to spend more time with him. She laughed softly. 'So the secret of a successful friendship might be simple—not to know each other well.'

'I don't let most people close to the true person I am, but I want you to feel free to ask me any questions you want. To talk about whatever you want.' His eyes were serious.

'Even embroidery?' she jested, wanting to lighten the moment, and hoping to feel closer to him.

'Well, perhaps most things. Not all.' Then he moved

closer. 'On second thought, don't tell anyone, but I would even take up embroidery to spend more time with you.'

'You don't have to,' she said. 'But it might be enjoyable to watch you struggle with a needle and thread.'

'I would not want to imagine how the stitching would appear.'

'I suspect you would be good at anything you tried.' And it was true. He just seemed so competent, assured. Not even flustered when things erupted around him. Sturdy.

'If I ever take up embroidery, I will be sure to let you know.'

They stood so close she could hear the slightest rustle of his clothing, and note the soft scent of his soap.

'What I would really like to know is what your skin feels like.'

'I already know what yours is like.' He leaned in but stopped just before his lips found hers. 'Soft.' He kissed her, and it was not the kiss of a man wanting a brief encounter. His lips caressed hers and she felt the warmth begin to spread about her body. He had a gentleness about him and she touched her hand to the side of his face. She felt the growth of his beard and the firmness of his skin.

At that touch, his kiss strengthened, his body moved to touch hers and he pulled her against him. She felt the length of him touching her.

His arm ran down her back and he pressed her to him, but the movement did not seem to please him.

'This is not so dangerous for me, but it is for you. You must consider where this will take us,' he said.

'Does it have to lead anywhere?' She could see the

look in his eyes, and put her two hands on his chest to still him, to keep him from pulling away.

'If we are intimate, it will change things between us. It cannot help but do so. We have already begun baring our thoughts to each other. When our bodies become involved, it will alter things. And no one can tell in advance if it will be for better or worse. We could wake up in the morning disliking each other intensely. Our bodies pounding us with regret for being so close with someone we do not know well.'

'I may have been wrong about you,' she said. 'This isn't a frivolous conversation.'

'If we were two people like that, it would be. But we aren't.'

'I'm willing to take the risk with you.'

He bowed his head, the tendrils of his hair brushing her face. Touching the spot over his heart, she put her hand over his and held him. 'Are you closing your heart to me?' she asked.

'I'm trying. It's not working.'

She had the body of a sylph, a delicate figurine, and she had the magic dust to go with it. He could feel it fluttering around him in the air, making everything intense, and his skin burned with a response to her.

He kissed her again and paused, hesitating. He'd never hesitated between kisses. He wanted to say something to her but he wasn't sure what. And then he realised—he wanted to tell her he loved her.

The words stopped in his throat. His desire for her was fogging his thoughts, ruining his intellect, turning his brain useless. Putting ideas of togetherness inside him, for ever togetherness—something unfathomable to her.

And, if he had mistakenly whispered it to her, it would have changed even more between them than the act of love-making would. No matter if he said it or she did.

The word 'love' built expectations, added promises not spoken. Created a commitment of a thousand words hidden among the four letters. It would ruin what friendship they had. Put chains around them, adding a layer of unspoken assurances that each would interpret from their own views.

They were enormously attracted to each other, or at least he was to her, and he believed she felt the same way. When he looked into her eyes, he could see it.

But he couldn't fall in love with her. She was too pampered, too wealthy and too used to having her own way.

'Don't ever think you aren't special to me,' he said, grazing her lips. 'You are.'

He was amazed at the vitality he could feel vibrating into him with just the merest touch of her clothing.

'That sounds like something a man says before leaving.'

'It is.'

She put her arms around his waist and he knew then that, if he was to get out without losing even one more part of his heart, he could not make love to her. He could not. It would be sending himself into an abyss of love. She would be able to crush him with rejection.

He stepped away, giving her a kiss on the forehead. He couldn't get more entangled. He'd never be able to regain himself. She would be lodged in his heart for ever, a memory that would resurface throughout his days. He would hear whispers of her new romances, and he'd feel the stab of pain that reminded him of what he'd felt for her.

'I have to leave,' he said. 'Leave without you. I don't want you to think I don't care for you. I do.'

He imagined their bodies intertwined, like two separate flowering plants in a garden growing higher, around each other, climbing together to reach the sun, yet being pulled apart, separated and left hanging to fall to the ground alone.

'We can sit. Hold each other. Talk, if you want. Or not, if you wish,' Marianna said.

'I would not be able to stop kissing you. Wanting to hold you. Nothing else would matter to me but holding you in my arms. And the memories would tarnish and either bring a sense of loss, or possibly of being used. I don't want that for either of us.'

'Of being used? She stepped away, silent at first. 'I don't like the sound of that. Do you think I am using you to get over my broken betrothal?'

'You may be.' He somehow understood that and accepted it. He did not want her suffering or longing for someone who could not give her happiness.

'I am not.'

'You're a woman who has been sheltered at every turn, and you always have pillows around you when you stumble.'

'You are looking for ways to end our encounter.'

'I see it blowing up in our faces. Causing more harm than good. Hurt feelings. Loss.'

She stepped back. 'This is you bringing an unhappy end to a meeting, not me.'

'Better to have a little unhappiness now, and one night of lost sleep, than months of it because we stumbled into something and it caught us too close.'

She took in a deep breath and stepped away, her voice becoming tight. 'You are trying to force me from you. I cannot believe you are doing such a thing.'

'I don't want a mindless encounter with you. It wouldn't be on my part, but I don't believe you are willing to make a true commitment to anyone.'

'How dare you pretend to know me so well?' Her voice rose and she paced back and forth. 'I have been completely honest with you. That I haven't found the right person is not my fault.'

'Whose fault is it?'

'You are blaming me. It's no one's fault.' Her voice rose again, and she put her hands on her hips. 'Father scared off the first one with talk of the marriage settlement, and Jules wouldn't sign the marriage agreement when Father produced it. I never expected that. Father finally decided to allow more funds to be left at my husband's disposal in order for Jules to sign, and when he told me that I called the marriage off.'

'Finances shouldn't have been a part of the agreement,' he stated, hearing the emotion that flowed through the words.

She should be wed for herself, and she shouldn't choose her mate based on his wealth. If she did, he would have no part in her life.

'They very much are,' she said. 'In my case, I have seen it proven.'

* * *

He took her hand. 'I don't know that it was a good idea for us to meet. Since I am leaving tomorrow, it might be best if I told you goodbye now and I went to my room instead of being alone with you.'

She didn't answer at first, trying to read the expression in his eyes. 'Is that really what you wish to do?'

'No, but what I wish to do is a mistake, and I know it. I'm not a youth any more, and I'm responsible for my actions. I can't blame it on inexperience. And I don't want to begin something that will only cause more loss when it ends.'

'Don't expect me to make promises to you,' she said, tracing a heart shape with her finger over his waistcoat. 'I have learned my lesson. No more betrothals.'

'I believe that. You like things to proceed in the way you wish. This is safe for you. In your home, where mostly everything happens in the way you direct it.'

'And I do not see myself changing,' she said. 'And you are no different in your house, I would imagine. You are an earl, and you wear it like a cape around you, separating you from others. An extra layer.'

'I don't agree with you. When I see you, I don't wish to be separate from you. You are making me a different person, and I don't understand it. I change a little bit every time I look in your eyes.'

She clasped his hand tighter.

'I will miss you,' he said.

'Are you certain?'

'I am. I see you like a fragile flower. And you draw me to you.'

'Do not think of me as delicate,' she said. 'It means

you don't know me. I must be stronger now than I was. I have more experience.'

'If it doesn't bother you when friendships end, it means you didn't care.'

She touched his coat front. 'I do care. I just don't know how much. If it's enough.'

'That's fair.' He clasped the hand she had put at his chest. 'I hate the thought of leaving you. I feel you need me to watch over you. To keep your matchmaking father from introducing you to the wrong person.'

'Like you?' she asked.

'I don't know which category I fall into.'

He watched her and she lifted her face closer to his, almost kissing him but stopping at the last moment. Instead, he used a fingertip to trace her lips. Then he touched the door, holding the handle. 'Goodbye.'

'Wait,' she said, holding his arm. 'Is it that you consider me the wrong person?'

'I don't know.' He stilled in front of her.

'But perhaps…two wrongs can make a right.'

'Possibly.'

He took the back of her head in his left hand and then he brushed a kiss beside her eye, and the bristles along his cheek made her aware of his masculinity. Of the scent of leather, strength, well-worn wool and of how much his caress could mean to her. And how many regrets she would have if he left her life, and how many regrets they both might have if he stayed.

He moved forward enough that she could feel the wisp of his breath on her lips, not touching her mouth but breathing so that his exhalation caressed her.

At that moment, his heart felt bigger than it ever had

and he didn't want to leave her. She was different from the women he'd met before. They were all like Cecilia or simpering misses who held no attraction. But Marianna was different. She intrigued him and made him not want to leave her. She'd taken his iron will and made it no stronger than a blade of grass.

His hands at her shoulders, he leaned to rest his forehead softly against hers. 'You don't have to do anything, Marianna. Just be with me and let me hold you.'

She stepped back and ran the back of her hand down his jawline, stopping to rest it on his shoulder and watch his eyes taking her in, separating them from the rest of the world.

She could not let him go, and she wanted to experience as much of him as she could. She kissed him, tentative, exploring, moving into unknown territory.

His clasp tightened, pulling her closer. In that moment, the kiss became moist and blended her with him. He caressed her mouth with his and she felt his hand move so that his palm was against her neck and his thumb at the back of her ear. He held her softly and she felt the gentle kiss, a nip of his teeth grazing her lips, and then a return to the kiss and the hint of his tongue.

A longing unfurled inside her. She melted into him, her arms around his neck, holding herself upright with his body.

Again his lips found hers and this time everything bloomed stronger, making warm her lips, her breasts, the skin on her arms where he touched her and where his legs brushed hers.

Then he pulled away. 'I want you to see my life. The true world I live in. I have already sent Dinsmore ahead with my things. I really must leave and have no plans to stay longer.'

'Is your life so different from my own?'

'Yes.'

He took her hand. 'I've met your family. And you really should meet mine. I have seen your world, but you have not seen mine. It do not want to lead you into a place of mystery; it would be wrong.'

She understood then that she knew nothing of the private Adam. She'd assumed his life was much like her own, but it couldn't be. With him having the title, his father couldn't be alive, and that meant he was the head of his family. But she knew nothing more about him and, from the stcel in his eyes, she knew she must discover what his world was like.

Curiosity lapped around her and she couldn't bat it away. True, she had just escaped one entanglement, and she had sworn never, ever to let that happen again. She had not planned to make another betrothal.

Once she had accepted the last marriage proposal, it had been as if they'd started sparring with the details of the marriage. He'd had such determined plans in place. She'd been crushed but determined to go through with it. He had wandering eyes, she'd suspected, but she'd pinned her hopes on everything getting better after he made a vow to her.

He had announced their betrothal to all, had made certain everyone knew, and she had started to notice things about him that she didn't think he'd let her see before.

She appraised Adam. His family? She wondered who that consisted of.

'Find a maid who can chaperone,' he said, 'And walk with me into my world, or I can leave right now. Just say the word and I'll return home. This moment. We have nothing to bind us together if you don't wish it. It can end now, while it's safer for you. I've barely kissed you.'

Her pulse pounded. He called that 'barely kissed'…

Footsteps sounded in the hallway and they stepped apart.

Cecilia opened the door and strolled in, momentarily pausing when she saw Adam. 'Oh,' she said. 'I certainly *hope* I'm interrupting something.'

'Nothing that can't be resumed,' Marianna said, a challenging lilt in her voice.

'Good on you, little cousin,' Cecilia answered, giving her a salute.

'Sorry to steal her, Adam, but she and I have long-standing plans to replenish our wardrobes. I just reminded Uncle that we're leaving. The seamstress will have the fashion plates ready, and we will be able to get orders in place for dozens of new dresses.'

'I've changed my plans,' she said, darting a glance at Adam and seeing understanding in his eyes. 'I want you to go on without me. I'm going to meet Adam's family.'

'Do tell,' Cecilia said, almost purring. 'Well, I suppose I must go alone.'

'I expect to be back long before I would have returned from a shopping trip with you,' Marianna said. 'So don't let Father know. You must promise.'

Cecilia tossed her head back. 'Fine. I promise.' Then she bit her bottom lip, gave her cousin a wave and left the room.

'Let's go now. Alone,' Marianna said. 'While everyone thinks I'm leaving with Cecilia. Even the maids won't know I've left.'

Chapter Twelve

The carriage trip passed quickly, and neither spoke, but Adam had plenty to think about. His brother was a blast of activity, and it wouldn't be fair to a wife not to know what her future held. He wasn't sure of the outcome of his plans, only that he wanted to keep his brother near.

After his father had died, Adam had taken responsibility for the child. He'd sent Dinsmore to act as a go-between, but his uncle had brought the little one home with him from time to time. Nathan had been a bundle of energy and curiosity and had enlivened the entire household. Nothing had been the same since.

Adam's stepmother had realised the connection between the two, and had often used it to her advantage, but she hadn't overplayed her hand.

Adam helped Marianna disembark at his stepmother's home, and for a moment they stood together, and she stared at the house.

'Do you live here?' she asked, and he heard the surprise in her voice.

The house had a modest front, no gables, porticos or

elaborate windows. It was not an estate by any means, nor was it a hovel. It contained cramped quarters for eleven servants—the absolute minimum his stepmother agreed she could make do with—plus his stepmother and half-brother. 'My stepmother does, and I provide for her.'

He walked to the door and the butler opened it and gave him a bow.

'Please let Lady Rockwell know I am here.'

The servant turned away, and at that moment a bundle of boyhood energy appeared at the steps, and didn't touch the handrail as he plunged ahead like a wild cat and almost headfirst down the steps.

'Adam,' Nathan called.

'Slower,' Adam barked out, but it was too late for the child to slow. The body continued forward until he reached the last few steps and his feet stopped, but his upward body did not, and he hurled himself at Adam, who caught him.

'Be careful,' Adam cautioned, and gently put him on his feet. 'Slow. You know the rules.' He ruffled his brother's hair.

'I am slow. Compared to how fast I want to run.'

A man appeared at the top of the stairs, the boy's tutor. 'My pardon, Your Lordship. There was no stopping him when he heard your voice.'

Adam nodded and greeted him, and the tutor left.

'What is the rule for the stairs?' he asked Nathan.

The boy smiled. 'No running. No jumping. No sliding. Not even backwards. But you didn't say no flying.'

'Nothing fast down the stairs. You must remember that.'

The boy nodded, and stared at Marianna.

'Marianna, this is my brother. And Nathan, how do you greet a lady?'

He gave her a bow and turned to Adam. 'Are you taking me home with you?'

'Not today.'

'I was going to save a dead mouse I found for Inky, but Mother said I couldn't. It might make him sick.'

'Good.' He turned to her. 'Inky is our ferret.'

Nathan bared his teeth. 'And he can bite if you make him angry.' He smiled, devilment in his eyes. 'I try not to make him angry.' He held up one finger that had a mark on it. 'He doesn't like it if you pull his tail.'

Marianna studied the youth. He could have been a younger version of Adam, except his features were softer and his hair lighter. He hadn't yet reached the age for a young man's growth spurt, but he appeared close.

'Could you tell your mother I'm here?' Adam asked. 'I'll be waiting for her in the sitting room.'

'Yes,' the boy said, and he grabbed the handrail and hopped up the stairs. At the landing, he glanced over his shoulder. 'Hopping is slow. And hard.' He scampered away.

She went with Adam to find a sitting room with two large windows, with closed heavy draperies. Adam opened them and the light burst in on a medium-sized room with large seating places rounding the room, each looking comfortably used. Wall decorations surrounded the room. She could imagine a salon of people sitting around, regaling each other with stories.

'Adam.' A woman walked into the room. Marianna

had never heard his name said with such devotion. She held out both hands to him, walked forward and turned her cheek so he could kiss it. 'So happy to see you again. It's been far too long.'

She wore a day dress, but it hardly appeared a day dress, because she wore a sleeveless wrap over it that hung like a royal robe, stopping both just short of the floor.

'Lady Rockwell, I wanted you to meet Marianna,' he said.

She turned, mouth half-open in surprise, but then she caught herself and oozed warmth.

Marianna was speechless when Adam introduced her to his stepmother. The woman had liquid azure eyes, lashes that could have swept out a room and a welcoming smile with perfect teeth.

At that moment, Marianna remembered reading about her in the society papers, but they had not done her justice.

'Pleased always to meet any friend of Adam's.' The woman took Marianna's hand in both hers, surrounding Marianna fingers in a delicate clasp.

'And do tell me for what reason I have the pleasure of your company today?' she asked Adam.

'I wanted Marianna to meet my family.'

'Oh,' she said, beaming at Marianna. 'This sounds serious.'

Then she returned to Adam and slipped her hand over his arm. 'You've never brought anyone here to meet us before.'

Adam stepped away, but she remained entrenched at his side.

'Nathan's older now, and I thought Marianna would be strong enough to weather his turbulence.'

'Then you must indeed be sturdy,' she said, her gaze taking Marianna in. 'As I would wager he is as active as Adam must have been when he was a child. He is a darling little boy. I shall miss him intensely when he goes away to school. You must visit more then, Adam, as I do not wish to die of loneliness.'

'I am sure you have plenty of friends to keep you company.'

'None as precious as you. We are having a salon next Tuesday, and I would love you to be here.' Her words caressed him. 'And you are welcome to bring Marianna, of course.'

'I do not know what next week holds.'

'Well, do stop by if you have the chance,' she said. 'Mr Weathers and I are becoming closer, and he will be here. In fact, you just missed him.'

'Adam!' The boy ran back into the room, holding a slingshot. 'The tutor helped me make this. I wanted to show you.'

Adam took it, using the chance to extricate himself from his stepmother. He held the slingshot, proud of his brother. 'Looks excellent to me. Reminds me of one I made when I was small.'

'Want to try it?' Nathan asked.

'Perhaps on the next visit,' he said. 'We could have a contest.'

'I can't hit much with it.'

'Doesn't matter,' Adam said. 'I'll teach you.' He put his hand on Nathan's shoulder. His brother's chest poked out, full of pride.

'I have a cravat to show you,' Nathan added. 'It's my first one.' Then he bounded out of the room again.

Adam couldn't wait any longer. Now was the time to ask his stepmother what he had been considering for a long time.

'If he wants to stay with me, would you agree?' Adam asked her. He tried to show no emotion, but bit the inside of his lip, waiting for the reply. He wanted this to be smooth and work in everyone's best interest, but most importantly Nathan's.

'That is a serious loss to me. I don't know how I could bear it.'

'He is growing and will be needing more education soon. I will see that he has the best instruction possible. And I will pass the house to you.'

She stilled and, while the eyes didn't lose their beauty, they stopped being liquid and became a whole different substance before they melted again.

'And a stipend for the servants?' She touched the ties at the top of her robe. 'You do know how I want to care for those around me.'

'Yes. A small one.'

'What about a large stipend?' She moved closer to him and gazed at him with all the innocence in the world. 'No house. Just the amount equal to it, and then double for the servants, and I can visit him when I want?'

Marianna could hardly breathe, watching the transaction of a mother regarding her son.

'You are not to visit my house. But he would be able to visit yours, with a servant, when you send for him.

And while he is at your home you must be there, and he is to spend time with you, not servants.'

She adjusted her robe, then raised her knuckles to her jaw, rubbing it once before dropping her hand. 'And will you speak badly of me?'

'No. His opinion of you should be his own. You are his mother, and that should mean something good to him.'

She laughed. 'Interesting.' Then she waved a hand. 'Get things in motion and he can go to your house after that. I may be having another child soon, and this could work out very nicely.'

Adam didn't move, except for a brief upturn of his lips. 'I wish you all the best.'

'As I do you.' Then she turned to Marianna, and again Marianna was struck by what appeared to be sincere warmth in her face. 'Do take care of him. I'm sure I will miss him.'

Then she left, her skirts swirling at her feet.

Marianna wasn't sure if she meant Adam or her son. Adam patted over his waistcoat pocket when he looked at Marianna. And, when the dowager countess's young son passed her on the stairs, she didn't even acknowledge him. Nathan bounded to his brother, waistcoat and cravat in hand. Adam tied the neckcloth for him and helped him with the waistcoat as they discussed Inky.

'How would you feel about living with me?' Adam asked.

Nathan jumped into the air and gave a pretend punch at his brother's midsection. 'Can I feed Inky? And Bags? Can Bags stay in my room?'

'You can feed Inky, but Bags is not to stay in your

room.' Adam tousled his brother's hair. 'It is up to your mother about whether you live with me,' he said. 'It will be a few days before the final decision is made. But now Marianna and I must be leaving. I want you to think about it. It's very important.'

The boy nodded. 'I don't have to think about it. I like your house.' He paused. 'And can I bring the tutor?'

'Yes.'

'Good. I'm helping him learn too.'

'Now, will you see us out?' Adam asked. 'I have new lanterns for the carriage.'

'Green ones, like I asked?'

'Yes.'

He darted past them and, when they reached the carriage, he was inspecting the new lanterns from all sides.

'We have to leave.'

'Can I go with you now?'

'It will be a few days.'

'Ah,' he grumbled, then he brightened. 'Tell Dinsmore I am going to feed Inky all the time,' he said. 'And tell Cook I will need biscuits because I am a growing lad.'

'We'll see.'

'I'll go tell Mother I want to live with you,' he said, rushing back to the house.

They settled into the carriage and Adam thumped the top to let the driver know they were ready to leave.

He didn't say a word, and the air around him seemed impenetrable. And she wasn't certain she wanted to intrude on his thoughts. Adam had shown her the place his brother held in his life, and she understood it.

'I'm not surprised you're pensive,' he said. 'My brother is a bundle of energy and excitement. He's important in my life.'

'I understand why you want him to live with you.' And she did. Their bond was obvious.

'It is best that a family is around him. My stepmother is growing attached to her beau, and he will not fill the house with a family air. I heard it said that her beau wanted her, but "not the brat". I knew I must consider Nathan's future. My brother is not a brat. He's spirited, isn't always smiling and moves constantly, but he is a good child.'

'He's your brother. You can't desert him.' She wasn't sure she liked the idea of Nathan living with his mother, and definitely not with a man who considered him a brat. Adam had his heart in the right place.

'My stepmother drops him off at my house often, and he has been spending more and more time with me until recently. She had begun talking about him needing an inheritance. When I made the agreement with Driscoll, I knew I would have enough money to satisfy her. And she's really a better mother than I expected. I thought I would have to go much higher.'

'Today, she made the best choice for her son.'

'She did. She could have continued on as before. If I purchased the house for her to live in upon my father's death, it is unlikely that I would toss her from it, and I have no plans for it. I will bring some of her servants into my house so they will not be without employment when it is sold. With Nathan at my house, they will likely be needed.'

'You are kind to them.'

'It's responsibility, not kindness. I inherited duties and they mean something to me. Possibly because I saw how little they meant to my father. But with Nathan it isn't about duty. It's something else.'

He wasn't the person she'd thought he was. The one Cecilia's chattering friends had spoken about. 'You don't enjoy the events you attend as much as you appear to.'

'I do enjoy them. But, when Nathan is at my house, I try to make sure he is asleep and being cared for before I leave for the night. I had been thinking of asking for Nathan, but didn't want the tug-of-war that could distress him. When she mentioned her suitor, I saw it was the right time. I couldn't wait any longer.'

The vehicle rolled to a stop in front of his home. It was an estate, larger than his stepmother's house. The first thing he noticed was a worn path over the grass from the workmen moving about, an unattended wagon with a side plank missing and a shovel handle sticking from the side of it, and a sad horse that smelled of a hay field, whinnying at them and expecting a meal. Some day it would have abundant gardens in the back, once the workmen stopped treading over the area.

'And this is where I live,' he said, watching her reaction. She appeared as if she'd never seen a horse before.

Or perhaps a dog like Bags. Bags started barking and ran up to the gate. At least the workmen had managed to keep the dog within the boundaries. The once underfed animal had appeared one day and Nathan had started feeding it. Cook had claimed the dog would look more handsome with a bag over his head. The name stuck, and the dog hadn't left. Now Adam knew it was unlikely he'd ever have the truly beautiful gardens he'd imagined, but Nathan liked the animal. Adam had never been able to have one as a child, and in hindsight his father might have been right on that one.

Marianna leaned forward, peering out of the window. But she wasn't frowning. He was surprised at how much that meant to him.

As they stepped from the vehicle, he wrapped her hand around his elbow, then they moved forward and he opened the door.

Suddenly, she reminded him of a little girl, with the same anticipation as if she were about to untie the ribbon on a gift.

'Let me take you to meet Cook and Tilda.'

'Are they special members of your household?' she asked.

'I would say.' He didn't want to tell her the two of them were the only other members of his staff.

The house was mostly bare, except for the few rooms now needed to live in. He hoped to fill the structure with pieces that would stand the test of time, and knew he would, but it would never be the mansion of riches she was used to. He had nothing to be ashamed of, he reminded himself. He'd worked hard to put the household on an even footing after he'd inherited.

He took Marianna to the kitchen door and peered in. 'Marianna, this is Cook,' he said, walking in.

The older woman was stirring a pot, which gave the room a spicy aroma. Cook gasped, dropping the spoon against the side of the pot, wiping her hands on her apron and greeted Marianna. 'I was not expecting guests. My pardon. This will not be done until later. I will get to work cooking a…something for you both.'

Marianna shook her head. 'Please understand, I am here to meet you. I did not expect a meal.'

'I will be happy to serve something delicious to you.'

Then, behind them, Dinsmore strolled in. 'I heard the carriage and—' He stopped. 'Emory's daughter!' Dinsmore gasped, grasping a hand at his heart and moving back as if he'd been hit. 'What are you thinking?' He put a palm on his head. 'Oh, let's just make one of the most powerful businessmen in London angry at us. That will make everything smoother.'

'No one knows I'm here,' she reassured the man-servant.

'This is not going to end well.' Dinsmore retreated one step. 'This is not going to end well,' he repeated.

'I probably should leave soon,' she said.

'You are right, miss.' He glared at Adam. 'She's right. Listen to her.' He waved a finger in the air. 'This is not a puppy or a raven or a ferret. This is a woman. An heiress. You cannot keep her without a wedding. I forbid it. I cannot tolerate such behaviour. It is wrong.'

Adam's chin jutted forward. 'I will do as I wish.'

'Even your father did not bring his female friends into the house, and I know what you thought of him.'

Dinsmore put a hand over his eyes. 'I thought I raised you better than this. You were the son I never had. I stood at your side when your half-foxed father married the girl you loved, and then he died and left you holding his empty purse, and you had to support the woman and Nathan, who is always scraping either a body part of his own, someone else's or a piece of furniture. He almost stepped on Inky the last time he was here, and then they got into a scuffle.'

Dinsmore slapped his forehead. 'I have to get Tilda out of the house. Now. She can't keep a secret. And Mr Wilkins wants to speak with you.'

Adam raised a brow. 'Is the work going to take longer than he thought or has he unexpected expenses?'

Dinsmore lowered his chin and gave him a stare that said he shouldn't have asked.

'Or both?'

A nod.

He chuckled to himself. A fact of his life.

He led Marianna towards the sound of hammers, and he asked her to stay inside while he spoke with the workers. With that, he gave a nod to Marianna and departed.

When he had finished and returned to her, he was amazed at how quiet she remained.

She studied her surroundings. She appeared like someone who couldn't read a foreign language and been given a book and asked to explain the story printed in it.

He felt he and his home were on trial, and he didn't like it. But it had to be this way for both of them. She had to know what his life was like. And perhaps she'd see more of him by looking at his household than she would ever see by watching a sunset, dancing a waltz or taking a carriage ride with him.

His house was his respite, his haven.

Or at least it was when everyone had turned in for the night. There were the problems Inky caused when he escaped. And sometimes the carpenters stayed late to work and Dinsmore would let them have an evening meal inside and spend the night; and the maid of all work would be in tears or sick or have family illness; and Cook would need someone to go for more food; and Dinsmore would have to get the carpenters to help out. But everyone always seemed ready to assist.

He knew his world could be chaos but he could not keep himself from letting her inside his world.

'All settled,' he said. 'But the house, even with so few people, is not always as calm as it is today. Cook can be threatening Tilda with her life if she doesn't stop hiding from her work, and my brother doesn't take a breath between sentences or pause between steps. Some days the hammering is incessant.'

'How long before you expect the house to be finished?'

'It was supposed to be finished last year, so it is going better than I've grown to expect. Perhaps a year and a half.' He touched the wall. 'It's solid. Since my father passed, I have had a plan to make everything as lasting as I can around me. And it is.'

'I like the thought, and it appears you have done magnificently.'

His words stuck in his throat but he hid it with a bow of his head to compose himself. He'd not really known how she would react.

'High praise,' he said, and meant it.

Their eyes stayed on each other long enough, he knew she'd meant the words.

The approval had meant everything to him. He'd considered her much like warmth on a cool night. Something almost intangible, yet it stayed in front of him, and was so close he could feel her smile and her sadness in a way he'd never experienced before. And that had changed everything. How could he explain what he felt about her? He didn't think there were words. At least none he knew. But mainly he didn't want his words to influence her feelings.

Yes, he loved her. He truly loved her. He hadn't wanted to. He hadn't meant for it to happen and hadn't known it could envelope one so fast.

But he had loved another woman once, and that had been like tossing himself into a pit of ash, regularly watered down to make caustic lye. He had seen what one-sided love did. It was like swallowing a bellyful of that lye and not being able to escape from it until it leeched out of his stomach, one drop at a time. One slow drop at a time.

Now he wondered if the problem was inside himself. Perhaps he truly did not wish to wed, and discovering a woman who had a history of the same made her more appealing to him.

A star who lived in a galaxy of other celestial beings would not be impressed easily. And nothing he could ever create could match the world she had grown up in.

'Would you like to see the rest of the house?' he asked.

'Of course.'

'There is no music room that adjoins a grand ballroom. I have many empty rooms, and there will be another set of rooms large enough for another family to live in, but it will be years before I have the funds to furnish them the way I would like.'

'How many servants do you have here?' she asked.

'Less than you have at an evening meal,' he said. 'Inside, I have Dinsmore, who I suppose is more relative than staff. Plus, Cook, and someone who was to be a maid of all work, but Dinsmore says she is a maid of little work. And then I have the stablemen, who take care of the horses, carriage and the grounds. The carpenters and workers completing the repairs will eventually leave. But now I plan to sell my stepmother's house, and I'm sure many of her staff will be absorbed into this household.'

'I would like to see the rest of your home, if you don't mind.'

Adam took her to the ballroom, which had no draperies. The floor shone like glass, but it had recently been installed, and a bucket and mop sat in the corner. He didn't know if the maid had left it about, or the men who had put the flooring down. He'd not noticed it before.

She took in the room, her eyes resting on the pail, then the windows. The scent of paint lingered in the room which was half the size of her father's ballroom. But then, he'd never seen a ballroom as big as the one at her home. His feeling of pride vanished. It had taken so much work just to get to this point.

He saw her take in the empty walls. He didn't explain. The sale of the artwork had funded the restoration, not just of this room, but also of the dining room and most of the rest of the house.

'There is a dining room,' he said, and took her to it. Again, no artwork on the wall, but the table had been made to fit the room. He had kept it, and the sideboard.

She went to the sideboard and opened the door underneath, a move that surprised him.

'Oh,' she said, pulling out a broken branch and holding it up, examining it before putting it back.

'Probably my half-brother, making a nest for Inky.'

She knelt, reaching deeper into the sideboard.

'One plate is broken.' She pulled out the two pieces and showed him, before tucking them back inside.

'Probably happened when he put the stick in. If he doesn't break a window, I consider myself fortunate. He's harder to keep up with than the ferret is. You saw how boisterous he is, and he's calmed down now that he's older. But he needs me in his life, and that is what family is. Not the names we place on people, but the people we allow in our lives.'

They walked to another room, the main sitting room he used, the one between his master bedroom and a smaller bedroom on the other side.

He opened the door, holding out his hand to indicate she enter.

A large table dominated the room, and stacked upon it were the plans for the house—the drawings, the changes. If they had been able to see behind it, she would have seen the sofa pushed against the wall and out of the way. His desk sat in the corner, where the light flowed into the room and he considered his business endeavours. Another desk sat at the other side where he worked out the house plans.

She picked up a stone paperweight and studied the papers underneath.

He'd often acted around others as a person who pursued enjoyment above all else, but he truly considered duty above all else. He questioned himself, seeing the room through her eyes, and wondering why he had not rolled away the drawings. But studying them in the evenings, when he was tired, gave him a feeling of solace. Of creating a new beginning for his family.

He knew he didn't need an heir. His brother would take care of that if necessary.

His childhood had been divided into two worlds— those people who lived for the social activities, and those who were in the background. The ones who ignored him and the ones who'd watched over him.

'Your life seems all planned out, a kind of summit to climb,' she said. 'And my plans are only to stay the same. To let my life continue on as it has in the past.'

'You never have made a decision that your father cannot undo for you,' he said.

He stood near her and gently lifted the paperweight from her hands. 'What you have to do now is chart your course. Either happily, in the same direction you have been going, or onto a different path.'

'You make it sound as if I am not a person in my own right.'

'No. But you have to consider your future—with no thoughts but of your own strengths and weaknesses. Your romances in the past, and a marriage, would have kept you in the same direction.'

Even though he did not want her to hide from others, in a sense the shadows were the most he could promise her. Her father's home was easily four times his own. And he suspected, living within the walls, were more servants than the population of many small villages.

'My former marriage plans included remaining in the house. It was one thing we could all agree on.'

'I plan to live the rest of my life here. I have been rebuilding my heritage, one brick at a time. And, even if I were never to wed and have children, I have my brother's heritage to preserve. Yet I don't regret it. It has been my quest, although I have never admitted it to anyone else.'

'I understand,' she said.

But he wanted more—to be joined with another person more completely than he had ever been before. And he wasn't sure she would understand that. Neither of them had truly seen a good marriage.

'I'm not sure I've even lived in a house with married people,' he said, realising the truth of it as he spoke the words. 'Or at least in the same wing, now that I think of it.'

'Well, I have married servants, so perhaps I know more about it than you.' She stepped closer, studying him as closely as any artist ever studied a painting.

'Perhaps you do.'

He ran a finger along the side of her jaw, stopping at the seam of her lips, impressed with the intensity of feelings that thundered in him. She felt so delicate, softer than a whisper, but delving into him more warmly than sunrays on the shortest day of winter.

Then she looked away, recoiled, screeched and followed that by jumping closer to him. He saw the tail, the short furry legs as they disappeared behind the table holding the drawings. He held her at his side.

'Don't worry. It's Inky.'

'A rat?' she asked, her nose wrinkling. 'You have a rat in the house? Named?'

'Inky,' he said. 'The ferret. With all the work going on, it was easy for rodents to enter from the fields, and I thought Inky would be better than having a cat in the house.'

'I'm not sure of that,' she said.

His was almost an entirely male household. At first, only Cook and Tilda had expressed any gentle reservations about the ferret, but the men had thought Inky the solution. And they all hated mice.

'Sometimes Inky is allowed into a room at night if we find evidence of a rodent. I approved of it at first, because it was said to be the best way to rid the pests. But Inky has her own problems, and I insist that Dinsmore keep her caged, except on rare occasions. Inky is good at finding rare occasions.'

He saw the house through her eyes. He thought of the vast expense of the workmen and the supplies, and the endless need for more funds. But now he saw the masculinity in it—his papers spread about; no fripperies on the walls; simplicity.

He put his arm around her and moved to close the outer door. 'Now that we know where she is, Dinsmore will collect her and put her back in the cage.'

'It appeared very much like a rat. Though I don't know that I've ever seen one. Never in a house.'

'Dinsmore is fond of it. It would be difficult for him to get rid of it.'

'Do you like it?'

'It's a trial, but it can be amusing. It entertains my brother for hours. Dinsmore tolerates it. It always seems to find a way to escape because Dinsmore is so gentle with it. When my brother visits, it can be a problem, because he likes to carry it about, and when they tire of each other Inky usually does not want to go back into the cage.'

'Yet you allow it to stay?'

'It seems a necessary evil. I don't like poisoning rodents. I like nature's way better, even if it seems sad at first.'

'You could have got a cat.'

'We saw the ferret when my brother and I were out, and he wanted it. The man selling it said it would rid any place of rodents, so I relented. And then all three of us became attached to him.'

'I see what you mean about marriage joining two different households. I don't know that I would like a ferret better than mice.'

He put a hand on the small of her back. 'A ferret isn't for everyone. But I don't want to get rid of him. I don't plan to have another one, but we try to work around the problems Inky causes, and we don't have mice any more.'

She considered his words.

'I'd like to see the other rooms.'

He opened the door, and Inky was no fool. He darted out and ran around her feet, causing her to jump back and Adam to steady her.

The slender rush of fur and four legs disappeared.

Adam held Marianna in his arms, shutting his eyes, resting his cheek against her head and letting the soft scent of her hair caress him. Suddenly he saw the one burst of femininity his house needed, and he held it in his arms. A treasure like no other.

He stepped away, leaving a part of himself behind, a part that he could never regain except in her arms. And that was the way he wanted it. He accepted the knowledge that he would never be whole again if she was not in his life, and he would never want to be without her.

He remembered the tiny house she had for her dolls,

and how sheltered they were inside the little structure, with heat for them in winter and shade in summer. A delicate place for them, and one which kept them pristine and secluded away from disasters. Much like the life her father had created for her. If the dolls were left about in the weather, they would crumple and lose their lustre. He didn't want the same for Marianna.

He would rather not be whole than to see her crumple.

Chapter Thirteen

He strode to the room at the end of the hallway, opened the door wide, thinking Tilda had overdone it, with the smell of a strident soap in the room. It still didn't disguise the lack of effort she'd put into her cleaning. Removing the pristine dust cloth might have helped. At least it didn't smell like wet fur. He studied the room, surprised to see that it did feel welcoming. The bed appeared freshly made. The plain nightstand had a lamp filled with oil. There was a wardrobe.

'This would be the room for the lady of the house. The door is to a shared sitting room, and on the other side of it is my room.'

'No artwork on the wall,' she said, her attention seemingly more on that than anything else.

She meandered over, running a palm over the coverlet on the bed, somehow making it appear tidy. It was as if a second heart had wound itself into him—hers—and hugged him close with all its might.

'Dinsmore was right. I will get my carriage and I will return you to your father.'

She squared her shoulders. 'I do not want to be *returned* to anyone.'

'You have to. You've seen my house now. My family. We're unmarried, you're getting a history for indecision and your father claims you to be seeing how many broken betrothals you can have. You must leave before anyone discovers this. Otherwise, you will not be the heiress, Marianna, but the woman who leads men to the alter as if it is all a jest to her.'

His voice softened. 'It will appear that your father's money affords you to act as you wish, and others will not like that.'

'You are jumping to conclusions.'

'The same as everyone else will.' He stopped. 'We really haven't had time to learn much about each other. But today is not the day for that.'

But he knew he wanted to learn more about her. He already missed her and she'd not left yet.

Yet it wouldn't work if he couldn't make her happy. And making an heiress happy who had been pampered beyond belief, who'd had everything she ever wanted at her fingertips, and had never had to share anything with anyone she didn't want to would be difficult if not impossible. At the smallest disagreement, she would be able to run back to her former home and command a battalion of servants to bring her handkerchiefs to dry her tears. She could have so many diversions to distract her.

'It feels as if you're angry for having me in your home, but it was your suggestion. Since you have offered to take me home, it's a good idea.'

'If you wish.'

His home did not appeal to her—a woman used to hothouse flowers and servants watching out for her every need. A choice between two mansions, her father's or her uncle's. And her father's country estate, and likely various other properties.

She was more pampered than any princess.

It was best he make a clean break and take her home. She could not be happy with the household he had. He didn't want her to feel trapped into a marriage with him. He loved her enough not to want that for her.

And he wanted something for himself too. He had his heritage, the title his father had passed to him with little else. And he'd wanted to right the memories of his ancestors and not leave the world behind him in ruin. He wanted a legacy.

She would never understand how hard he must work to get his home back onto a stable foundation and keep it there.

And he didn't just owe it to himself. Dinsmore worked for him, and Cook and Tilda lived here too. His half-brother would be growing up with them, and he wanted the boy to have a good foundation, a home. He had to provide their living. It was his duty. And he would be less than his father if he didn't provide.

'I can take you home.'

'And is this the only house you have?'

Not a question anyone else in the world would have asked. 'Yes. I will be selling the house that my stepmother lives in so I will have enough to give her the funds she wants.'

He watched for her reaction, but her face was turned away from him. Even though he knew she pondered his statement, she appeared more fascinated by the room, the bed cover that wasn't hanging straight and a coal smear on the floor. He wondered if she'd ever seen a bed that hadn't been made perfectly this time of day. He doubted she had.

'Does your room have art on the wall?' she asked.

He chuckled and led her to his bedroom.

Several framed drawings were on the wall, ones he'd done. There were some sketches of the completed house, one of a hare that had visited the gardens many times, plus a winsome drawing of Bags and a separate one of Inky.

He supposed the portrait of his father and his mother at the edge of a woodland could be considered art, painted at the time of their marriage.

'Your parents?' she asked.

'Yes. I don't remember them like that at all. I'm not even sure I ever remember seeing them in the same room together, but the portrait is a nice one. Done by a good artist.'

On the other side of the mantle was a painting of a little boy wading in a stream, holding a stick with a string on the end.

'You?' she asked, pointing to the boy.

He shook his head. 'Just a painting I saw. It reminded me of how much I enjoyed playing in the rain and puddles when I was small.'

'This is the only room I have seen that says anything about the person who lives here.'

He didn't tell her that this room wasn't as much of a reflection of him as the remainder of the house was, the adjoining sitting room with papers scattered about and the rest of the house with its stark lines and lack of furnishings.

'I did not live in this wing of the house when I was a lad,' he said. Something in his voice must have been different, because she turned to study him.

'The wing I lived in has been demolished. I hated doing that. That was the hardest part.' He'd had to make the decision which part of the house to save and which to let go. He'd been torn. He'd not wanted to save the main part, where he'd not lived, but it had been the logical choice. The additional wing wouldn't have stood well on its own, and the upkeep there had been most neglected. It had been like watching his past being torn away. Dinsmore and Cook had celebrated. He had mourned.

But now he was so pleased he'd done so. Everything had been refurbished. Nothing appeared the same. New memories had replaced his childhood ones and, while he'd not really wanted to move into the most elaborate part of the house, it had become his home as the furnishings had slowly begun to reflect who he was. And, when called to remember his childhood, he could walk among the gardens, watch the bees and butterflies in the summertime, frost in autumn and icicles and snow in winter.

And. when he thought about it now, he didn't care at all that it was not like the elaborate Emory estate. His home was right for him and for his servants. In fact, he would not choose to live in any other place in the world. Not for any sum of money.

He'd spent his childhood on the grounds, and had run in the gardens or followed along with stablemen.

He'd found birds' nests and snakes and had enjoyed the freedom. He'd made friends with the stableman's dog and even the cat. He'd even travelled with the man-of-affairs to the tenants' farms and followed along with the families as they'd done their farming and crops. The tenants had treated him much better than any of his parents' friends.

He supposed that was why he'd kept the dog. His father would never have allowed such a thing. Pets were dirty. Yet his father had had guests too drunken to stand and had thought it a huge laugh. Adam had heard the servants talking about cleaning up after the guests, windows being shattered, bottles being thrown and a guest had broken a leg and nose when sliding down the stair railing. But pets had been too dirty.

Dinsmore had once told him to be thankful they had lived among the rotting timbers rather than the rotting people and that his grandfather would have tossed his son out.

'You tore down the part of the house you lived in as a child?'

'I wanted to keep the front façade,' he said. Then the words reverberated inside him.

The façade…it represented the earldom. That was important to him. Dinsmore had told him over and over how important it was, his legacy. He could restore the house, the name. The family. 'I did make sure the house remained large enough that one or two other families could easily live privately in it. I'd thought my brother might eventually live here.'

She clasped his hand again, and that almost startled him. 'It's good that you help take care of your brother.'

'I have to,' he said. 'It's my duty. I don't begrudge a second of his care, or the efforts it has taken to make this house the home I wanted.'

He lifted her hand, and again held it clasped over his heart.

'It's your choice, Marianna. It really is all your choice.' He reached to brush her hair back from her face. 'I will take you home.' He gently kissed her cheek. 'You can't stay here without a marriage taking place.'

When he looked into her eyes, he realised he'd never been closer to a woman. He'd held them, he'd had some long-lasting romances, but by touching him Marianna connected with him in a way that he'd not before sensed with anyone.

He received the answer he'd expected—downcast eyes. Thoughtful silence.

'The place you want to go is yours to choose,' he said, sensing her departure even before she said a world. He wanted to make it easier for both of them. 'I'll take you there.'

'I'll send Father a note to have my things sent to Cecilia's parents. I will live there for a brief time. I'll deliver the note in your carriage and go on to Cecilia's. For a time. I want to chart my own path.'

'I'll get the carriage.'

'Please. No,' she said. 'I want to stay here for now. At least for a little longer. Long enough to be with you.'

'You can't. You can't be sure society will not discover that we are together.'

'Please.'

It was too late for him to tell her no.

He put his arms around her. 'I will take you back to

your home afterwards. But this is not the solution you think it is. This is the beginning of the end.'

He could not continue to see her. He couldn't feel the pain of knowing he was prolonging the end—the moment she would become tired of him and send him on his way.

'Marianna. Do you understand that I am not prepared to enter into a romance of stolen moments, carriage rides, waltzes and meandering through the darkness and gardens for quick kisses and touches? I am not going to live like that. I am no longer a youth. Nor am I going to enter into a courtship as a pretence. It is all or nothing, for me. I want something I've never had before. If we are to stay together, I want to state it to the world. I have worked hard to make my house a home for the people who live here. And I will do whatever it takes to keep them secure in their home.'

'But you don't wish to court me?' she asked.

'No. Until recently, I had never kissed you, and it turned out to be a wondrous thing. I am not opposed to trying new things. We will all make mistakes on our journey and should face our decisions with courage. The risks of too much hesitation are just as large as the risks of charging ahead without thought for the consequences. But I don't think we should court. It is always the beginning of the end with you. And I don't want my heart so tied to you that I have to say goodbye.'

'And what are you doing now?' she asked.

'Charging ahead without thought, but at a slow pace. This is a change of direction for both of us. Either a move to separate or to a marriage.'

She lifted his hand, holding it to her face. 'I understand. This moment is important to me. I want to have this memory of our time together. And, if this will end our companionship, then I grasp that. But it feels that I can't let you go without touching you. Without becoming a part of you.'

He led her outside his bedroom. His hair brushed against her skin, tickling her and sending vibrating brushes against her.

He touched the tip of her nose with his lips. 'I want this to be special for you, Marianna.'

She cupped his cheek. 'It will be. Because it's us.'

He placed her onto the upholstered clothing stand at the end of the bed, and sat beside her.

He slipped off one of his boots and then the other. The leather creaked and he scooted them aside with his foot. He slipped the cravat from his neck and tossed it aside, onto the boot rack.

He reached out to her and she settled onto his lap.

'You always make me think of flowers when I am this close to you,' he said, holding her loosely in his arms. 'I don't know what kind of flower it is, and then I realise it's a Marianna flower, the most precious bloom of all.'

'Your talk is what's flowery,' she whispered against his skin.

'When I am talking of you. Only then.'

On the last word, his head turned and his lips touched hers. They were moist, tender, longing. And she hugged him tight, feeling his intensity through his clothing and the vibrancy that seemed jump from his body into hers and make her have as much strength as he did.

Then he kissed her bottom lip and she breathed in the scent of his skin. Nothing had ever touched her in the same way. He was chocolate and spice, morning and light.

Her body only lived where it connected to his. And she knew, she just knew, if they made love he would change his mind about courting her. He seemed happy to be unmarried, and she imagined a happy courtship for them. Her first one ever.

He stood, setting her on her feet, and held her waist, kissing his way down her neck and over her collarbone, and then with one finger he slipped aside the shoulder of her dress and chemise and his lips lingered against hers.

Marianna shut her eyes, aware of the warmth of him surrounding her. She put her arms around him, trying to hug him so close she would never be able to get the imprint of him to leave her body.

'May I?' he asked, touching the buttons at the back of her dress.

'If you have to ask, you do not know me as well as I think you do.'

'I just wanted to hear you say yes.'

'Yes,' she answered. 'How many times do you want me to say it?'

His forehead touched hers and his breath lingered against her lips, seeming to put a caress inside her, and filling her with a wondrous, magical sense of floating. Of being away from the rest of the world and on an island, just the two of them.

'As many times as you'd like,' he said.

He clasped her shoulders, slid her dress away from her body and put it on the upholstered bench at the end of his bed, finishing with a kiss to the hollow spot at the base of her throat and refreshing the tingling sensations inside her. He turned her round so that he could unlace the ties of her corset.

Within moments he'd removed his shirt and his trousers, dropping them on top of her dress, then he lifted her again, the same as when he'd carried her over the threshold, and gently placed her between the covers of his bed.

Next, she slipped her chemise aside and he joined her, rustling the covers, stretching alongside, holding her in a close embrace, the masculine scent of his skin warming her own and bringing her senses even more alive.

The kiss was soft, caressing and caring, brief in touch but not in emotion. He pulled away and their eyes locked. 'I've been missing you my whole life,' he said. 'I just didn't know it.'

She pulled him closer, running her hands over the muscles of his shoulders and slipping an arm around him so she could caress the bare skin of his back.

Their legs intertwined. She could feel the pressure of him against her leg and shut her eyes. His lips moved to kiss under her chin.

Then she slipped beneath the covers, and he lay beside her. His long body stretched against her and she felt his hand begin a tease against her body as he pulled up her chemise and two fingertips moved up to brush over her breast. The sensation of his hand against her bare flesh was so strong, she could experience nothing else.

Her body began to control her thoughts and her hand touched his bare chest, trying to memorise the feel of him with her fingertips. She flattened the hair against his skin as she rubbed her hand over him.

He did not speak, but his lips found hers, and his kiss was soft, almost teasing. He kissed her and she wrapped her leg around his and let his hands roam her body until she could feel nothing but the touch of him. She was consumed by the magic of the sensations he could create in her body. Her feet pushed against the bed, and he held her as his teeth grazed her lips and his hand touched her most sensitive area. His hand rose, and she gasped as he caressed her. Her feelings peaked, leaving her out of breath and aware of a tiny kiss at her ear.

She felt the surge of passion surround her, and she lived in it, and then her body relaxed—she could not have summoned enough strength to have moved a muscle, relishing the aftermath of her passion—as he rose above her.

He positioned himself between her legs then lowered himself, joining with her. She did not feel a kiss, but his breath touched her and she felt him move rhythmically into her.

She was pressed to the bed so that she could only pull herself closer to him, and she realised that his breathing had become ragged and his movements were intense. She had never felt so wanted, or so alive.

He brushed the hair from beside her eye and dropped a kiss on her cheek, whispering her name from the depths of his soul.

She cupped his face, letting the moments of his desire caress her. She would always remember this moment of closeness, and intensity, and the awareness he'd created inside her.

He was above her, buried, and she knew the passion soared in his body. She saw the tension of his face and he pulled aside, the tendrils of his hair brushing her face.

He touched her hair, brushed it back from her face and kissed her.

He lay beside her with his head resting on his crooked elbow, silent, contemplative.

Marianna gave him another squeeze. Hugging him made her feel stronger—complete, alive.

He caressed her body in return, and she felt he was trying to put her impression into himself, deeply, where he could hold her in his memory for ever.

When his breathing returned to normal, he held her.

She couldn't believe the serenity in the room. Nothing had been calm about it, but now it was as if she could hear every movement of the covers from his chest rising and falling, and see every sparkle of the sunlight in the room stretching all the way back to its origins.

This was the way to be ruined. The only way.

Chapter Fourteen

Adam stood alone at the window, one arm braced against the frame, his shirt opened, fluttering in the breeze, cool air flowing into the room overheated by the coals.

He was aware that she was lying in bed behind him. A part of him felt he touched her still, and a part of him felt he never had. They seemed alone in the world. They weren't, but for this moment no one else mattered. The feeling surrounded him, and he closed his eyes. He was alone with Marianna in a world full of people.

The first true moment of peace he'd ever felt in his life.

He had grown up in a house that had been in his family for generations, and everyone had expected everything to remain as it was, just as they'd expected rain and sunshine, day and night. A house that had held the babies of his grandparents and their parents—all without much warmth, he suspected. His forbears had increased the size of the house, adding on and adding on. Bigger had been better, and they'd never noticed the rotting wood in the windowsills, or even the draperies becoming threadbare.

His father had found other ways to amuse himself rather than concern himself with upkeep: revelry; over-abundance of lifestyle; one carriage after another; more stables; more rooms; more events. More…always more.

Yet, no matter how much coal had been burned, the house had always been cold in winter. Until he'd made changes.

When his father had resided in it, the Earl's room had reeked of tobacco, spilled drinks and boots that had been left in the rain. The smoke-tinted walls had reminded him of the inside of the fireplace. Nothing had been maintained properly. To him it had been a disgrace, but to his father it must have been comforting or invisible.

He'd only been in his father's rooms a few times while his father had been alive. Now, the walls had been repainted white, with a slightly darker lily pattern stamped around the top border. The cleaned windows, with draperies that could be slid aside completely from the glass, gave the feeling of openness. Of freedom.

He'd kept only the bed and one nightstand, and had added a small shaving stand, in addition to the mon-strosity in the dressing room, which was still often cold in the winter and warm in the summer. And he'd added a large dressing bench at the foot of the bed, and every morning he sat on it while he put on his boots and re-alised how much progress he'd made.

He'd been a child whose mother and father had truly been strangers to him. Yet Dinsmore had been a parent, and had refused to wed when he'd known he could not take his nephew with him. He'd stayed with the sister and brother-in-law he'd detested, making sacrifices and taking on most of the running of the household, and never caring that the house wouldn't become his own.

When Adam had inherited, Dinsmore had refused to drape the mirrors with black, and had spent his time poring over financial tables and ledgers and making careful plans that he'd showed Adam.

Slowly, the home had become Adam's own. The responsibilities, his own. The title, his own. The trials of maintaining everything, his own. But restoring it had been easier than watching the decay.

On the first day he'd looked at all the records Dinsmore had been able to locate, he'd not really understood the enormity of the undertaking in front of him. Dinsmore had, but he'd not been deterred. The house had been starkness itself at first, but Adam had been free to create a home he could find comfort in.

His room was the only place he frequented, as well as the sitting room and the library, which wasn't devoted to books but his ledgers and maps, with a desk for Dinsmore, the man-of-affairs and him. He had kept the huge case clock.

Carriages had been sold. The wine cellar—his father's pride, what was left of it—had not been replenished.

Adam had got rid of wagonloads of fripperies. He'd sold the spears and the armour, which needed polishing and appeared to have been on the losing side, though he knew it wasn't.

Selling them had allowed him to have the funds to make sure the floors were solid, the plain walls were freshly papered or painted, to replace the window frames and mend or purchase floor coverings. He'd only kept the pieces he liked—nothing with serpents' heads or dragons' flames—and those had apparently brought good prices which amazed him.

He did not miss the dark artwork. He was sure neither of his parents had realised the worth of it or the paintings would have been sold long before.

His home was secure, but had little more than walls and places to sit, not that he minded. In fact, it pleased him. Nothing was gilded or silver. Everything was sparse, sturdy, strong, cared for.

It was not a house of squabbles and upheaval—even the former artwork had been contentious—but a house of serenity. Everything was as plain, solid and sturdy as he could make it, and the emptiness usually made him feel orderly.

But now it just made him feel empty. And he knew he would for a long time after Marianna left. She could not stay. There would be too much attention on her. Things would be exaggerated. She would be ruined in society. Her life as she knew it would end. Her father would still be welcomed, but she would be talked about. She would be diminished if she had a romance in public.

Their encounter had already been discovered once. One could only push the boundaries of society so far, and then a title, a fortune or anything else would not be enough. Odds were that they would be discovered again if they continued meeting. And not necessarily by someone who had her best interests at heart. He was certain all their luck had been used on that front.

He flexed his muscles, gathering his strength.

The day had to end, and it was best for it to do so soon. He pushed himself away from the window.

Marianna rolled over, watching him through tousled hair. 'You're so pensive.'

'Yes,' he said, walking to the side of the bed.

He kissed her and stayed just a moment to give her a caress. 'I have to get you back home.' He moved to the fireplace, opened a decanter and held a glass out to her, but she shook her head.

He turned, poured himself a drink, took a sip and let the taste linger while he listened to the sound of her leaving the bed and gathering her clothing.

He set down the glass and she stood beside him, holding her stays in place. He laced her up.

'Will you court me?' she asked.

He shook his head a minute amount. 'I will marry you. But that is my only offer.'

'No courtship?'

'No. If what just happened between us doesn't reckon as something meaningful, then no amount of strolls and admiring the beauty of the clouds will ever matter.'

'I feel like I am being jilted,' she said. 'Like I am being left at my wedding.'

His eyes had such a faraway look, and at first he didn't seem to hear her.

'I know.' He lifted the glass, but set it down again. 'I know how that feels.' He put the stopper onto the decanter, and she heard the small slide as he pushed the container away.

'I don't know if I made the biggest mistake of my life or the wisest decision. I don't know up from down at this moment, and it is because of you.'

'But you don't want to court me?'

'It would only lead to a dismal end, not a marriage. That could only lead to more sadness for us both. If we are to end it, today is a good day for that. While there is no real chance of a babe forcing us to marry, or move away, we need to quieten the whispers about you.'

She sat down on the side of the bed and thought about what had happened. It had been true love-making, an experience she had dreamed about, and it was as beautiful as her dreams. A hollowness filled her. She couldn't imagine life without him.

She watched him at the wash basin as he splashed the water about and sluiced it over his face. She wondered that a few drops didn't hit her. He slapped the towel over his face and tossed it aside.

He sat on the bench at the end of the bed, putting on his boots, appearing to carry silence on his shoulders and yet remain at peace with himself and those around him.

She moved to him, not wanting to feel the emptiness between them. He was closer than he had been when they had danced the waltz, although he didn't touch her. And, even though he didn't clasp her, she felt he was as near as if he still had his arm on her waist and her hand in his. Only more so—because, at the dance, other eyes had been there to keep propriety. Now there was only the two of them.

She was so relieved that he was so calm. She needed a chance to tell him goodbye. To tell him that his friendship meant something to her, even though she wasn't entirely sure they were more than acquaintances. She would find a way to carry on alone and at peace with the decision.

He walked away, but didn't comment, and then moved to the window.

She breathed in, realising she'd been looking for an excuse to avoid marriage. It hadn't felt right to her, and she'd just meandered along, but she didn't want either of them to feel pushed.

She did not speak at first, following him.

'The act of marriage. Is that a commitment you want in your life?' she asked. 'Something you cannot walk away from?'

'I have thought of it more recently.' That she asked sent cold shivers throughout his body. The question told him that she wanted to continue her ability to leave any encounter.

'You don't need an heir.'

'No. I have a brother.'

'So you wish to marry me so that you might have a…' She searched for a word.

'Wife,' he suggested. 'It's an old custom. Possibly from the beginning of written or spoken history.'

'It has never been my true goal, and perhaps that is also why I balked.'

'So what do you want in life? What is important to you?'

'I'm not sure. I've always had everything I wanted. The only thing I've never had is a husband, and I don't know that it is the answer for me.' She bit her lip. 'But perhaps it isn't the husband I am unsure of. It could be the prospect of being a wife.'

'Why wouldn't you wish to have your own home?'

'If I wed, I planned that my husband and me would live with my father. The house is already staffed and we have plenty of extra rooms. Nothing would really need to change.'

'I could not leave the Earl's estate. It has been in my family for generations. It is not just a home. It is a heritage.'

'But if I were to move…it would be into your home.'

'You think it would be moving from one man's home to another, but it wouldn't be. It would be your home as well as mine. By making the marriage vows, we would be vowing to go forward as one. To accept each other's heritage.'

He studied the sadness in her eyes. 'You don't plan to marry. It is not the person you are concerned about, it is the commitment. I understand.'

He helped her finish dressing and led her to his sitting room, hoping to truly understand what she was thinking.

She studied the room, seeing evidence of his presence everywhere. Someone had even left a neck cloth on top of a drawing. It was little different from his library.

She didn't want to be a wife who was only privy to the parts of her husband's life that he wished to share. Or neatly be tucked into a house with the label of '*wife*' metaphorically hung on her. And there would be another label with '*leisure*' written on it, and those actions would only concern the husband, in his opinion.

And she was certain that his leisure could touch her as well.

'I wouldn't want to be a wife whose husband goes about and does as he wishes, while she is at home with her sewing and the children. I want more than that. I want more of a promise than that.'

She turned her face away from him.

'I understand that, if we're married, we would be one another's companion to attend public events,' she said. 'Rather like a nice carriage one could park away and then bring out to jaunt around town on special occasions.'

'At least you are not blinded by the lure of a marriage of sunbeams and moonbeams.'

'No. I felt it when I was younger, but no longer.' She met his gaze.

'I felt it once too,' he said, surprising her.

He looked into her eyes. 'I wished to marry,' he said. 'The first woman I ever truly noticed. I never kissed her. One does not kiss a fairy princess….' He paused. 'I thought she felt as I did. I was a lad, and I thought she was the moon, stars and the best of the world. And then she started courting my father. But luckily I am soon to get that millstone from around my neck.'

'Do you still care for her?'

'No. I tolerate her because she is Nathan's mother. Barely.' He tilted his head. 'She is a stranger that I must watch over. She doesn't even look like the same person to me. Now she appears a fraud every time I see her. A woman who uses her appearance to get closer to the men she wants. I'm thankful to be the one she overlooked.'

'Did it make you cautious of marriage?'

It had made him cautious about love. But just because one was careful… Well, sometimes the warning wasn't really heeded. He studied Marianna. He had not been careful enough. He had let his passion for her override everything else.

Now they would be together for ever, in a way. Bound by this moment, which meant nothing in society's eyes as a promise, but had tossed him into a maelstrom.

'It made me cautious of love. And I was right to be.'

With only the barest of movements, he reached out to the ink pot on the desk, tapping the top of the stopper. Then he slid it aside, lifted the pen and began twirling it between his two fingers, causing a dance of silver.

'I don't think my stepmother loved my father. She wanted to be a countess and have a family. He was the conduit she used to get what she wanted.' He flipped the pen upwards and caught it. 'After a few years, she became immersed in being a countess and I was relieved that I had escaped my father's fate. Once she got what she wanted, she was happy to revel in it, and didn't seem to care about anything else.'

'I sometimes wondered if my suitors tried to impress me because I am an heiress. I would be contrary, and they would laugh it away, but it would make me wonder. It irritated me that they didn't complain. I could do no wrong.'

'Perhaps that is what you and I do to suitors,' he said, eyes on the pen, holding it where she could see it. 'Perhaps we hold them close for a while and then put them aside for a different one. A shinier one. Newer.'

'Is that so wrong?'

'It might be, with people. We are more than cold objects with nothing inside but working parts. I see men entranced by women who want them only as a purse and men who only want a beautiful possession. Although I suppose that is fine, because both get what they want.'

'How do you know you're different?'

He didn't answer the question at first, sitting the pen down by the ink pot.

'I wanted to rescue you,' he said. 'And yet, you don't need rescuing, because you are an heiress, so I don't know why I feel that way.'

'I think, if I irritated you, you'd always let me know. I don't think you would fume and hide it from me, and then tell your problems to another woman.' She stood and moved to him, clasping his hand.

'I will miss arguing with you,' he said.

'It's easy to find people to argue with.'

He didn't speak. 'Is it really? Particularly for you or me? Or do you tend to banish anyone who disagrees with you?'

'You would be long gone if that were the case.'

'You might make an exception for me.'

He didn't say it, but he meant because of his peerage.

'But what kind of miserable person would fill her life with people who only add to unhappiness? That wouldn't be logical.'

He tapped the pen on the desk. Then he challenged her with his constant gaze. 'Without realising it, were you choosing suitors who might throw obstacles in your way? Suitors who your father could force away?'

'I don't know.'

'You like your treats, Marianna, and you don't want to give them up. Even if you aren't sure you want to keep them, you want them at your fingertips in case you change your mind later.'

'I don't think that's fair.'

'Are you sure?'

'I am.' She took in a breath. 'And, if I am wrong, it is only human nature to want as much as is available to you. We all like treasures and treats and choices, if we can have them. That doesn't make me a bad person. And are you any different? You've not rushed to wed but you've not lived a celibate life, by your own admission.'

'I may not be different,' he said. 'I only pursue women who have let me know they're interested. It's almost as if I don't want to waste time on a pursuit that will not end in success.'

'Did you care about the women in your life?'

'Of course. I liked them or I would not spend time with them.'

She raised a brow. 'But did you like them as pretty dolls, or were you interested in being with them because you enjoyed the conversation? Tell me a deep discussion you had with them. Do you remember any?'

He hesitated. 'At the time they were all intense…or frivolous. I have no complaints. Besides, if a woman told me something in confidence, it should remain in confidence.'

'And if you did have a grumble, did you immediately walk away?'

She watched his eyes and could see him consider her words. The silence between them wasn't unfriendly but was powerful.

'If I always walked away when I had a complaint, now would be the moment I would leave.'

'But you're not.' She stopped directly in front of him, trying to read every movement of his face and take in an awareness of every fibre of his being.

'It depends on you. Is part of the reason you don't

want to wed me because I don't have the resources you are used to?'

'That you think such a thing proves how little you know me,' she said, moving closer.

'Are you misleading yourself?' he asked. 'Are you using the fact that you had bad experiences in the past as an excuse for not stepping into a marriage now?'

'That would be intensely shallow of me.' She clasped his waist. 'And I hope you will miss me, even if it's only for a brief moment in which you think of the walk we took, or even the fight with my father.'

'You didn't know it, but you knocked me aside in the fight. When you burrowed around my arm, you surrounded me, trapped me. The fight in me was lost, trampled under footsteps you didn't even know you made.'

'I didn't plan it.'

'Nor did I.'

A knock on the door startled her. He reached out, calming her.

'What is it?' he called out.

'Adam.' Dinsmore spoke through the door. 'Might I speak with you a moment? Privately.'

'I will be out in a moment,' he said.

'Could you hurry, please?' Dinsmore continued. 'You're needed.'

Before he left, he collected the cravat, slipped it round his neck and found a waistcoat. He bent to give her a quick kiss and said, 'I'll be back soon.'

He didn't know what would happen next, but when he returned, he knew things would be different between them for ever.

Chapter Fifteen

Adam stepped out of the room.

'Her father is here,' Dinsmore whispered. 'And he asked where his daughter is.'

'What did you say?' Adam said, running a hand through his hair to straighten it.

'I said, i*s she supposed to be here?*' He waved an arm. 'That was my most coherent reply, other than *yes*. I could not tell him that.'

'Did you offer him a cup of tea?'

'No. He said the cousin's maid told him she did not go with her cousin. That she left with…'

He was certain Cecilia was behind this.

They heard a thumping noise from downstairs, then another thump.

'But you'd best get dressed—completely—before you see him.'

'I will have a discussion with her father. I will calm him down. They can leave together. It will be all nice and proper.'

'That horse has already left the stables and he shouldn't

be looking back now. You are ruining her life if you don't marry her.'

'That horse may have left the stable with the first one.' Adam walked away from the door. 'She would not agree to marry me,' he said quietly, while Dinsmore did a few quick flips with the cravat, then he slipped on his waistcoat. 'So, don't make those faces at me. If we don't marry, it's not my fault.'

'The poor girl was in a state.'

'I'll repair the damage done,' Adam said. 'If the lady will let me.'

'You had better,' Dinsmore said, holding his chin up high. 'One cannot pretend one does not know what is going on when one nearly trips over it, and her father has tripped over it.'

'Well, close your eyes and tell her father I will be down immediately. Show him to the library. There are not many books he can throw, and he likely can't lift the clock in there.'

Adam turned and went back to his room. He knocked— on his own door—and then opened it.

Adam didn't speak but stepped back into his room.

'What is it?' she asked.

'Sweeting. We have a slight problem. A guest—your father. You might wish to straighten your hair if you plan to talk with him. I suspect your cousin directed him here through her maid.'

Shock registered on her face. 'No reason to rush. Whatever he's decided, he's already firm into believing it.' He watched as she ran to the mirror.

'Really. It doesn't matter,' he said.

'It might,' she said. 'He's already attacked you once.'

'I survived. And so did you. I expect your father is furious. You're fortunate to have a father who wants the best for you.'

At the mirror, she twisted her hair and put it in a knot on her head. It still appeared as if it had been treated roughly.

'Wait,' he said. He couldn't call the maid to help with her hair. Tilda couldn't keep a secret, if she was still in the house. 'It's important that you are confident now. And for ever.' He held the comb out for her, but when she clasped it he didn't release it.

'You are an adult. You make your own decisions about what is best for you.' Then he let her take the comb and finish correcting her hair.

When she finished, her hand shook.

'I didn't believe Cecilia would do this.'

'Marianna, I will go and speak with him and I will get this corrected, although perhaps we should give him a little time to digest the news. I will make sure he listens.'

'He doesn't listen to anyone but me.'

'He will.'

Adam reassured her with his eyes. 'When twenty years have passed and we see each other at an event, I will not ask you to dance, but I will give you a smile. I want you to remember this day with humour, and the best moments we had together, and for you to give me a genuine smile in return.'

'You are hopeful,' she said. 'If I am not still in gaol for throttling Cecilia.'

'It is the two of us who created this, and the two of us will make it right.'

* * *

They moved downstairs, and Adam saw Emory pacing to and fro. He raised his hands and gesticulated wildly to the heavens. He pounded his fist against the mantle.

'Blast it. Marianna, I did not raise you in such a way. You have lost all semblance of propriety. Both of you.'

Marianna saw a fair amount of fire in his eyes. She had never seen him look like this. His hair stood on end, and she worried that he might cause himself injury with his wild movements.

'I cannot— I cannot— I will not—'

Her father was as angry as she'd ever seen him.

Adam stood still, rather like he'd been taking a country stroll, and his jaw was tight. She could hardly believe this was the same man who'd kissed her.

She interlaced her fingers, turned her head the barest bit to Adam and spoke softly to him. 'You can leave. Father and I will talk this through.'

'No,' Adam said.

Her father growled. He moved quickly and slammed the library door shut then turned the latch.

'He thinks I should stay as well,' Adam said calmly.

'Father,' she said. 'We were talking about commitment.'

'That would be marriage. Did he ask?'

'He suggested it.'

'Fine,' her father said. 'That is what he will do. Today.'

'No. I have changed my mind. I will not have a wife who has no other choice. Not in my lifetime,' Adam said.

Marianna swept her hand over her hair. 'I have choices. I will always have choices because I will make them. But Adam thinks I cannot follow through with a marriage.'

'I don't either,' her father said. 'Why do you think that, Adam? I believe she needs to hear your view explained.'

'She has led such a sheltered life that she fears stepping a foot out of the door of her house and moving into the world.'

'Nonsense.' She turned to Adam.

Her father shot him an evil glance. 'Both of you are at fault. And both of you will correct this.'

She sat delicately on the edge of her chair, smoothing out her clothes, but her movements were quick. 'We came here to see Adam's house. To discuss whether we wished to court or not.'

'Yes,' her father said. 'I'm sure. I'm sure. A gentle discussion of courtship. Which of course could not be conducted in a room such as…' He studied the walls. 'A library.'

'I had…' She paused.

'I don't care what the reason was for your so-called discussion,' her father said. 'Your trials with suitors are getting to be a habit. Marianna,' he continued, and his voice was as cold as she had ever heard it. 'If you were to choose at this very moment—which would you choose? To marry by special licence, or to marry by special licence. Those are your only choices.'

'I would, of course,' she said, 'Choose not to make a decision rashly.'

'That is not an option,' her father said.

'That is preposterous,' she said, standing. 'I will not marry him.'

'Why not? He has a title. I have money. You'll have everything.'

'I mentioned marriage but she declined. And I liked that about her,' Adam said.

'I could be a spinster for ever. I don't have to wed anyone—ever. You said so.'

'That was before today,' her father said. 'How old are you, Adam?'

Adam answered.

'The perfect age to wed. And I need it for the special licence.'

'Father,' Marianna said, barely controlling her voice, standing and moving to the desk. She put her palms on the wood, facing him. 'I cannot believe you would do this to me. I do not want to be a wife. Do not I have any say in this?' Marianna asked.

'You have all the say.' Adam turned to her, eyes level. 'You can easily say no at this moment. End of our discussion and our meetings. I give your father my promise on that.'

'You keep talking about our parting. I thought I had trouble with commitment, but you are on the cusp of leaving all the time.'

'He doesn't have the right to disappear any more,' her father inserted. 'You will wed. I will go for the special licence so this conflagration can immediately be ended.'

He paused, hand on the door. 'I did not mean to say the word "conflagration". I meant to say "betrothal". Consider it a business decision, if you wish. And, if you don't feel you know each other now, I assure you, if you marry that will be resolved.'

He fumbled with the latch and opened the door. 'And

whatever you decide, you are not to return home, Marianna, without being wed. I will be back with the special licence. I have friends in the proper places and they will help me get this resolved.

'Oh, and one other small thing,' Emory said, standing taller than he'd ever seemed before. 'If Adam does not wed you, I will ruin him financially. With my last breath and if it impoverishes me, I will use every penny I have to block every venture he tries.'

He glared at them both. 'I will be back.'

He stomped out.

Adam turned to her. 'Let us have a cup of tea.'

'Tea?' she asked. 'Tea?'

'There is no amount of any drink that will solve this. And Cook makes better tea than anything else.'

'I will go to my cousin's house,' Marianna said.

'Not while your father is on the loose,' Adam replied. 'He needs a chance to calm.'

'Are you going to try to convince me to wed you?'

'Absolutely not.' He ushered her to the kitchen, and she appeared surprised to be expected to enter the room.

'Tea,' he said, walking in. 'It's been a long day.'

'Going to get longer,' Cook said, reaching for the kettle. 'If all the slamming about was any indication.'

He helped Marianna to sit and noticed her fingers trembling. He reached out and clasped her hand.

'I don't think I've ever asked you,' he said to Cook, grasping at the first thought of conversation away from their predicament. 'How did you become a Cook?'

She studied Marianna, then turned to the kettle and started chattering on about her days in the scullery.

When the kettle boiled, she poured them both a cup and scurried away with the pot.

Marianna squeezed his hand.

'Don't worry,' he told her.

'I've never seen him so angry,' she said. 'I think it's all my ruined betrothals adding up, and he has lost sight of reason.'

'You can't live your life for others,' he said, 'Or mislead yourself into thinking you're doing that. Every step you take is a choice of your own. No one is moving your feet, or your mouth, but you.'

The instant he sat near her, he knew they were doing right not to marry. She reminded him of a flower gone too long without being watered, but still alive enough to become vibrant again if treated well.

'There will be smoke boiling out of your father's ears. But he is an adult as well.'

He smiled, imagining he might need to carry a bucket of water with him for a time, just in case Emory needed to be doused.

'Father will banish me to Cecilia's,' she said. 'And I will likely have to live with her parents, as she will not want me underfoot.

'Is that your wish?'

'No. That house is rather a frightening place. Uncle Cleo is a naturalist and the house always smells of wet animals and dirt. Not flowers.'

'I prefer flowers.' And it seemed he could see them when he looked at her.

She always did something like this—she either made him angrier or feel like the whole world was abloom.

He'd never had anyone in his life that could change the world around him in the way she did. A thundercloud or sun only created anything inside him when she was at his side.

'Marianna,' he said quietly. 'You smell like a garden full of blooms.'

'Keep your charming words to yourself,' she said. 'But I appreciate the effort to cheer me.'

'You do smell like flowers, but not ones I am aware of. Something exotic,' he said. 'I was merely noticing it. And it's so appropriate, as you are so many things to me. A flower. A rain cloud. A tempest in a teapot. A wonderful thorn in my side, and the balm to ease all the trials.' He shook his head, laughing. 'I am acting like I have never a seen a woman before, and perhaps I haven't truly. Until now.'

Cook returned, and put the pot back on the stove. 'It's been a quiet few moments,' she said.

'I don't expect it to stay that way. Cook, will you stay with Marianna until her father returns? I don't know if it will be today or tomorrow, or when, but I know he will be back for her.'

'If she doesn't mind listening to my rattlin' pots and my rattlin' words. And I can find her a spot to put her head if she needs it.'

'I would love it,' Marianna said. 'This appears to be one of the most comfortable, relaxed rooms I've ever been in.'

Cook studied Marianna, walked over and gave her a pat on the shoulder that was more hug than tap. 'It will all work out.'

Instantly, Marianna brightened.

Even though Cook wasn't the best at food preparation, she'd created a haven around her and gave peace to everyone she smiled upon.

Then Cook studied Adam. 'And you will be on your best behaviour, young man,' she said, repeating words she'd said to him over and over as a child.

Then she looked over her shoulder and said something she'd not said before. 'And, this time, I expect it.'

Chapter Sixteen

He heard banging on the entrance door. Emory had returned as promised, but Adam had been surprised at how long he'd left Marianna with him. Adam suspected Emory was trying to make it harder for them to part.

'I will get it,' Dinsmore shouted out from within the house.

'Not alone,' Adam said, hurrying to the entrance.

Dinsmore opened the door and Emory rushed in, a crumpled paper held high in one fist. "I managed to get some help from my friends, and speak with the Archbishop yesterday." He straightened the paper and still held it aloft. "The special licence, and it is now ready to be used." He scowled.

'I have the cleric with me, and he can wed the two of you, or act as my second.' The words were growled out. He stared at Dinsmore. 'And you will be his.'

The cleric stepped in, a book under his arm. He was a man with completely unlined, plump cheeks and thinning hair, who looked as if he'd been smiling since his first peek at the world.

Marianna rushed out from the kitchen, a half-eaten biscuit in her hand. She popped it into her mouth and swallowed, eyes wide as she dusted her hand on her skirt.

'I brought a prayer book, not a duelling pistol,' the cleric said, raising the book. 'Mr Emory, I have told you—a marriage must be joined into with all good thoughts.'

Her father gave him a withering look. 'You are here to convince them to marry, and then get it taken care of."

The cleric studied the faces in front of him, nodded to them and said, 'We are prepared for a happy occasion?'

No one spoke.

'We will not proceed,' the cleric said, 'Until the couple is in agreement.'

Adam stepped beside her and clasped her hand, and she thought her knees would leave her.

The cleric stood solemnly, as if he were to begin the ceremony, but his eyes still twinkled. 'Before we start the conversation,' he said, 'there is something I feel I must ask first. I wish to know if anyone here has reason for this couple not to be married?'

He slowly looked at her father' face, then Adam's, Dinsmore's and hers.

'We are all in agreement, then?' he asked.

He looked at them. 'I am sorry for my lateness. I was visiting a grieving family. I am reminded of that as I look at your faces.'

'They will smile afterwards,' her father said.

'That isn't always how it works,' the man said. The cleric raised his hand, silencing all, a gentle smile on his face. 'I will say a prayer with you, and we will proceed to the church. If you are both absolutely certain this is what you wish to do.'

Neither answered.

The cleric took in a deep breath. 'Wedding concerns are usual before the ceremony. It is not necessarily bad. It can mean an awareness of the seriousness of the commitment.'

Adam glanced at Marianna. She appeared to have shrunk in stature. She shivered. He knew people getting married were nervous, but still, he couldn't bear the thought of her shaking.

The wedding had to be stopped.

'Let's call this off together,' Adam said to her.

The cleric was silent, waiting.

Adam ignored the man and pulled her away from him. 'I can't let you go through with this, Marianna. You are being coerced.'

'But I can't back out now. This would be the third time. I have to see it through.'

'The third time?' the cleric repeated. 'See it through?' He shut the prayer book with a thud. 'No one is going any further.'

'This is the closest she's made it to the ceremony,' Adam explained, holding her arm.

'I'm not changing my mind.' She put out a hand to the cleric. 'But I would like a moment to think. I don't know if I can agree to this.'

'Then this is the wrong place for me to be,' the cleric said.

'No. It's right. It's the right place,' her father spouted. 'He gets money. She gets a title. That is the way it works. And whether it is or isn't—we call it a love match.'

The cleric lowered his head, shaking it. 'I can't continue. If the couple needs time to think, then they should not speak their vows. Especially if each person in front of me has either money or a title.'

'No. No. No!' her father shouted.

'No is correct,' Adam said, taking Marianna by the hand.

'No,' her father said. 'They're both destroying their lives.' He waved the licence. 'Let them at least be married before they start causing more grief.'

The man took the licence from her father's hand, folded it and put it inside his prayer book. 'This is not for you or I to decide. I will pray with you but not witness a duel or force a couple to wed.'

Her father's eyes were bloodshot. He did not look in control of his temper, and definitely not of his fists.

'Father,' Marianna said, appearing to regain her strength. 'Father. I am not to be coerced.'

'Marianna, sweetness…' Her father stepped away, touching his cravat. 'I understand completely. But it is not my fault that you will be ruined.'

'That is wrong. Wrong. I am making my own decisions. The outcome of my life is my own.'

Her father drew in a deep breath. 'You are making terrible decisions, Marianna. Everyone will talk. I cannot have your name sullied so.'

Adam cocked a brow. 'This is her life and her decision. She must make it. And your insistence is only pushing her away. You have pushed her towards marriage her whole life. And she rebels because she is used to having her own way.'

'You can't talk to me like that.'

'We've been down this path before and a clock was broken.'

Her father studied the cleric. 'You'd best begin to pray for him. I can't outfight him but I have enough of a fortune to bury all his dreams.'

'Father, you cannot do that.'

The cleric's shoulders rose and his eyes widened. 'The two people who have all the sway in this decision seem unwilling to sway and should not be pushed.'

Her father said to the round-faced man, 'You were brought here for one purpose and one purpose only. You had best not forget it.'

'I came to follow the rules of righteousness. And keep you from losing your temper.'

'No.'

'I will be on my way until this is decided,' the cleric said, moving towards the entrance. 'The couple will know where to find me.'

Then, Inky ran from one side of the room, across Adam's boots and darted forward.

'The door,' Dinsmore said, jumping forward, moving the cleric aside. 'Do not open the door. We'll never catch Inky.'

Then Inky changed direction and ran to the hallway.

Emory gaped. 'Marianna. You cannot live here. I forbid it. The man has overgrown rats living within these walls. And they're named.'

'Emory,' Adam said. 'That was not a rat. It was a pet. But you do not have to worry about seeing Marianna home. I will take her where ever she wishes to be. You may leave now.'

Her father spluttered and made a fist at his side. 'I should have pummelled you when I had the chance.' His eyes narrowed and his voice became a low growl. 'Rockwell, I will destroy you. You will not even be able to feed your rats.'

Adam smiled, but his teeth were mostly hidden. 'You may do your best. I assure you, I will prevent it. Dinsmore, escort him and the cleric out.'

Dinsmore stepped in front of the cleric. 'We may need you here to accompany the young woman home and give a semblance of respectability.'

'No one can give this home such a thing,' Emory said. 'He will be fighting those rats for a crumb when I finish with him.'

'It's the way of it,' the cleric consoled Emory. 'Children must be allowed to follow their own paths because they will go on no other.'

'You're on their side.' Emory's fists balled.

Dinsmore touched Emory's elbow. 'Hurry, Mr Emory. Inky will be back. And he bites.'

Her father snapped a nod at him and strode out.

Dinsmore indicated the cleric precede him. 'Come with me and I will make sure you have tea and some pie. It has a sturdy crust, and once you toss that aside, the rest is tasty. The Earl's carriage can take you home when it takes Miss Emory, and it will certainly be best if it is thought… Well, it might be best if it was thought you are here to oversee things. Plus, I have some good wine instead of tea, if you'd prefer.'

He led the man away.

'I thought I was going to get married today. Get it over with.' She shook her head.

'No sense in ruining your perfect record,' Adam said, hugging her close for an instant.

'Yes. What a disgrace.'

She found the nearest chair and held the back of it. 'Father is in such a temper. Such a temper. I don't know if I've ever seen him so upset, except when he lashed out at you. And this time it is more seething than striking.'

'I understand. I might be the same if I had a daughter.'

'He will try to destroy you.'

'No matter. I have had to fight to get where I am now. Fighting makes me stronger. I will go forward and take care of my household.'

'Your brother…'

'Yes. He will be fine. We will be fine. And if my stepmother suffers a bit…' he gave a one-sided shrug and smiled. '…that is just a vail for me.'

'I think I should marry you.'

'Are you saying that because you mean it?' he asked.

'I'm tired of wondering about who I should marry and when I will marry, and now I am beginning to think a man would have to be dented to want to wed me.' She shook her head. 'Think about it. Wouldn't you wonder what was wrong with a man who might suggest marriage to me after such disastrous courtships?'

'I suppose I am flawed,' he said. 'Because I want to wed you.'

'Perfectly flawed,' she said.

'Don't say you weren't warned.'

He stepped away from her and noted the claw marks at the base of the door frame. The house was sturdy, but scars were a part of life. And he didn't want Marianna scarred in any way; he wanted her to make her own decisions.

'You are so used to having your own way that you don't even think of it. You have to understand, in a marriage, compromise is usually required.'

'Compromise?' she asked.

'Mutual concessions.'

'Both sides lose.'

'Win. In a marriage there should only be one side. Together. What is best for the future of the couple. We shouldn't consider a marriage, because neither of us knows anything about that,' he said. 'Perhaps a partnership. Like in business. We could be a partnership, sorting everything out as we go along.' He paused. 'Scars and all. Slights, real and imagined. Standing strong against the world, backs together, and sometimes nose to nose in discussion about how things should be handled.'

'Do you think it would be a happy union?'

'I don't know what happiness is, or if it should be a word that we consider. Or something we should look for. My father searched for happiness in idleness and frivolity, and that is what I believe the word to mean, and what I believe many people think it. So, if you wish to sit at the helm of the household, chat idly with other ladies and attend dinners, and if that satisfies you, then that's what you'll do.

'I don't think that's what happiness is, though,' he continued. 'If you want to take on a task bigger than you have ever managed before, then at my side you will have a challenge. Not because I will be cruel, but because I will be honest, unflinching and will expect you to be the same.'

'That sounds daunting.' Marianna smiled. She knew that her father did have the power to weld a lot of grief Adam's way. She'd seen it before when he'd felt he'd been wronged. He would not back down easily. And Adam had worked so hard to take care of his brother and set the house in order. Her father would truly destroy him, so she had no choice but to marry him. She'd set this in motion without thinking about how her father would react. She couldn't risk Adam losing so much because of her.

'What is wrong?' Adam asked.

'Nothing,' she said. 'I am just concerned that you don't regret this.'

'If I didn't think you were capable, neither of us would be standing here. And I assure you, I will not be like the men in your past. And you would not be like the women in mine.'

'Why do you think that?'

'While we had tea, I thought of how you would be an interesting person to wed. A person who might seem to be the most agreeable in the world, but who actually agrees up until the moment she no longer wishes to go forward and stops with feet firmly planted. Who tells herself a variety of reasons that she can't go forward in marriage, but it is just because she is scared.'

'Scared?'

'Not just scared of marriage but scared of trying new things and meeting new people. Scared of stepping out of the shadows and beginning a new life. If you want to be a part of my life, you can continue to live behind the façade of my house. To live behind the façade of a marriage.'

* * *

His words startled her.

'You are saying I could make it another façade to hide behind.'

'If that's what you wanted. You're not doing as well hiding behind betrothals any more.'

He would be at her side. That would make it easier to greet people. And she could not let him lose all he had accomplished because her father was vengeful.

'When I fought with your father,' he said, 'You shouted at me that he was all you had. This is a chance for you to have a larger family in your life. Even if you continue to stay in the background, it's possible that you will have more people to share it with you. And perhaps it will mean more people in your father's life also.'

'I will.' Her heart started beating rapidly, and each beat filled her with excitement. 'I am willing to go forward with the marriage.'

She understood she'd just agreed to be wed. And she understood she was doing it for the right reason. She was protecting Adam.

But perhaps she was beginning to respect Adam, as she saw how he treated others. And she wanted to be one of the people he wrapped his devotion around.

'I'll find the cleric and see if he still has the special licence.'

The sound of Adam's voice invigorated her even more, and he stood, reminding her of a protector, a shield against the world, and a shield which made her stronger.

He took her hand and they walked into the kitchen. The cleric sat at the table, a half-finished piece of pie in front of him, watching Cook wave her rolling pin. She regaled him with a story of a mouse sighting in the kitchen, explaining how they'd collected the ferret and let him take charge, and then that she'd dreamed about a giant ferret chasing her into the cupboards and locking her in.

Dinsmore stood at the side, half-propped on a stool, finishing his pie.

'Where is the licence?' Adam asked.

The chatter stopped, and everyone froze except Dinsmore. Crumbs still on his fingers, Dinsmore reached behind him and retrieved the licence from the prayer book on the cabinet, then he dusted it off and held it up.

'We would like to wed,' Adam said. 'As the wedding celebration is already taking place.'

'I can take care of a marriage,' the cleric said, after wiping his mouth with a napkin. 'It appears we have wonderful witnesses. But do we have the couple?' He tossed the napkin onto the table.

'We do,' Adam said and, when he nodded Marianna's way, their eyes caught and he reached out to her, and clasped her hand. She put her other hand over his, and he tugged her to his side.

'There will be no coercion,' the cleric said, taking the licence and putting it beside his napkin. 'Unless both are coercing equally.'

'We are,' Marianna said. 'We have decided.'

'I don't have to tell you that this will significantly alter the course of this household,' the cleric said. He asked Cook and Dinsmore, 'Are you in agreement with this?'

They nodded, and Cook's cap wobbled on her head.

The cleric studied Marianna. 'Is this acceptable to you, Miss Emory?'

'Yes.'

'We need to get the marriage completed,' Adam said. 'But I don't have a ring.'

'No need,' the cleric said, dusting his hands. 'You have the licence and me.'

The cleric collected his prayer book. "And to give yourself an added chance, let's get this conducted somewhere a little more spiritual. And if you have any concerns, then bring along Dinsmore and Cook for witnesses. I'm sure they'll enjoy a chance to see a marriage taking place."

Adam agreed, then he regarded Marianna, not dressed as he'd expected his bride would be, but in every day clothing with her hair barely hanging in place, a sense of completion filled him.

This was not normal. In the past he had felt relief when leaving his sweethearts behind. And, now that he was marrying a woman, he was afraid of losing her.

He was aware of his home, and his world, in a way he had never been before. He felt ready to wed but, more than that, he felt he had found where the grail of completion resided. It didn't reside inside him, as he'd expected, but in her grasp.

He had lost his mind and he did not care.

He softly stepped away from her, then without his awareness he reached to hold her hand. She looked at him in surprise, the same surprise he felt, and, he saw her blush.

He took the hand to his lips and kissed it.

But he did not release it. For that instant, he wanted

to feel complete—married. He blinked away a feeling of wetness in his eyes. He was in love…for ever. Nothing felt the same. Everything felt warmer, more intense, and to have Marianna at his side seemed to complete him in a way he'd not expected. He'd not known himself incomplete, but that had all changed. He needed her at his side—in a place where he could see and adore her, and do all in his power to give her pleasure. That was the secret to his happiness.

The cleric looked at Adam and began to read the words slowly, lingering over each one. Yet, they flew by, with the quick question for each of them, then he closed his book.

He spoke over his shoulder as he neared the door. 'We will get this recorded in the parish register after the proper signatures are in place. And I generally visit you in about a fortnight to present each of you with a paper cross which has the names, date and a prayer about forgiveness.' He coughed slightly. 'The prayer about forgiveness is perhaps more important than a ring, in my view.'

'Is this a true wedding?' Adam said, interrupting the cleric's departure and the man's last praises to the cook on the heartiness of her pastry and the flavour of the apples.

'A licence with your names and ages on it.' The cleric looked at him. 'As good as carved in stone. Witnesses, words and it will be written in the parish register.' He tilted his head and gave a wry smile. 'Then, just try to get out of it and you'll see how legal it is.'

Dinsmore took a handkerchief and dabbed at his eyes. 'I think it's dusty in here.'

'Yes,' Cook said, also brushing her eyes. 'The hard part is over. Who knew a wedding could be so easy?'

'I don't feel married, though,' Marianna said, not really understanding their emotions. 'I feel the same as before.'

'Don't let that bother you,' Dinsmore told her. 'The two of you seem as if you've been married my whole lifetime. So, if you feel no different, it is because you were already wed in your actions, and really nothing has changed. The world continues on as before.'

'Don't believe him,' Cook said. 'He's full of pie. He's a real talker after he's been in my kitchen with the treats. It's a ploy he uses to stay near me."

'Of course, my sweet Cooktress."

Behind Cook's exaggerated choking motions, a smile lingered.

Marianna walked with Adam out of the room. 'It was that simple to get married,' she said. 'Isn't that dangerous?'

Adam laughed. 'I considered it anything but simple.'

'The vows… I would have thought a gong should have pealed after each one, or a clap of thunder. Or the ground should have shaken—loud winds…'

Adam put his hand on Marianna's waist and she stilled. Feeling the protection from all the storms of life was standing around her.

He took his hand and gently held her chin.

He kissed her, slowly and feather-soft. As he pulled his head away, he looked into her eyes again, and she saw a bit of an upturn to his mouth. Then he bent to her ear and touched his nose to it. 'We'll survive,' he whispered.

'I hope so.'

'We are the only two who can make it happen, now let us get Cook and Dinsmore home, and have a true wedding breakfast.'

Chapter Seventeen

Cecilia strolled into Adam's house after the banging on the door alerted them that someone was at the entrance. 'Nice butler here, Marianna. He looks amazingly like Adam.' She shook her head. 'Oh, wait—it is Adam.'

She entered, swinging a parasol that stirred a cloud of her perfume.

'I'm here to talk some sense into you. Which is something I never thought I'd hear from my lips.' She pretended to pull something distasteful from the tip of her tongue. 'But I forgive you.'

'What are you doing here?' Marianna asked.

'Uncle sent me to collect you. He truly is desperate if he's resorting to my help. And, truly, you do need to leave. A dozen chaperones won't be able to put a positive speech on this if you stay.' She tapped her parasol against the chair leg. 'Surprisingly, I just discovered my maid informed him that we did not go shopping the other day, and he found you here.'

'I'm married,' Marianna said.

She tilted her head to the side. 'You?'

'Yes.'

'That's a laugh.' She peered at Marianna's finger. 'No ring.'

'We wed. We had a special licence,' Marianna said.

'Then it's time to get a ring, if you truly did get married.'

'We did,' Marianna said. 'Have you ever known me to lie?'

Cecilia extended her hands, palms raised. 'That is wonderful. I never thought you would wed for a title, and not even get a ring out of the deal.' She blinked. 'I could see me doing it, but not you.' She tapped the parasol against the nearest chair. 'But it is wonderful. He gets your money and you get a title. This is the best thing that could have happened to me. I have a cousin who is a countess. Darius will be impressed.'

'We did not wed to impress your suitor,' Adam said.

'Yes, I'm sure. Certainly.' She raised her brows. 'Uncle will be so happy. He thought he couldn't pur-chase a title.' She laughed. 'Money can buy anything, I suppose.'

'He did not purchase a title,' Adam stated, eyes nar-rowing. 'His funds had nothing to do with this. Noth-ing.'

Cecilia stepped back. 'Well, I don't have a problem with it.' Her chin rose. 'Better that than the talk be that she is unable to form an attachment unless uncle pays for it.' She scowled. 'Everyone knows uncle purchases all he can for her. I don't see that as a problem at all.'

'Cecilia, this is none of your affair,' Marianna said.

She chortled in disbelief. 'Who is your cousin? Me. And who has been a sister to you? Me. And who tries to catch everyone's eye and ear throughout London? Me.

Of course it's my concern. Who do you think will be talking to everyone in London and telling them about the Earl that is now in the family?'

'I did not wed her for her father's funds.'

Cecilia wobbled in disbelief. 'Did you get marriage settlements drawn up before the wedding? I think not. One suitor darted when he saw the settlement Uncle proposed, and the last one pretended he was going to sign the agreements up until he thought it was too late for her to bolt.'

'We did not have time.'

'He swept you off your feet and right into his title, and you rushed through it so he could be richly rewarded and not have to sign anything that kept your money out of his hands. True love.'

Cecilia rolled her eyes. 'In my opinion, it is perfectly acceptable for you to wed her for her funds and she to wed you for the title. Everyone can believe that and will understand it. The other two were not titled and had little to bring to a union.' She shook a finger. 'What other reason do you have? The two of you are obviously not in love. And then it becomes a case of Marianna saying, well, time to go through with it.'

She turned her back to them. 'It's ridiculous that you would wed on such short acquaintance for any other reason.' She held out her arms and turned to her cousin. She pursed her lips. 'Uncle wanted the Earl of Rockwell for a son-in-law. That was too sweet a deal to pass up.' She shook her head. 'I will be on my way. Uncle needs to hear of this. He will be so happy to know that the two of you will say he didn't purchase a title.'

'He purchased nothing,' Adam said, his voice tensing with hidden emotion.

Cecilia waved her hand, waltzing towards the door. 'Forget I was here.' She sighed, heaving, and tapped her parasol against the door as she left. 'I suppose it may be discussed when I return to Uncle. I will tell him that he purchased not a son-in-law, or a husband, for Marianna, and that he is to keep quiet about it and let everyone come to their own conclusions.' She twirled. 'Of course, I may not be able to keep quiet.'

'I really don't need a wedding ring.' Marianna sounded wistful, examining her ringless finger after Cecilia left.

'You do need a wedding ring,' Adam said.

'I'm sure there's one in the safe at Father's that I can wear.'

'Absolutely not. You will have one of your own. We will have matching rings.' If he had to mine the metal and melt it and shape it himself.

'I have jewels inherited from my mother which are in my father's safe. I rarely wear them, but they are precious to me. One of those will do.'

'This is not a time for your mother's jewellery. It's a time for your own. We will get matching rings ordered now.'

The rings were important to him, and he believed to her too.

'Rings always seem heavy on my hands, so I don't wear them much.'

'This one won't.' He spoke softly. 'We'll pick out something light for you, heavier for me. I want to feel the ring.'

He trod out of the room and she heard him shout out for Dinsmore to retrieve the carriage.

'It should mean something to us. Like our vows. But, even if they didn't mean a word, it doesn't change the truth that we're married. And the first step of our union is to get rings to wear each day of our lives and show people that we are committed to marriage."

When the carriage rolled up in front of the goldsmith's shop, the moment felt sincere to him. Walking into the tiny shop was as meaningful as the actual marriage.

An old man put aside his polishing cloth and file, and moved to assist them.

'We wish to order rings.'

The man gave them a smile. 'Certainly.'

'Can you create a design for us?' Adam asked.

'Of course.'

'Do you have any preferences?' Adam asked Marianna.

She shook her head. 'So long as it is not weighty and does not catch on things.'

'Two strands of gold, intertwined, side by side,' Adam directed the goldsmith. 'Smooth on the back and engrave today's date. One for me, just like it only slightly larger.' Adam held out his hand for a pencil. 'I'll sketch it up.'

The clerk gave Adam a pencil and paper. Adam quickly drew the two strands of gold linked together in front and melded into one band in the back. 'The date on the inside here,' he said. He glanced at Marianna, and then drew again. 'I want the rings first, then matching ear rings, with the two strands hanging about this long.' He swiftly drew a pair of earrings. 'And a match-

ing teardrop necklace, but with the strands meeting at
the top where it clasps onto the chain. And make sure
the necklace and earrings are light, because she doesn't
usually wear much jewellery.'

He held the drawing out to Marianna. 'Do you want
any changes?'

She studied it, surprised at the quickness of his drawing, and shook her head. 'I will be happy with it.'

Adam nodded to the jeweller and gave him his name
and the address for it to be delivered. They let the man
measure their fingers, and suddenly the truth of the
wedding hit Adam. They'd wed. They were together,
ordering the rings they were to wear as a symbol of
their union. And their wedding date would be engraved
inside.

When he stepped outside, she said, 'I just realised I
didn't even know the date.'

'You shouldn't have to worry about forgetting it now,'
he said. He knew he would always remember, as soon
as he found out what it was. 'It will be engraved on the
back of the rings, so it should be easy to recall.'

He wished he could have walked out of the shop with
a ring, but it would take some time for the jeweller to
fashion the pieces. He could hardly wait to see it on her
finger. The thought made him feel proud, content and
part of a union.

The pieces of his life had intertwined in the marriage
with Marianna and, whether they stayed in the same
home or went their separate ways, she would always be
a feature of his life. They had secured that with simple
words repeated side by side, and no other ceremony that

he'd experienced had carried such weight. A quick ceremony, a fcw words and they'd entered into a contract.

They stepped into the carriage, and to him even that simple action seemed different now. Part of a bigger event. A man and his wife on an outing. A statement of their first day of marriage.

'It concerns me that everyone is going to think I wed you for your father's funds,' he said, settling into the carriage.

'Don't let it bother you,' she said. 'It has always been a consideration in my life. I cannot tell you how many times I have been warned about it.'

He swung his body away from her so he could peer into her eyes.

'Do you believe it?' he asked. 'Do you believe that is why I married you?'

'No,' she said.

'Pardon?' his voice rose. Her answer was a little too quiet, a little too hesitant.

Pain shot through his body as if he had suffered a mortal wound. How could he convince everyone that he hadn't married for the money when she believed it herself?

Marriage was bringing out a side of him he didn't know existed. At that moment, it was all he could do to keep from turning the carriage around, returning to the shop and selecting something so weighty she'd feel it with every movement. But he couldn't. That would only be an outward display and prove nothing. She had to believe it from the inside, and he had to convince her. He had to shape the forward path of their marriage, and he had to do it soon. He had to show her that they could have a marriage of deep, caring feelings—of sincerity, kindness and innocence.

He didn't want to ruin the innocence he had believed in her at first, but to take it as a cornerstone of their marriage. To share in it with her.

He was more than his title, and she was more than her money, and she had to believe it. If she didn't believe it to her core, the idea could linger in a crevice of her mind and, whenever disagreements arose, it could flower like a seed stored in the ground throughout the winter. Bit would burst into bloom to add discontent, little words of anger spreading like a creeping ivy into the heart, surrounding it, choking out any chance for love.

In his view, marriage disintegrated easily enough. Almost naturally, to hear the men in the clubs speaking of it. Just as the seasons changed, many marriages seemed to flower at first and then fade on the vine, only the passion was never replanted. The marriage stayed in place, but the couple moved through the motions, often living in the same house but inhabiting different places for the most part. Joined by a vow and a commitment, but nothing else.

He had heard of a few men who were devoted to their wives—a few. He wanted to be one, and he wanted her devoted to him.

A cool breeze brought the scent of street refuse into the carriage, and for the first time that felt better than the awareness of his thoughts. Someone swore in the distance, and he pulled the window closed and ran his fingertips over the freshly painted sill, trying to keep out the oaths. But he couldn't. Because it wasn't from the outside but the inside that the distastefulness invaded him.

He saw the damage tales could do to their future if she was thought to have purchased a title. No one would believe them in love. In fact, he wouldn't have himself. It had been so sudden. It would follow them throughout their life. Their children would hear of it, and most likely the tales would be expanded upon.

He'd been wrong. He'd told her to ignore the rumours others told, and only let her feelings come from inside herself. But he imagined the rainstorm of words that could be unleashed about them—particularly from her former sweethearts. Particularly if they did not attend events together; if they stayed home, it would be noticed.

If he wanted any hope of a true marriage, a true partnership, he had to convince her that he'd not wed her for financial gain, and he had to show her that he was more than a title. He had to find a way to make society occasions enjoyable for her, but they wouldn't be if she sensed others talking about them.

He should have waited to wed her, but he'd been unable to. He'd glimpsed her moving away from him, and he'd not wanted to risk a chance of losing her. He'd known he wanted her in his life. He'd wanted to protect her.

He admitted he was a fortune hunter—but the fortune was her smile, her happiness.

He couldn't bear the thought of their union being perceived as only a marriage of convenience. Dissatisfaction would set in…resentment. The talk in society would eventually cast a cloud over them. And the cloud would rain down upon both of them, covering them in mud and mould, and from that brambles would grow.

Chapter Eighteen

He helped her out of the carriage, and together they walked into his home—their home—the woman who held his heart and happiness in her clasp, and believed he had wed her only for money.

He walked with her to the shared sitting room between their quarters.

She looked around. 'It doesn't feel I belong here. Everything here was chosen by someone else.'

And he almost felt the same way—about her. Truly, he had chosen her, but she didn't believe it. She believed he'd wed her for other reasons.

'I would like it if you added some things you prefer. Things that reflect you. And I will have the drawings for the house stored away in the attic, the extra tables removed and the sofa pulled into place.'

'That will be nice.' She viewed the walls. 'I can take some of the servants shopping with me.'

'Tilda?' he asked.

'I cannot leave behind the maids who have been helping me every day. I will bring them from my father's house if they want to leave. I can't abandon them.'

He had known he would be adding more servants, particularly if he absorbed some from his stepmother's house. But he hadn't really considered Marianna bringing her own staff. He hoped they blended well with his but, even if they didn't, a way would be found to accommodate them.

He moved to the picture he'd drawn of a waterwheel. He straightened it, even though it immediately slid back into the slanted position.

The best leaders led by inspiring the people around him. The leader gave people faith. He was there to let them see all was right with the world.

'I am anxious to see the ring on my finger,' she said.

'Yes.' He took her hand. His wife's hand. The action stilled something inside him, awed him. 'I don't think it will be cumbersome. If it is, we're doing something wrong.'

Marianna stood, eyes fixed on the plans at Adam's desk, but not seeing the lines on the paper. 'Did you ask me to wed out of rivalry?' she asked.

'What are you talking about?'

'A rivalry with Jules? After all, you told me we are all animals in human clothing.'

He laughed softly. 'No. To have a rival you must feel challenged.'

Then he realised it was starting—the questions about why they had married.

'I married you for one reason and one reason alone. You.' Simple words, and easy for him to say. The hard part was going to be convincing her. She had to believe him. Their entire future depended on it.

Vows wouldn't erase the question. A ring with the

date on it wouldn't make a difference to the questions that would bubble inside her. To the whispers she might hear at an event.

If she had disliked attending events in the past, she would thoroughly detest them if she thought people were talking about her.

She'd not responded when he'd said he'd married her for one reason alone—herself—but it was the truth. He'd seen her innocence and happiness in the folly and her joy in simple things. The little doll house hadn't meant as much to her as the simple stone shelter where the bugs had been swept out.

She put her hand on her chest. 'I wanted to shield you from Father. I know how powerful he is, and he does not make threats lightly.'

'He did nothing to your former sweethearts.' He sat down at the desk with the drawings scattered over it, and began to roll them up one at a time. 'I would have no trouble going toe to toe and nose to nose with him. I had to use strategy to deal with my father when I was a child.'

'Was our marriage part of your strategy?'

He put the rolled paper into the case he'd had made and he didn't answer right away, continuing to collect the other plans.

'To have you in my life, I suppose it was. I mentioned that to you earlier when I told you that if you didn't wed me our lives were going to go in separate directions.'

He felt the need to touch his pocket when he said that. For better or worse, they had said vows to each other, and more importantly had made a vow in public. They had changed the path of their lives for ever. They had bound themselves to each other. And he did not regret it. No matter if they never spent another day together in their lives, they had pledged themselves to each other and that meant something to him. More than he had ever expected. This marriage was a true one.

'Would you not agree your father sheltered you?'

'No more than any other caring father.'

'Your father deeply cares for you, but he is also manipulative and weak where you are concerned.'

'Weak?'

'Yes. It would have been no true effort for you to attend events with him, and have more confidence among society, but he let you stay in your room and avoid them. Perhaps you would have had a good time. You might have. I feel you would have.'

If everyone saw him as falling deeply in love with her and remaining so, then it would all appear to make sense. But if he attended events alone, and didn't have any with her at his side, they would never be able to convince society they cared for each other.

He could only do so much without her.

'You are the person I want to welcome our guests here. It doesn't have to be many. And it should be people you are comfortable with.'

She shuddered and shook her head. 'I cannot stand with a smile affixed, speaking when I have absolutely nothing to say. I thought you understood that.'

'I do.'

'I won't,' she said. 'You will invite everyone and then tell them I am unwell. My father has done it for years.

No one will be surprised. They will all assume I have some illness that prevents me from being able to attend.'

'But you don't. And this is the perfect time to begin opening up to people that you like.'

'You cannot make me into someone I'm not.'

'I only want you to be the person you are.'

'Well, perhaps Cecilia can help me. And we can host something small at my father's house,' she said.

'No. No. Absolutely not.' Anger boiled inside him at the thought of her cousin's methods.

He minded eternally that Cecilia had meddled in her cousin's life. He didn't know if she thought she had Marianna's best interests at heart or not, but he would not risk her playing her tricks any more. He would stand up for Marianna and keep Cecilia at a distance.

'I would prefer you to keep her at a distance. Her machinations are far reaching.'

'She is my cousin.'

'And I am now your husband.'

'I am to have a husband at my side. But you are not to dictate my family to me.'

'I am only concerned for your best interests. And, while she may have saved your life and she has been close to you, she is not to be trusted. She does not care about truth or respecting you.'

He paused, hearing the words that he'd said. 'That's the problem, Marianna.' He spoke softly. 'She does not respect you as a person. She may love you. She may care deeply for you. But, to her, you are the toy she can bat around for amusement. Perhaps she is jealous that you have so much. I don't know. Perhaps, in her mind, she means no true harm. But harm you she does.' He stared directly into her eyes, daring her to contradict him.

'You cannot keep the two of us apart.' She clasped her hands together. 'We have been together much of my life.'

'But you are married now. And I want you protected.' His voice rose.

'This is no different.' She matched his volume, thrusting out an arm. 'You claimed my father protected me too much, and now you wish to do so more than even he did.'

'The one place he failed to protect you was from your cousin.'

'That is preposterous.'

'I'm speaking to you as a friend, not a husband.'

'No,' she muttered, her teeth clamping together after the word. 'That is not the case at all. Not at all. You are speaking as a husband. You are not asking me. You are not compromising. You are commanding.'

'I may be, that's true, and you should listen. When someone tells you truths, you should listen, even if you don't like them.'

'Here is a truth for you. At my first opportunity, I am going to select some comfortable items for the house, in the part far from you. I am going to make myself a comfortable little nest there. A space for me and my personal staff. I will be completely in charge.'

'Feel free to do so,' he said. 'I thought you were too innocent for marriage and I see that you are turning your back on it our first day. Well, I am turning my back too.'

With that, he slammed into his room.

He'd provoked her. He'd just not been able to help himself. He'd been thinking so heavily about marriage and Marianna that he'd not really considered how Cecilia had hurt her and, when he saw it plainly, he was furious and he'd been unable to tether his words.

He'd made a bad mistake. Anger had fuelled what he'd said. He knew nothing about marriage.

The night was going to be a long one. Because he wanted to be with Marianna, but the problems they had not sorted out before their marriage were still festering between them. He had to protect their future, he had to give them a chance at happiness, but he wasn't sure how.

He knew of only one person who might be able to help him, and it was the last person to whom he wanted to go for advice.

Adam lay in his bed and stared ahead, jaw locked, watching the shadows turn to night and darkness envelope the room. He wanted to shout to the heavens and rail at the stars, because only something so strong could give him such a weakness for her. He not only had an Achille's heel for her, his entire body was consumed by weakness for her.

If he went to her, it would be temporary, and settle nothing deep within him. It would be a balm, but the distress inside would not ease.

And he would be risking their future because their start had been unsteady. If he understood one thing about himself, it was that he didn't have the strength to stay in the house without holding her.

He got out of bed and dressed. He left the room and did not look to the right as he passed her door. He would walk to the stable and saddle his horse. He needed to move, to leave his house and feel the air on his face, in order to think.

The walk warmed him in the chilled air. He called out the stablemaster's name, shouting loud enough so the man would know he was taking the horse. He heard the mumbled reply.

He put a woollen pad on the gelding, then tossed the saddle on next. Then he slipped the prong of the belt through the buckle on the saddle, and looked at Mercury, the contented horse. Obviously, Mercury wasn't married... Adam led the gelding out of the stall, securing the stables behind him, put a foot in the stirrup and jumped astride.

Marianna completely took up his thoughts.

She'd not said she loved him. He'd expected her to, though he'd not truly expected she could understand what it meant. It couldn't mean as much to her as it did to him. He'd never said those three words in that order to anyone, ever.

Because it had been a foreign language to him. One he couldn't comprehend. He couldn't put the words together in a way that made sense. He'd been told he was loved by women and he'd been as kind and sweet as he could. He'd answered, '*you too*,' or something else, like the last sentiment on a letter to a friend. He'd never wanted to cause unnecessary pain to anyone expressing a tender emotion, particularly one that had escaped him.

But now it overpowered him, engulfed him, weakened his knees. Tossed him about in a sea of uncertainty.

This was love. It entrenched itself in him, and suddenly he welcomed it. Welcomed the helplessness he felt and the power it had over him. And in that instant he became empowered by it, emboldened. He was in love, and it felt better than any emotion he'd ever felt before.

He'd had a hasty betrothal, if you could call it that, and an even hastier wedding—if you could call it that. But they were married, and he'd wed the right woman, even if their marriage had had a jagged start.

He discovered he didn't even care if she had wed him to become a countess. But he didn't believe it meant enough to her to have made it a consideration.

He laughed on the inside. A courtship would never have survived between them. Neither of them was good at courting. A courtship interrupted life and put a false frame around the encounter, almost assuring a marriage to follow, or a dissolution that tended to create friction.

He'd been so careful for so many years not to become infatuated with a woman. He'd taken such care around women because he had not wanted to propose and marry anyone not suitable to be a countess.

He had not wanted to take the same course his father had— although in truth, now that he thought about it, his stepmother Linda had made his father as happy as it was possible for the man to be. In hindsight, he would have to consider their marriage a success. They'd both relished the distance of it.

He only wished that, when his father had died, she'd hid her happiness better.

He'd really not wanted to live a life where, when he died, his friends were momentarily sad, but made due with a rousing celebration in his memory, with the widow joining in, and no one even missed his not being there.

The event had lasted for almost a week after his father's death. It had been fortunate that Dinsmore had finally had enough of the revelry and insisted it end, or the celebration might still be continuing and his father might still be waiting to be buried.

The country house his father owned hadn't been entailed, and he'd been able to sell the residence for more funds to purchase a cottage for his stepmother and brother to live in, and to enable him to afford their expenses.

He'd not realised it, but that had been the final nail in the coffin on his views of marriage.

He had forgotten all his caution when Marianna, a twice-betrothed woman, had awoken in front of him. First, it had been about saving her from the scandal. Then it had become about her.

Understanding why she had been proposed to was easy. Understanding why others hadn't was more difficult.

The knowledge that his status had made a difference simmered inside him. But then he thought of her, his first proposal, and he had done such a poor job of it. He couldn't remember even truly proposing.

It caused a catch in his breath. A weight settled around his shoulders, causing a pressure he felt so strongly he wondered that the horse could keep carrying him.

He didn't want to think about it any more. The night was crisp, and a little colder than he'd expected, a lot colder, with more wind. But it might be his imagination, a result of the way he felt.

Then a drop of rain hit him in the face. Another splattered his hand.

It was just his damnable luck. He was going to get drenched, the wind was picking up and the night was turning colder.

And the horse was taking him closer to Emory's house. His father by law or by default.

The rain was tapering off when he reached Emory's. Of course the drops would slow as he reached shelter, almost shivering!

He dismounted then banged on the door. After a second series of raps, a butler's voice called to him through the wood.

'Rockwell,' he answered, and waited. The door opened and a lit lamp was held aloft while two weary eyes studied him. 'I would like to talk with Emory.'

The man took Adam's hat, as if a drenched earl was expected in the middle of the night.

'I will see if he is available,' the butler said. 'And I could get you a dressing gown, if you'd like.'

'I'm fine.' He ignored the puddle pooling at his boots.

'Please follow me to the sitting room, your lordship.'

Within a few moments, Emory appeared in the doorway in a dressing gown with a collar that would have looked suitable on a king's robes.

'I was expecting Marianna,' Emory said when he saw Adam. 'Not you.'

Adam answered. 'What? You did not remember you had a new son?'

Her father went to the decanter, put it on the side table and put a glass beside it. He offered to pour a drink, but Adam waved it away.

'And did you tell your bride where you are?' Emory asked, waving a hand to the servant in the doorway, saying, 'Tea,' and sending the man away.

'She does not know I have even left my bed,' Adam said.

Her father nodded.

'I was her third betrothal.' Adam paced in front of the cold fireplace. 'And I knew that, if I waited, she would find a reason not to wed me.'

'I wouldn't consider you her third betrothal.' Emory spoke slowly, the new growth of his whiskers rasping as he scratched fingernails over them. 'I think it was too hasty for that.'

'That irks me. I should have waited, just to see if she would go through with it. But now I know I had nothing to worry about. She would have married me. You would have insisted.'

'So? Did she? She's not standing here. You are. What is the problem?'

'I didn't say there was one.'

'I'm sure there isn't.' He paused. 'And why are you here in the middle of the night?'

'I want you to talk with a lawyer. I want it duly noted and recorded—and I will be happy to sign it— that should my wife inherit a penny from you, or more, it is all to be in her control and I am not to see even a halfpenny of it. I know we didn't get a marriage settlement drawn up, but I wish to make a will, and also to make certain you have one and I am not in it.'

'I generally don't like people telling me what to do,' Emory said. 'But you have a valid request.' He rubbed his eyes and yawned. 'Cecilia must have told you that

Marianna's last betrothal fell to the side because of the marriage settlement.'

The butler returned with the tea.

'I'm not thirsty.' Adam waved it away.

'Well, I am,' Emory said.

The man poured tea, but again Adam refused it. He put his hand flat over his cup.

Emory hesitated. 'The house seems so quiet without Marianna. Though she and I rarely spoke in the middle of the night.' He took a sip of tea. 'Is this going to become a habit?'

'I do not know.'

'Very well.' He waved away the butler, and the man left as silently as he'd arrived.

'You wanted the marriage because you thought you could get the title, and your daughter would leave me and return to your household,' Adam said.

'You think too much.' Emory raised his teacup in a silent toast. Then he held it close in both hands. 'You're forgetting the part about grandchildren. I knew you would have the rights over the grandsons, but I thought I might get a granddaughter as well. I saw my empire increasing. And my family.'

'I will never give you my children.'

'You may have to share them, to get my child.'

'That's cold. Marianna's happiness should be first.'

'I agree.' Emory put down his teacup, interlaced his fingers with both index fingers pointed upwards and studied Adam. 'And now you have a chance to court her. To court her from your heart. A married man doesn't have to court his wife, but when he does it shows he wants to. Is she worth it to you?'

'Yes. And she is worth putting up with you in my life.'

'Good.' He lowered his hands and touched the cup. 'Because she is worth putting up with you in my life.' Emory stared at him. 'Don't worry about the repercussions of the wedding. They will happen. It's nature. You can't put two people in the same room and expect them to always see things the same.' He stretched and smiled. 'It only matters that you listen to me.'

'Rot.'

He lifted the teapot and poured the liquid into Adam's cup. 'Yes. You should always listen, even if you don't always agree. I have some experience. Some favours to call in. And you are the same.'

'You envision a family empire?'

'A dynasty. And you were the only one I saw, besides Driscoll, that could do such a thing. I invited you both, and I was surprised at how well it has worked out.'

'That is yet to be seen. She wed me for my title. You thought you were purchasing a title for her, and so did she.'

He shook his head. 'A mere earl? If I were going to purchase a title for her, I would definitely aim for a duke.' He clucked his tongue. 'You underestimate me.'

He relaxed back into his seat, interlocking his fingertips over his girth. 'I expect a lot from you. You have a keen intellect for business. I have seen how you turned your father's estate around, and how you managed to get Driscoll involved in your business before me. Not that Faraday one, but the other. I didn't sense that swiftness.'

He held out a hand in a placating gesture. 'We are

human,' he continued. 'If we treat each other decently—
and we are decent people—both of us will have much
more power than either alone. And Marianna is not a
piece of embroidery floss. She is not comfortable in society. She is not comfortable among many people. But
she can sort out a business path so quickly that it makes
me envious. Truly, she is the one you should listen to.'

Then he sighed. 'She doesn't have a lot of true heart
experience, though.' He paused, considering. 'But perhaps that is also one of her strengths. Only time will
tell.'

'You think she is scared of society?'

'Very. She has never truly warmed to it, like Cecilia
has. Yes, I should not have let her hide away. And the
two broken betrothals caused her to doubt anyone could
love her for herself. She sees Cecilia prancing around
and compares herself to her cousin. Never noting that
she is the better of the two.'

'That woman must quit meddling in Marianna's life.
It is unthinkable, the things she has been doing.'

'I agree. It has gone on too long. Together you and I
will be able to put the brakes on that.'

'What chance do you think my marriage has?'

Emory continued to sip from his cup. 'Every chance
in the world.' Emory nodded. 'I have already seen some
of your strengths. When you didn't fight back as I attacked you. When you refused to wed my daughter as
I insisted, but you took her in and made a vow to her.'
He looked down, a smile on his lips. 'By the way, Cecilia did stop in to tell me of the marriage, and she was
going to continue on to share the news with her friends.
I would say half the town knows of it by now.'

'As long as they don't think it was a transaction.'

'I don't know that I can like you easily, Adam, but a father does not always like his son.'

He stood. 'I will make sure to confide in all the wrong people once the financial documents are signed. And I will add in a few details to make it too good to keep quiet.'

He thumped the robe. 'Help yourself to the brandy or whatever drink you can find in the house,' he said. 'We may end up liking each other or not. It doesn't matter that much. It only matters that we both care for my daughter.'

He stepped towards the door.

'Don't you wish to stay and entertain your guest?' Adam stared at the liquid in the cup.

'As you said before....' Her father gave him a slight smile. 'You're family now. Entertain yourself. I've got things to do—sleep is one of them. Rest in Marianna's old room. I will send my valet for your clothes and he will hang them by the fire and return them in much better condition. With your clothes soaked, you look like a mere baron at most.' Then he laughed heartily.

Chapter Nineteen

She rolled from the bed and, for a moment, she didn't know where she was. Then the memories returned.

She pulled the counterpane from the foot of the bed, wrapped it around her and walked to the door. She reached to pull it open, but realised it was latched. She fumbled with the mechanism and turned to release it. Then she opened the door and walked from the room.

She went through the sitting room, studying it. She could see Adam's influence in the room. It was plain and masculine, but in the most wonderful way. Once the sofa was positioned better, she could imagine herself cuddling up on it. She walked to the table and ran her hand over the wood. Pencils were strewn about on surfaces, along with papers with notes.

The room made her feel comfortable. Secure. Safe.

She saw a dark spot near the back of the sofa and hesitated, wondering if Inky or a mouse were there. On closer inspection, she found a man's stocking.

She could see that no servants took care of the room, only Adam.

She had become a part of him. Something had changed, even without a ring or a true wedding night. Just seeing his things scattered about made her heart warm.

She wanted to go to him. Without knocking, she opened the door to his room. The bed appeared as if a bear had tussled in it. She had no choice. She had to touch the covers and hold them in her hands. Lifting his pillow, she put it against her face.

Returning to her bedroom, she dressed as well as she could.

She went to each room on the floor and opened the door. She went downstairs and saw the cook. She did not know where Adam was, nor did Dinsmore. When called for, the stableman said a horse was gone, but he could manage to get her wherever she wanted to go.

He had left her and she had no idea where he'd gone.

She would not stay here. Let him find the house empty when he came home. She would visit her father. She would leave Adam and return to her old home. She could always send someone for her things.

But before she left she went through the entire house except for the servants' quarters. She had to make certain he had not relocated within the house, but she couldn't find him. Her imagination reminded her of the jaded friends men could have who would pull them from their families, and she feared she had stepped back into another mire.

Then she went back to the sitting room with all the plans and drawings, and a container filled with pencils and chalks, in it. She looked at the sketches on the wall more closely, including the one of the ferret, and saw the signature 'Rockwell' written in the bottom-right corner. She shuffled some of the papers on the table and found a sketch of Dinsmore, complete with a twinkle in his eye. A drawing of a desk. A rosebush. And what she supposed were the gardens.

She imagined him sketching in the room, and she embroidering, and thought of the peace she would feel. And she realised the house was achingly empty without Adam. It was a shell. And so would her life be.

After first light, Adam had not returned. She sent for his carriage and left.

When she got to her old home, she found her father in the dining room, an almost empty plate with a solitary piece of toast on it beside him.

She put her hands on her hips. 'Adam has left me,' she stated.

Her father took the cloth and wiped his lips. Then he went to the pull and rang for a servant. 'I daresay you will find suitable words for him.'

'Do you think I made a mistake?'

'As to whether you made a mistake or not...' He smiled. 'Wait to decide on that. It doesn't seem so.'

He looked at the plate on the table. 'Please excuse me, as I am late for a meeting with my solicitor. And I am going to visit Cecilia to explain that, if she continues to meddle in your life, she will have the wrath of you, Adam and me to contend with.'

'I am not so certain he will remain in my life.'

'I am.' He patted her shoulder. 'At this time, you must concern yourself with the two of you learning how to disagree properly. To discuss things between yourselves. There is apparently an art to it, and I have been thinking heavily on that this morning.'

He straightened his cuffs. 'I have talked to Darius and Driscoll. I have been trying to buy out his shares in the business with Adam, but neither wants to sell. And Mrs Driscoll hinted that she hopes the two of you might wed.'

'Think twice about going into business with Adam.'

'I have,' her father said. He touched the back of her head and kissed her forehead, then left the room. 'Three times and then a fourth. He might not like it, but we are to be partners. I will find a way.'

Marianna noticed the toast her father had not touched. She picked it up and left the room with it. Even if she hated Adam, it was no reason to starve herself. She took her reticule and went upstairs. She had slept so little in that strange bed at Adam's, and had cried so long that she had exhausted herself. She might lie down for a bit.

When she got to the door to her bedroom, it stood wide open. She took one step inside. Boots... A man's coat... And a man asleep, her covers pulled up over his chest, arm lying out, and obviously not wearing a lot of clothing. Did he have no mercy?

'You left me...to go to my father's?' She rasped out the words, and he kept his arm flung out.

He opened one eye. 'I knew you would appear here. I wanted to be with you but I was too tired to return home. I thank you for finding me.'

'You must leave my room this instant.' She tapped his boot.

He put a hand over his eyes. 'I don't think I wish

to stand up.' He rubbed his forehead. 'I think I have caught a Marianna megrim. It is caused by thinking about you too much.'

'That is preposterous.'

'No.' He drawled the word. 'It's painful.'

He pulled a pillow out, rolled away from her and put it over his head.

Marianna threw her reticule to the floor and raised her eyebrows. 'What are you doing here?'

'I left you.'

'But I am leaving you.'

'You didn't expect marriage to be easy, now, did you? Not after that courtship?'

'We didn't court.'

'Perhaps we should.'

'I had a good life and I ruined it.' Marianna sat on the side of the bed, her head in her hands. 'Well, I would have had a good life, if I hadn't kept getting betrothed.'

He reached for another pillow, fluffed it and put it under his head. 'I had some thinking to do.'

'You can't leave me and come here. I'm leaving you to come here. This is my house, Adam,' she said, walking to the side of the bed. 'Father thinks we should learn to disagree.'

'Did he tell you we are to have paperwork prepared so I will not be able to touch any of the assets he might give you, or leave you as an inheritance, and I will sign whatever is needed to make certain of it?'

'No.'

'It's true. And I did it after the marriage. After. No one can say I was cajoled into doing it. Or that first your father drove a hard bargain and created a dowry for you that I could not touch. I did it willingly, and no one can question it. As my wife, I will be certain you have funds set aside that will always be yours.'

'That is very dear of you,' she said, touching his bare shoulder.

He moved the pillow to put it back beneath his head but didn't open his eyes. 'You can leave me. You will still be a countess. It is yours and without reservation. I want you to be free and the only strings to bind you to be heart strings. As I said, I don't have to worry about having an heir. I have my brother for that.'

'What are you thinking?'

'I want to court you, every evening for the rest of my life. And I want you to love me.'

'You want me to love you?'

'More than anything I have ever wanted in my life, because I love you so much.'

His long lashes rested against his cheeks and he had the look of innocence of a boy. She wanted to brush her hand over his cheek.

She slid across beside him and, when she put her hand on his chest, he put his arm around her and she put her head on his shoulder, moulded her body against his and felt his breathing. She could feel the muscles beneath her palm and she felt comforted in a way she could never have expected.

'Marianna. Do you realise that it truly is difficult for us to stay apart from each other?'

She did not answer.

He stopped talking and she wondered if he'd fallen asleep.

He spoke again. 'It's as if neither of us wish to admit

we want to be with the other, but we are pulled together by our hidden wills as strongly as any force can pull.'

'Desire?'

'I think it's not desire,' he said. 'Desire would keep us in the same bed. It would make all else seem trivial. I love you. I don't believe in love at first sight, but it may have happened. You were throwing things at me and, I when I got up from the floor, I knew I'd never seen anyone as lovely as you. All I cared about was that things did not explode around us and you would continue to speak with me.'

'I don't believe in love at first sight.'

'As I said, I don't either. I'm sure when the book hit my head I probably blinked, or when I slid to the floor. And then I saw you a second time and I was smitten.' He touched his head. 'Where you smote me. It didn't leave a scar but I wish it had.'

'You are a romantic.'

'No. I am in love. I am willing to move into your house to be with you, or I will happily hire more servants to make you happy in my own home, although I enjoy the silence of it.' His eyes opened briefly.

'Do you like to be alone that much?'

'Yes. I think better alone, except when I'm with you. And I think you're the same. You created the soirees for your father, and did the work, but then let your cousin host the events. You became betrothed as expected but did not wed. You appear as a woman who lives in the shadows of others, but I believe you are not living in shadows, but doing just as you wish.'

She sat up and moved to the foot of the bed, turning so she could see him. She pulled her knees up and wrapped her arms around them. 'I don't allow the servants into my rooms much, except for my lady's maid. It isn't that I don't like them, I just like to be alone more. But your Dinsmore and your Cook seem different. Like family.'

'They are. I cannot tell you how many times Cook ruffled my hair when I was small and told me I must be a good boy. And when I let the horses out, my father never found out who did it, but she didn't let me have any treats for three days. And she made sure the whole house smelled of my favourites. She said that, even if I didn't get caught, life punished me, and I believed her. But more importantly I wanted the biscuits and puddings and pies. She prepares my favourites, just as she has all her life. And no one else even likes them. Don't be surprised if you think her a failure at her job, but she is the perfect cook for me. I would like to leave her be, but we can employ someone to assist her and cook the things you like.'

'I will try to get used to her recipes.'

The room was silent for a bit, then he opened his eyes. 'I wanted you to find me.'

'I woke up and didn't know where you were.'

'I like you in my house,' he said, shutting his eyes again. 'I could not bear the thought of you leaving and my being there without you.' He rolled towards her, and laid his hand on the cover, fingers open. 'But I changed my mind. If you wish to live here, I will try it. For you.'

She scooted closer to clasp his hand. 'I studied your home. I could see my embroidery pictures on the wall in my room. And more of your sketches framed. It needs more furniture, though.'

'If you would like to select it, even if you don't live there, I would like it.'

'When I walked through your house alone, I could see the work you put into. The care. I was impressed. If you can put that much care into a marriage, you will be a wonderful man to be wed to.'

'Do you think so?'

'I know so. I talked with Cook and she sings your praises. And Dinsmore says you are the son he never had, but he claims that doesn't say much for his fathering.'

'Did you ask them about me?'

'Yes. I just wanted to talk about you.'

'Do you think you can fall in love with me?'

'I think I already am. When I saw you were gone, I was devastated. I didn't want you to be away. I wanted you with me.'

'Good,' he said. 'I missed you terribly.'

'Do you think I am falling in love?' she asked. 'I don't feel all fidgety with you as I did with my other two suitors.

'You could be. But I don't think we are in romantic love,' he continued. 'That creates happiness. People swoon for each other. They cannot wait to steal away to gaze into each other's eyes.'

She watched his lips move as he spoke. 'Well, love is a good thing.'

'If you say so,' Adam said. 'I suppose it is. But the feeling of not being able to exist in my own home with anyone else is a sobering thought. The feeling of being willing to change everything I have worked for in order to help your happiness is a new experience for me.'

'And how do you feel at this moment?' Marianna asked, watching the crinkles at the side of his eyes. The warmth of him reached deep into her.

'Unsettled—if you are not at my side.'

'Lost—without you,' she whispered.

'Wretched not to feel your lips,' he added, and his own turned up.

'Melancholy—not to see your smile.'

'Dismal—in the hours we must sleep and not be together.'

He gazed at her. 'I've never really felt this way before. But it also seems that a kiss from you could erase it all.'

'It's wonderful that something so pleasant could make another person happy.'

She curled forward, wrapping his arm around her and snuggling closer to him. He lifted his other hand and held her in a soft clutch.

'Well,' he added, and moved slightly so that he could place a hand on her stomach. 'Even if the head symptoms are vexing, the body seems quite pleased. Having you close to me is a treasure. It seems, if I could hold you like this the rest of my life and neither of us needed to move for anything, it would be the happiest a human could be.'

His touch worked like a flame against her skin.

He pulled her so that she lay on his chest and her face was near against his. One of her hands was against his shoulder, the other against his pillow.

With that, his hand touched the back of her head, and he did not have to press her against him as she kissed him briefly.

His eyes opened and seemed to look into her soul.

'And, if love is wanting to be with you the rest of my life, and of wanting to make a family with you and see you each morning for ever, then this is love,' Adam said, whispering the words.

'I don't want you to say that just to make me happy.' Marianna closed her eyes tightly and hugged him.

'It is making me happier,' he said. 'When I slid into this bed, it was as if I was in the room with you. The covers smell like you, and I felt enveloped in a hug that I'd never experienced before. I knew even then that, if I stayed here, you would find me.'

He stopped. 'And, if you didn't, I wasn't worried. I would find you. Most of all, I want a true friendship. Not one created by marriage or closeness or anything else. I like being with you. I like arguing with you. I like just the knowledge that we are married.'

'Then are we friends?'

'I believe we can be the closest friends. There is a kind of a strain in some friendships. Truly, the smiles are there and the camaraderie, but the person drags on you. They cause distress that you don't even know you're feeling. If the friendship wanes, you have a feeling of relief. That isn't a true friendship or a marriage I would want. I want togetherness. Sharing. An openness that can't be felt with anyone else. Disagreements that raise the roof, but a moment of the heart clutching when you see the smallest pain in the expression across from you.'

'You are thinking very seriously.'

'This is what I want from you,' he said. 'I don't want you to care about my leaving your life, if my absence will make your life better. I don't want our togetherness to be an equation based on whether you will miss me or not. If it is just that, then give in to the emotion of missing me. I want our marriage to be more than that. I want to be a part of you. I want us to be a part of each other. Not a romance or an affection.'

'I don't think I understand what you mean.'

'You do. In the past, when the others left your life, I think the loss eased you, in a sense. After you recovered from the original concerns about ending the connection, you didn't have to worry about making them happy any more.'

'I felt selfish when they left and I was relieved.'

'You should not. That isn't selfishness, that is wholeness. You have to be whole yourself. I've thought about it. Wholeness is what I want in a marriage. A joining of two people which makes both of them whole and better.'

'That is quite a task.'

'Marriage is quite a task. I want the way we feel whole when we are together to free both of us. I want to carry a part of you inside me as I move about my day, and the same for you. I want to have a closeness with you that I don't have, and can't have, with anyone else. I want us to be joined in the truest, most whole, sense of the word. I want faithfulness on both our parts, in our hearts and with our bodies. Two halves that make a whole heart.'

He clutched her hand. 'That first night you saw me, you woke up willing to defend yourself. You defended your father, even though you were more dangerous to him than I. If you were to have children, I could see you fighting for the best for them. You act as a timid mouse, pretending to be hiding away. But I believe you inherited the will, when pushed into a corner, to come out with ferociousness. And, with me at your side, I suspect you can be very ferocious any time it is needed.'

He chuckled softly. 'I expect, without even meaning to, I will bring out that side of you.'

'I've never been married before, and I see what I was missing now. But only because the marriage wasn't to you.'

Epilogue

The stones were all in place and the mortar had dried. A small stairway encircled the exterior of the castle-like structure and, when she reached the top, Marianna had a feeling of freedom—even though it only reached to the bottom storey of their house and no more than a few people could have fitted at the top.

Marianna stood against the parapets and studied the trees, watching for birds. Wind blew over her face while she waited for Adam.

The stonemason had done just as she'd requested, and she couldn't have been happier with the little castle. Nathan had been thrilled to help her plan the structure, and he'd designed the flags for it, one now snapping in the wind with a large R in the central part of it. The one he'd designed with a N in the middle was used when he returned from school and was in residence.

The cobbled-together parts of the estate were a thing of the past. Now the structure was smaller, but was cared-for, and had the appearance of more prosperity, instead of less.

She loved it more than her old home.

She heard Adam moving up the steps. He came into view with two large cushions in his hands and he spread them in the centre of the structure. Then he reached into his pocket and gave her the new spyglass he had promised her, steadying his elbow on the stone walls and peering out into the trees. Once he adjusted it, he gave it to her and she did the same.

'This telescope was created by the best craftsman in the world.' He touched the smooth tube and tapped it. She saw the engraving of her name.

'It appears good for viewing,' she said 'I'll be able to see birds' nests in spring, if the leaves don't block my view. I'll enjoy ending my walk in the gardens with a chance to come up here and look over everything, and watch new life. I want to see the future, and not the past.'

'And the pillows?' he asked. He smiled, and his eyes gave that special twinkle only for her.

'I want to see the sky with you. The clouds or the stars…afterwards.'

He put an arm around her and pulled her close. I think you planned this nest for us to be together.'

'I did,' she said. 'And I love it that you are interested in the skies.

'Truly, I'm more interested in the lady who is interested.' He chuckled, pulling her close. 'I am looking forward to standing here with you, keeping the chill from us with a warm blanket over both of us and feeling the serenity of the world.'

She could already imagine standing, looking over the gardens on a cold, dreary winter day and watching little birds scamper around, searching for bread crumbs she had dropped below.

'I will enjoy the seasons more, seeing them with you,' she said, holding her hand out, the gold band shining in the sunlight. 'I'll see the autumn colours, the winter bones of the trees with birds flitting about in them, the new growth of spring and I'll possibly just stay in the shade below in summer.'

'I never guessed it could be so beautiful here,' he said. 'I never imagined the tower. I just thought of the plants and the inside of the house. And when I was working on the house I never conceived I would have someone like you to share it with.'

'This will give us a place to sit and watch the sunset, or sunrise, and a chance to sit together in the evenings and look forward to our future.'

He put an arm around her. 'Rebuilding the house was a chance to correct the mistakes of my family's past. They added a room every time something was needed to distract them, to give themselves something to plan for and to keep their attention. But I have you for my attention and distraction…and I do love you to distraction.'

Wind ruffled his hair and she reached out, smoothing it back into place, the moment bringing them even closer.

'It all turned out well, though.'

'Two people in the same journey of life.'

She clasped his hand. 'Together. During construction and planning, and things going wrong, and righting them as best we can. It is more than the business you have been creating, it is the business of our lives.

Of having respite together. Of creating a direction and path just for us to travel along.'

He put a kiss on her forehead. 'I didn't imagine the contentment you could bring to my life and my home. But something happened to me when I saw you. I was so deeply aware of you.

'I could feel the spirit of you pulling me closer, even though you didn't know it. I have always been able to find the best people to settle around me and form a bond with. For that I am very grateful. At times it has meant that I have had fewer people in my life. But always the people closest to me have been the best. And you are.'

'You don't have to say that. I'm your wife, and I'm not going anywhere.'

'Oh, yes, I do,' he said. 'Because I can't help myself. I cannot believe my good fortune.'

'You've helped me feel more comfortable with others—standing by my side, your hand on the small of my back. It seems to infuse me with strength.'

'Seems to? I would hope it does.'

'It does. Every moment with you makes me stronger. And I've discovered I love your family as my own. It seems that the smaller staff makes us all closer, together. I didn't grasp when I wed you that I was bringing so many people into my life and I would love them all.'

'And my life is the same. You are the only person I could have ever proposed to. Do you feel married now?' he asked.

'Better than that,' she said. 'I feel courted, and safe and surrounded by your love.'

'And I feel your love,' he said. He held her hand and rested it against his chest.

'You don't worry that people will think we wed for all the wrong reasons?'

'No. They only have to take one look at us together and will know that love is the foundation for our union.'

She rested her head on his shoulder and closed her eyes, feeling nature around them, the magnificence of miscalculations which led to even better paths when one kept going forward, or round or over. The feeling of gaining a life with more intensity than she'd ever imagined. Of Adam. Of her heart's other half.

* * * * *

If you enjoyed this story, make sure to read
Liz Tyner's other great stories

The Governess's Guide to Marriage
A Cinderella for the Viscount
Tempting a Reformed Rake
A Marquess Too Rakish to Wed

Get 3 FREE REWARDS!

We'll send you 2 FREE Books plus a FREE Mystery Gift.

FREE Value Over **$20**

Both the **Harlequin® Desire** and **Harlequin Presents®** series feature compelling novels filled with passion, sensuality and intriguing scandals.

Get 3 FREE REWARDS!

We'll send you 2 FREE Books <u>plus</u> a FREE Mystery Gift.

Both the **Romance** and **Suspense** collections feature compelling novels written by many of today's bestselling authors.

YES! Please send me 2 FREE novels from the Essential Romance or Essential Suspense Collection and my FREE gift (gift is worth about $10 retail). After receiving them, if I don't wish to receive any more books, I can return the shipping statement marked "cancel." If I don't cancel, I will receive 6 brand-new novels every month and be billed just $7.49 each in the U.S. or $7.74 each in Canada. That's a savings of at least 17% off the cover price. It's quite a bargain! Shipping and handling is just 50¢ per book in the U.S. and $1.25 per book in Canada.* I understand that accepting the 2 free books and gift places me under no obligation to buy anything. I can always return a shipment and cancel at any time by calling the number below. The free books and gift are mine to keep no matter what I decide.

Choose one:

☐ **Essential Romance**
(194/394 BPA GRNM)

☐ **Essential Suspense**
(191/391 BPA GRNM)

☐ **Or Try Both!**
(194/394 & 191/391 BPA GRQZ)

Name (please print)

Address   Apt. #

City   State/Province   Zip/Postal Code

Email: Please check this box ☐ if you would like to receive newsletters and promotional emails from Harlequin Enterprises ULC and its affiliates. You can unsubscribe anytime.

Mail to the **Harlequin Reader Service:**
IN U.S.A.: P.O. Box 1341, Buffalo, NY 14240-8531
IN CANADA: P.O. Box 603, Fort Erie, Ontario L2A 5X3

Want to try 2 free books from another series? Call 1-800-873-8635 or visit www.ReaderService.com.

HARLEQUIN
PLUS

Try the best multimedia subscription service for romance readers like you!

Read, Watch and Play.

Experience the easiest way to get the romance content you crave.

Start your **FREE TRIAL** at
www.harlequinplus.com/freetrial.